the society

Entangled Publishing, LLC
2614 South Timberline Road
Suite 109
Fort Collins, CO 80525

Entangled Teen is an imprint of Entangled Publishing, LLC.
Visit our website at www.entangledpublishing.com.

Edited by Alethea Spiridon
Cover design by Louisa Maggio
Interior design by Toni Kerr
Photography credits:
iStock_000055720354
iStock_000050615880_Double

Print ISBN: 9781633753181
Epub ISBN: 9781633753273

Manufactured in the United States of America

First Edition May 2016

10 9 8 7 6 5 4 3 2 1

For Shay Wolfe, for always standing by your friends, no matter what.

Many people will walk in and out of your life, but only true friends will leave footprints on your heart.
—Eleanor Roosevelt

BEFORE

All things truly wicked start from innocence.
—Ernest Hemingway

My life changed forever exactly three years, two months, and seventeen days ago. Back then I still believed all people possessed redeeming qualities. Even myself. Talk about naive.

No thirteen-year-old should ever have to sit in a courtroom, scared and silent, waiting to hear if her father's going to jail. But nevertheless, there I was. My hands curled into tight fists against the lap of my skirt, nails digging small crescent moons in my sweaty palms.

I glanced over to where Jessica and her father sat in the row behind the prosecuting attorney. She must have felt my gaze, because she turned around and stared at me. I held my breath, praying I'd see sympathy for the situation, or remorse for what she'd done. Instead, the look she gave me was that of a stranger; she pursed her lips like she was biting a lemon and turned to face the front again. Her blow-off crushed me, although I guess it shouldn't have been a surprise.

Tears streaked down my face as I waited to hear the verdict. I couldn't remember ever feeling that scared in my life.

"Samantha, stop fidgeting." They were the first words my mother spoke all day. She didn't even bother looking at me as she issued her directive, her face a cold marble statue as she stared straight ahead. I forced myself to sit still and wondered what the jury would say. Feared what fate would throw at my dad, at my whole family.

I wasn't sure if Dad had actually done it or not. To tell the truth, I hadn't wanted to ask, although deep down amid memories of my parents shouting and my mother's tearful accusations, I'd known they were telling the truth. That he'd chosen greed over his family. Over me.

Once upon a time, I'd been a normal kid, one who hadn't even heard the term *insider trading*, let alone associated it with my father. But that was nothing compared to the "terroristic threats" charge the prosecution had also tacked on.

Maybe Dad *had* threatened the life of Jessica's father, but it wasn't like he would've actually followed through with it. My father had only been scared that Mr. Wainright was going to turn him in for the insider trading stuff—turned out he'd been right. But that didn't make a difference to Jessica. I was dead to her now.

And to think just five short months ago I'd been so excited to be leaving Trinity Junior Academy, ready to begin my big adventure as an official high school student. My euphoria hadn't lasted long, everything changed the day of my junior high graduation.

I was no longer the innocent, laughing girl who had friends and a real family. I could barely even remember what she'd been like. Remembering that day was like watching old home movies, the kind that you know must have happened because you see them on the screen, but you can't remember what it felt like to live it.

I'd sat waiting for the final bell to ring and glanced over at Jessica in the wooden desk next to me. She grinned and mouthed, "Ready, Sam?"

Like usual, I took my cues from her. Then again, so did most of the girls in our eighth grade class. But I didn't mind. She was more than a best friend to me; she was my soul sister. We shared secrets and planned to grow up and marry brothers and live in gorgeous houses next to each other in some exotic city far away.

One night when we were only ten, we'd gotten brave—or stupid—during a sleepover at her house and used a sewing needle to prick our fingers. We'd rubbed the tiny droplets of blood against each other's finger and sworn to remain friends forever.

We'd planned the best end of year prank ever for our last day of eighth grade. It was tradition to try to outdo the class before, and we'd nailed it. Of course, we had the perk of having some of the smartest kids in school help orchestrate the whole thing.

I covered my mouth to hide my giggle before turning my head to peek at Jeremy sitting behind me. He'd been another one of my best friends as long as I could remember. His hazel eyes twinkled as he caught my gaze, and he offered

the society

me an almost imperceptible nod.

Just as the dismissal bell began to ring, Jeremy reached inside his desk. My stomach did crazy little flip-flops, and I fought to hide my excited grin. Music blared from the built-in wall speakers used for school announcements. Mr. Mangelli looked up, aghast, as the opening beats of Nicki Minaj's "Super Bass"—the unedited version—shook the hallowed walls of our too-snobby-to-rock school.

On cue, all of the girls in the room pulled identical hot pink wigs from their desks and slapped them on their heads as artificial snow and shimmery glitter burst from a contraption rigged in the back of the classroom.

Mr. Mangelli's eyes bulged, and his mouth flapped like a fish trying to suck air. He burst from his desk chair, hands shaking, pointing around the room. "What is the meaning of this? I demand you stop this foolishness this instant." It was a bit difficult to take him seriously given he had glitter hanging from his moustache and had to keep wiping Styrofoam snow from his lips.

Of course, we ignored him. Sounds of cheering and clapping carried from the adjoining classrooms. A few brave students hovered at our homeroom door as they passed, peeking in and laughing when they saw the thirty of us in the room now standing and gyrating to the *boom badoom boom.* Jessica, always the leader, actually stood on her desk. Mr. Mangelli turned apoplectic.

"Get down from there right now!"

She blew him a kiss. I lost it. I grabbed her hand to pull her down, laughing hysterically. Jeremy's arm snaked around my shoulders in a quick hug, and he leaned in close to whisper, "Score. We did it." I turned, and my smile widened, including him in the moment.

Jer and his friend Pete were the brains behind the whole thing. Building the machine to shoot the snow and glitter when Jeremy pressed the button had taken them several weeks in Pete's garage, but they did it, it worked just like we'd planned.

I grabbed my backpack from the floor, and the three of us raced hand in hand out of the classroom, ignoring our teacher's shouted threats about this going on our permanent academic record. Really, what would it say? We made it snow in class? I wasn't worried; the school administration pretty much expected something like it on the last day of classes each year.

My heart raced in exhilaration as we ran together down the wide hallway toward the double doors that led to freedom. Summer vacation with the best friends in the world waited just ten feet away. Life was good.

I was still glowing twenty minutes later when I got home. Like usual, Jessica's mom had given me a ride, and Jess promised to come over early the next day to help decorate for my graduation party. I pushed open the front door and walked in.

"Mom, I'm home!" I tossed my bag on the stone landing and looked around when I didn't hear her usual cheery, "Hey, honey," welcoming me.

"Mom?" I called again, a little louder this time. It didn't seem like anyone was around. Granted, Dad didn't usually get home until after seven. He worked long hours with his job as a stockbroker on Wall Street. But I guess I kind of expected more of an excited scene walking in. My parent's usual go-overboard style should have dictated balloons and champagne, or *something*.

I trudged up the stairs to my room, still humming "Super Bass." I reached back to untwist my braid and shook my head when my long dark hair was finally freed. Just as I reached the landing at the top of the stairs, a muted voice carried from the end of the hall, from my parents' room.

"I cannot believe you would do this! What were you thinking?"

Mom had to be on the phone with one of her friends, though I'd never heard her sound like that, so bitter and furious. Curious, I crept closer, taking care to tiptoe as quietly as I could. Whatever she was talking about, it was probably a safe bet I wasn't meant to hear the conversation; maybe I'd get some juicy gossip I could share with my friends later. I giggled.

"Goddammit, Claire! It just happened. I…I don't know what you want me to fucking say."

My hand covered my mouth. That was my father's voice, but Dad never cursed at Mom; he always said that kind of language showed poor breeding and lack of intellect. And besides, my parents rarely argued, and even when they did, it wasn't like this, so heated. It was normally about where to go on vacation, or my Dad forgetting to pick up milk on his way home.

I crept closer to their closed door, determined to find out what had gotten them both so worked up. I couldn't even imagine my dad doing anything to make my mom that mad. He was my hero. He worked hard, and yet he still always made time to spend time with me: going to the skating rink or taking me to my horseback riding lessons. I think it bothered my mom that he and I had always had a special bond, one that she and I didn't share.

A loud crash sounded against the opposite side of the door, and I jerked my head back in shock and mounting fear; my stomach twisted and tears sprang to my eyes. I turned and slipped into my room across the hall and locked the bedroom door behind me with a firm *click*.

My hands shook as I crossed my large, pale lavender room and sat on the bed that was positioned between two chiffon-covered windows. A shadow fell across my previously bright and cheery room as storm clouds covered the sun outside my window. Somewhere deep inside, I was afraid of what was to come.

Little did I know at the time just how right I was to be scared.

I shook my head like that would get rid of the memories. I didn't need to relive one of the worst days of my life, not now, not when a jury of twelve strangers deliberated my father's fate. The knots in my stomach tightened until I was sure the pain would cause me to pass out. I looked to my mom for something—an encouraging smile, a squeeze of her hand. I got neither.

As soon as the jury foreman stood up, steely eyes and disapproving glare sent in my father's direction, I knew it was all over. Life as I'd known it up until that moment was gone. *Poof.* Like the flame on a birthday candle extinguished forever. Only I didn't get a wish this time.

My mother said nothing as the uniformed guard led my dad out of the courtroom in his orange jumpsuit, hands shackled together, making a clanging noise with each of his shuffling footsteps. Just as he was about to walk through the door that would lead him to the next ten years of his life, away from me, he looked up. His face looked tired, like he'd given up. His cheeks were more sunken in than they used to be, and his shoulders slumped.

I waited for him to say something, to call out that he loved me and it was all a big mistake. I jumped up from my seat, leaned forward against the bench in front of me, tears rolling unabated down my face. But after a heartbeat that lasted forever, he dropped his gaze and turned and walked through the door.

"Samantha, it's time to go." My mother's voice was cool, detached. I looked up at her incredulously. Her expression hardened when she saw I was crying. "Wipe your face. We'll go out the side entrance so we don't have to deal with the press. I'm late for a meeting." No hugs, no comforting words. I did as I was told and silently shadowed her out of the courtroom.

Watching my mother's straight back as she marched two feet ahead in her charcoal suit, something in me changed. The carefree girl I'd been on my last day of junior high was gone, life as I'd known it was over. Even at thirteen, I was smart enough to realize everything would change.

Turned out, I was right.

TODO

If you prick us, do we not bleed? If you tickle us, do we not laugh? If you poison us, do we not die? And if you wrong us, shall we not revenge?
—William Shakespeare

I pushed through the heavy oak doors leading into Trinity Academy, ignoring the groups of students milling around the wide steps of the ornate brick building. Not like it mattered. They were all busy talking, laughing, and fist-bumping each other, mostly jocks and their adoring fans, none of whom I had the time or interest to speak with.

"Out of my way."

Bren Fessler—bedazzled toady to my ex-best friend Jessica—shoved past, leaving me gagging from lingering fumes of eau de bitch. I rolled my eyes, hacked through the last of the stench, and headed toward my locker.

Trinity was founded like a hundred years ago, and if buildings really do have a personality, this one had the snooty air of old money. I mean, it was a beautiful campus;

it just sucked that I couldn't stand the majority of the kids who went there anymore. But since Trinity had a stellar academic program that looked great on college applications, I'd remained, even after everything that happened. Besides, my creative writing teacher, Ms. Kemper, had pretty much assured me a shining recommendation to Columbia, her alma mater. I think she felt sorry for me. So I stayed. I wasn't about to blow my chance at getting into my dream school even if everything around me sucked.

As I neared my locker, five or six members of the golden crew sashayed in a little blond bubble across from me, confident toothy smiles all over their faces. Since it was the start of Rush week, they were probably all certain they'd find a typed note covertly slipped through one of the vents in their locker, an invitation to rush our high school's hallowed cloak-and-dagger Musterian Society.

Even the name sounded decayed, like a musty blanket you'd find rotting in your grandmother's attic. I'd looked it up once. *Musterian.* Turns out it's Greek for "a mystery confided only to the initiated and not to ordinary mortals."

There would obviously be no note in my locker. I was way too ordinary, and mortal was putting it mildly. My hair wasn't blond and shiny enough. I didn't prance around in a cutesy little uniform with *TA* emblazoned across my not-quite-big-enough boobs.

The cheerleaders seemed to miss what just about everyone else recognized. The irony in the fact that our school's initials also stood for a completely different phrase. Then again, they'd probably be just as proud to wear the label, *Tits and Ass.* Yet these Einsteins were usually the ones chosen to pledge, at least to meet the female initiates quota.

Just about every kid at school dreamed of being invited to rush. Invitation to the Society wasn't only a guaranteed boost to your social standing, although that was a given. No, being in the Society offered even more tangible, life-changing perks. It pretty much guaranteed acceptance to the college of your choice—past members served on the admissions boards of some of the best schools in the country. Dream jobs tended to follow. The Society members helped their own.

We weren't supposed to know all that, but it didn't take a rocket scientist to figure it out when you saw school acceptance letters roll in. The Society was a who's who of the in crowd, guaranteeing a life we all fantasize about.

They didn't ask people like me to join. I wasn't cool enough, at least not anymore.

Steps away from my locker, the golden crew parted like the Red Sea. Whispers and giggles engulfed me—dark as smoke, and just as acrid.

"Oh my God, it's perfect."

"…her expression."

I tried to ignore them, just another day in Trinity paradise.

Until I saw it.

I stopped short and sucked in a breath. She'd gone too far this time. Heat burned my cheeks as I stared straight ahead.

Several black stripes made to resemble bars, drawn with what looked like thick Magic Marker, ran vertically from the top of my locker to the very bottom. A crude stick figure of a prisoner filled the center, with my yearbook photo pasted on as the face. In what I'm sure they felt was a clever play on words on our school's Musterian Society, they'd scribbled the words "Convict Society" above my photo.

I fought to hide my burning anger and embarrassment. *Jessica.* She'd taunted me on an almost obsessive basis since the trial three years ago. Jessica needed to prove she was done with me, that way none of the other kids would think she'd fallen from her Queen Bee pedestal and deigned to socialize with a convict's daughter.

Tears threatened, but I pushed them down and lifted my chin, ignoring the peals of laughter. They went on and on, new people joining in each second.

I yanked my locker door open and pretended to search for a book. I wanted so desperately to disappear, but no magic wand materialized on the locker shelf to help me. I shoved my bag in the narrow space and prayed for the ground to open up and swallow me whole. Unfortunately, those sorts of things never happen when you want them to.

Jessica sidled up next to me, eyes wide in mock innocence. "Looking for your invitation?" Her trusty sidekicks giggled some more.

"Please leave me alone." I shut the door and twisted away in resignation.

She reached out and grabbed my arm, pulling me back toward her. "You don't belong here," she hissed. "*You* know it." She poked me in the chest with a perfectly manicured fingernail. "And *we* all know it." Her icy stare dripped disdain, and she flipped her long blond mane over her shoulder in triumph.

I yanked my arm free. This time she didn't bother to stop me. I turned and walked down the hall before realizing I didn't have any of my books. It didn't matter; I couldn't imagine sitting in class knowing everyone was staring and whispering after Jessica's latest stunt. I needed to get out of there.

Tears scalded my eyes and heat scurried up my neck as I speed walked away, but it'd be a cold day in hell before I'd let her see me cry. I reached out to rip open the front doors of the school, but before I could make my escape, a hand clamped my upper arm. Not hard, but I jumped anyway.

"Sam! Where're you going?"

My heart rate slowed back down at the sound of his voice. My best—no, scratch that, my *only* real—friend in the world. Jeremy.

I bowed my head, allowing my hair to fall in a curtain in front of my face. I didn't need a mirror to tell me my pale skin would be all blotchy and gross from fighting back tears.

Jeremy's grasp on my arm loosened, and his voice grew softer as he took another step my way, leaning his head toward me, so close that I could smell the toothpaste he'd used that morning. "Hey, you okay?"

I bit my lip, stomach flopping all over the place, brought on by Jessica's words still ringing in my ears as well as Jeremy's caring. To be honest, I didn't know which was harder to take right that second. Both broke me in their own way.

The first, because three years of constant torture at the hands of someone who'd once been my best friend sometimes seemed like three hundred. The latter, because I was petrified that Jer would end up leaving too. Like my dad, and my mom shortly after that.

Kids rushed past, hurrying to get to class before the tardy bell rang.

Jeremy's hand slid down my arm to graze my wrist for the briefest of seconds. His touch always made me feel so safe. "Wait for me. I'll be right back."

I nodded, still unable to face him.

"Yo, Cody! Hang on." Jeremy crossed the hall and dug some papers out of his backpack before handing them to Cody Miller, a guy from our English Lit class. Cody shot me a quizzical glance before turning back and muttering to Jeremy while giving him an elbow jab and smile. Jeremy shook his head and said something I couldn't hear then clapped Cody on the shoulder and headed back my way and pointed to the door.

"What are you doing?" I asked. Jeremy wasn't the type to just ditch school, far from it. I didn't want him to miss class because of me.

He shrugged, and shaggy brown hair spilled into his eyes. "C'mon. Let's get out of here." He reached past me and pulled the handle.

"Wait! I'm fine. You don't have to come with me."

He turned and looked me directly in the eyes. "I know I don't."

My heartbeat sped up a little at his words. "Thanks, Jer," I whispered.

His familiar grin peeked through, breaking the spell. "Now let's go before Kurick comes and we both land in detention."

I couldn't help but laugh a little. He nodded his head toward the heavy door and tugged it open, motioning for me to go first.

As I stepped outside, the autumn air cooled my cheeks, and I glanced up at the overcast sky. Jeremy fell into step next to me. He glanced my way as I shivered.

"Here, take mine." He shrugged his jacket off and leaned closer to carefully slip it around my shoulders. I warmed instantly, partly from the heavy cotton and partly from him being so close. I inhaled, and his familiar scent enveloped me.

"Thanks." I smiled up at him.

His soft smile warmed me even more. "Anytime."

We walked a few more steps toward the student parking lot. "C'mon." He shoulder bumped me. "I'll buy you a coffee and you can tell me all about it. Besides, I owe you. All the times you've helped me with English papers and put up with my movie picks, it's the least I can do."

I shook my head and laughed again as I thanked my lucky stars I had him in my life.

three

Are you comfortable with the skin you're in? Are you screaming loud enough to be important? Are you following the path that you thought you would or wouldn't?
—*36 Crazyfists*

"So what's going on?" Jeremy stirred cream and sugar into his coffee across the small table.

I shook my head and blew on my own large coffee before taking a hesitant sip. "I don't know. The usual. Jessica." I shrugged, not sure what to say. How do you explain the culmination of years of torment? Everyone has a breaking point, and I'd reached mine.

"Did you see it?" I asked.

"See what?"

I filled him in on the locker art. He swore under his breath. He knew all the vindictive stunts she'd pulled, and couldn't figure out Jessica's problem anymore than I could.

"I'm sorry, Sam." He reached across the table to squeeze my hand. "It sucks, and she's a bitch. But just think, by this time next year you'll be in college, and all of this crap will be behind you."

At his words, the realization that we'd be apart for the first time in years slammed into me. I mean, I always knew the day was coming, but I'd never really wanted to face it—so I kind of blocked it out. While I couldn't wait to get away from this town, the idea of not being close to Jeremy anymore sent slivers of cold dread through me.

I offered a shaky smile and nodded.

"So, did you decide yet which school you think you're gonna go to?" I peeked at him over my coffee cup.

He lifted his shoulders and let them drop again before answering. "I'm not sure. But at least now I know that I have a decent chance of getting in to one of them, thanks to you." He smiled, and my heart squeezed in my chest a little bit.

A few weeks ago, I'd helped him with the essays for his college applications. Not that he really needed it, but when he'd asked, there was no way I could say no.

"What about you? Still intent on Columbia?"

I nodded. It'd been my dream for years. I couldn't even say for sure why. Maybe it had something to do with not wanting to go too far away from my aunt after all she'd done for me. Maybe a tiny piece of me still didn't want to move too far away from my father, even though I hadn't been able to bring myself to visit him the entire time he'd been in prison.

And in the back of my mind, I kept hoping that Jeremy would stay in state too. So even if we weren't a couple of streets away from each other anymore, it wouldn't be like we were just disappearing from each other's lives.

He looked down at the table for a second and then raised his eyes to meet mine. "I can't imagine not seeing you every day."

I blinked, fighting back the sudden tears that threatened. "I know," I said, my voice quiet. "Me either."

He took my hand once again and held it, not saying more.

$\mathcal{W}$e went back for afternoon classes. Jeremy managed to talk me down from bagging the entire day. Probably a good thing since we had a major test in chemistry seventh period; plus my aunt would kill me if she found out I'd skipped. Hopefully the school wouldn't call her given I'd faked a note saying I'd had a doctor's appointment that morning.

The rest of the day went by fairly uneventfully…until I ran into Jessica while I collected my books to take home at the end of the day.

"Hey, Sam." Her breath warmed my neck as she leaned in like a jackal hunting a rabbit.

I closed my eyes. One day. That's all I wanted. One freaking day without her constant needling. Over twelve hundred days…it had to be exhausting for her to exert that much energy making sure I—and every kid in school—knew I was a second, or third, or fourth-class citizen.

But I knew it wasn't going to happen. I'd tried, God knows I tried.

After dealing with the evil drama that is Jessica for about a year after the trial, trying to shrug it off and ignore it like teachers and parents always tell us to do, I'd built up the nerve to go to her house and ask her if we could talk the night before sophomore year. My version of extending the proverbial olive branch.

It hadn't gone well.

I'd tried the practical approach first—"can't we just get past this, after all, we were once best friends." After that, I'd moved to pleading to at least try to be civil to each other. I'd ended up crying—the ugly kind you don't want anyone to see. She'd laughed in my face.

"Sam, do you seriously think we can ever, *ever* go back to that?" Her face twisted into a familiar sneer. "It's *never* happening," she spit out.

"I don't understand. Why does it have to be this way?" I whispered, wiping my running nose and wishing I didn't feel so pathetic.

"Are you freaking kidding me? Your father threatened to *kill* my father. Your father was *sleeping with* my mother."

"*What?* No, no he wasn't." I sucked in air, eyes wide. It couldn't be true. Yeah, I'd known about my dad supposedly threatening Mr. Wainright's life, but the idea that he was unfaithful to my mom on top of it? I couldn't believe it. Wouldn't believe it.

Even as I protested, little things began to shift into focus. Bits and pieces of conversations behind closed doors. Jessica's parents divorcing about that time, and my mother's abrupt departure after the trial, dumping me into the care of my aunt.

Jessica took a step closer. "*Your father* destroyed my life. He took my family. So, *no*, Sam, I don't want anything to do with you." She stared at me, her normally flawless skin mottled with rage. "Now if you don't mind, I'd like you to get out of my house," she said through gritted teeth.

I'd nodded, mute, and fled.

If anything, things had only gotten worse after that. A Tumblr page had appeared about a week later, dedicated to posting altered pictures of me, or memes about secrets I'd shared with Jessica through the years. Mocking me.

Even worse was the time I'd dared to hope someone could actually still *like* me. Chase Latkin had come up to me about a month after school started that year and asked me out. Chase was one of the golden crew, and I'd been so shocked and thrilled when he'd smiled at me, flirted with me. It was the first time any guy had really shown an interest in me. I'd been so excited, thinking it was a sign of things to come.

I'd chosen my outfit with care, wanting it to be perfect. Aunt Lor had been so happy for me, knowing how lonely I'd felt recently. She'd driven me to the mall that Friday night, and I'd paced the food court where Chase and I were supposed to meet, palms sweaty in anticipation.

About ten minutes after I arrived, Chase showed up. Hand in hand with Jessica. They walked together to stand a few feet in front of me.

"You seriously thought he wanted to go out with you?" Jessica laughed. "Oh, poor little Sam." She'd slipped her hands around his neck and stood on tiptoes to kiss him while I'd stared, mortified, before running out of the mall and puking in the bushes next to the parking lot.

Her voice snapped me back to the present, where she once again stood just feet away, mocking me. "Still searching for your invite to rush?" She barked out a laugh. "It's not happening. Dig all you want, sweetie, the Society has standards."

My lips pressed together as I silently grabbed my calculus textbook and slid it into my bag.

She obviously didn't appreciate being ignored. Stepping around me, she leaned against the locker right next to mine, eyes narrowed. "Why don't you just take the hint? We don't want you here. Go crawl back under your little trailer trash rock and stay there."

A few students standing nearby snorted and giggled.

Teeth clenched, I squeezed the straps of my backpack and stared at my shoes. *Don't show her you care.*

Jessica grew bolder in the midst of her audience. "Your whole family is trash. From your convict father to that crazy old aunt you live with since even your own mom decided she didn't want you and took off."

She leaned in closer, sucking up all my air, leaving me sick and dizzy. "You're just like him. A nothing. *Less than nothing.* You could disappear tomorrow, and there isn't one single person who would even notice."

I slammed my locker closed and whipped around to face her, but one look at her triumphant sneer, and all the other kids smirking and whispering, stopped me cold. Because really, what could I say? How do you argue with the truth?

A part of me couldn't understand how she could hate me so much, how she could be so callous. After all, I hadn't done anything to her. It was my father, and he'd destroyed my family too. But thinking back, she'd always had a mean streak in her, I just hadn't noticed so much when we were friends since it hadn't been directed at me.

Loud laughter erupted all around me as I rushed down the hall to the exit. I walked down the school steps while thunder cracked overhead and rain poured. In seconds, my hair plastered against my face and neck, and I shivered. At least the heavy drops hid the burning tears that I could no longer hold back.

Waiting for my bus to show, I clenched my fists and swore. There had to be a way to stop her. If I didn't do something — soon — I was going to lose it. For real. I swept a hand roughly over my eyes and stood, wet, cold, and seething inside.

The counselor my aunt forced me to go to a couple of years ago had told me to let my feelings out, that it wasn't healthy to bottle them up. I'd stopped seeing him after four sessions, right after I'd snuck a peek at the papers he'd always scribbled on and saw "bipolar?" written below my name. What a load of crap. Being pissed off didn't make you bipolar. And with everything that happened, I had a damn good reason to be angry. Although...I couldn't deny that my moods flashed like quicksilver from depressed to angry anymore. But who could blame me?

I'd tried so hard to rise above it, to prove I wasn't like my father — I was good, honorable. But I couldn't just sit back and take it. Hell, even Gandhi said to be the change you wish to see in the world.

Out of nowhere, it hit. I half expected a lightning bolt to flash in the sky along with my epiphany. It was so perfect in its ironic simplicity that I couldn't believe I hadn't thought of it sooner. I tilted my head back and laughed, allowing the rain to wash away any trace of tears.

I knew how to get back at Jessica. And the best part? She'd have absolutely no idea it was me who planned her ruin.

Revenge would be so very sweet.

Last night I had a revelation. Somehow I have to make you pay. No one hurts me and goes free. I'll play on your fears; I'll leave you in tears. You'll never be the same, my friend.
—Red Delicious

I'd stayed up half the night writing down my ideas. It didn't matter what Jessica said or did next, I wouldn't let her get under my skin.

It'd bothered me for a long time how easily Jessica seemed to be able to walk away from our friendship. And not only walk away, but find enjoyment in tearing me down every chance she got. At first, I'd tried calling her over and over, begging her to talk to me. I'd left notes in her locker. I'd even left her a necklace with a charm that read BEST FRIENDS. I'd found it, chain broken, in my locker the following day.

I never knew for sure if Jessica's parents had told her she wasn't allowed to hang out with me anymore. Or maybe the pressures of starting high school and wanting to reign atop the social ladder, where I no longer fit in, made her treat me the way she did. I'd stopped caring. Well, I'd stopped showing her how much it hurt me anyway.

But now I had a plan.

Rush week offered the perfect chance to pull off the whole thing. Maybe once upon a time, I'd dreamed of receiving an invite to join the Society, but not anymore. Too many stares and snide comments completed my transformation into the little black butterfly that could.

And little did Jessica or the Society know, but I'd come up with a way to make pledge week blow up in their shiny Gold Card faces. To make them realize that despite what they thought, living in a mobile home park outside of town with my dad's older sister didn't make me stupid.

Because secret or not, I was pretty damn sure who reigned atop the Society's social ladder, and she was going down…in a big way. Jessica Wainright would regret all she'd done to me *and* my family.

Those times she'd slept over at my house, eavesdropping on my dad's phone conversations in his office just to report back to her dad? No real friend would do something like that. All of the horrible things she'd done to me since then— Jessica had no heart, and most likely, no soul either.

The custodians must have tried to remove the marker from my locker overnight. The picture was gone, and the lines were faded as if they'd been scrubbed with some type of industrial cleaner. Since I hadn't been called down to the office and asked about the tag-art, I considered it safe to assume the golden crew had gotten off once again. Shocker.

I grabbed what I needed for the morning's classes and shut my locker. I couldn't act on my plan yet; there were too many people around. But I could do it during lunch, when the halls would be mostly cleared of students. I turned to head to my first period class.

"Nice shoes." A body bumped into me from behind. I didn't need to glance back to know who the voice belonged to; Jessica's high-pitched cackle floated inches from my head. I half expected flying monkeys to zip past any second.

Warmth filled my cheeks as I marched on, spine held stiff, jaw clenched. I kept my head averted as I walked halfway down the hall and turned right to enter Ms. Sheppard's twelfth-grade English Lit class. I forced myself to take slow breaths, to calm down. *In through the nose, out through the mouth. In through the nose, out through the mouth.* Dr. Laroby would be so proud.

The classroom held twenty-five desks in five straight rows. Light filtered through the tall windows, catching dancing dust motes in its path. Heavy molding adorned the archway above the door, and as usual, the room held a note of wood soap.

Ms. Sheppard was busy writing, "Name three thematic elements…" in neat script on the wide chalkboard. Trinity apparently loved to hold on to old traditions that pleased the school trustees. Upgrade to whiteboards? Nah, the money was better spent on football uniforms. Go Titans!

I used to love school, the challenge, the ideas. Not so much anymore. But I still forced myself to play the role; college would be my ticket out, away from everyone who knew my family's sordid history.

Parents? Gone. I hadn't seen my mother since about a month after Dad's sentencing. She'd hightailed it out of the country and dumped me in the care of my Aunt Loretta as soon she could get the guardianship papers signed. I'd gotten a postcard from her about eight months ago. Apparently I had a stepdad I'd never met.

A yawn escaped my lips seconds before the bell rang to signal the start of class. I hadn't gotten much sleep the night before because I was too busy going over the plan again and again. Just three and a half more hours, and it would all finally begin. Well, laying the groundwork anyway. But next week? All hell would break loose.

"*Y*o, Sam! Wait up!" Jeremy's overflowing book bag slipped off his shoulder as he ran down the hall toward me.

I thrust the small envelopes I'd been studying back in my messenger bag before he could see them. I'd slipped out of class ahead of him, wanting to get started.

We'd shared most of our classes ever since the ninth grade. Students weren't supposed to know administration grouped us by ability for our core courses; instead, they made it look like we're arranged by grade and colors. Jeremy and I landed in 12-Red with our friend, Abby. Not to stereotype, but a lot of the cheerleaders were in Brown, which I found hilarious. The princesses in a crap color. A select group of students filled the Gold section. As if we couldn't figure out they were the shining stars of Trinity.

The Academy accepted kids in grades six through twelve, and the school board makes all prospective students pass entrance exams just to have the honor of paying their exorbitant yearly tuition. That is, unless you receive financial assistance, and I do thanks to dear old dad going to jail and losing everything. Which made me rank even higher on the *persona non grata* list. Didn't matter, even with the Jessica crap, I was thankful I still got to attend. The public school for my address left a lot to be desired.

A teacher stopped Jeremy. I shook my head and leaned back against my locker, offering a sympathetic smile when he glanced my way. Probably getting reamed out for running in the hall.

I played with my narrow tie as I waited. Our uniforms completely sucked. Think of those sweaters old people put on dogs. Now combine that image with plaid skirts and a tie, all in these god-awful shades of red and brown.

Who the hell picked *brown* for a school color, anyway? It's like they wanted to make us look as unattractive as possible, maybe to eliminate the chances of hooking up on school grounds. Like poor color choices would dissuade horny teenagers. Most of the guys would hump a troll if it had a nice enough rack.

Jeremy fought to suppress a grin as Mr. Reynolds bobbed his head up and down mid-lecture. The old Latin teacher sported a rather unfortunate toupee, and it tended to bounce when he moved his head too emphatically, which he did way more than he should. It struck me how cute Jeremy looked when he smiled.

Reynolds was on a roll. I sighed and glanced around. Bright posters dotted the ever-tasteful cream-colored walls in the wide hallway. *Latin Club, Photography Club, Pep Rally THIS FRIDAY!!!* My throat tightened. A multicolored bulletin board of my former life framed me with things I'd once been a part of. I averted my eyes and swallowed hard.

Finally released, Jeremy started my way again, slower this time, rolling his eyes. I noticed a group of girls across the hall sending Jeremy flirty looks as he passed. One of them, Sherri or Sierra…something with an S, even offered him a little finger waggle and hair toss. Jeremy looked confused, and just gave a halfhearted wave in return.

I suppressed a grin. He could be so oblivious sometimes.

"So, where'd you run off to after trig?" He stared at me curiously from behind John Lennon glasses. He wore them most of the time because he couldn't stand poking a finger in his eye to put his contacts in. Jer had amazing eyes, a mix of colors swirled together.

I bent and picked up my bag from where it rested next to my purple Converse on the gleaming wooden floor.

"I just had a couple things I wanted to get done."

He wrinkled his nose. "Like what?"

I headed with him toward the wide archway that led to the cafeteria, making sure to avoid his questioning eyes. "Uh, I was going to skip lunch. I need to print something out in the computer lab."

"Well, do you want to run over now before we eat?" He shrugged. "I don't mind. I'll go with you." His innocent gaze made me squirm a little inside.

"Nah, it's cool. I can do it later, but thanks." I smiled, wanting to change the subject from my mythical printing needs. "Hey, so how'd you do on Cooper's quiz this morning?"

He groaned. "I'm not sure, but I don't have a good feeling about it. I'll probably be lucky if I pulled a B."

"Yeah, me too." I frowned and picked up a tray as we entered the serving line.

Jeremy reached across me to grab some silverware. He set a handful on my tray before placing the other bundle on his own. "You're one of the smartest people I know. I can't imagine one history grade is going to affect your chances of getting into Columbia."

I selected a chicken wrap from the bin of assorted sandwiches, sniffed it, and plopped it on the center of my plastic tray.

"Maybe not, but it doesn't help when it comes to getting a scholarship. Plus, I have to fight twice as hard to get accepted, not having a daddy who's on the alumni committee."

He tipped his head grudgingly. "You'll still get in." He placed his hand on my shoulder. "You have all year to make up for a few bad quizzes." He smiled at me as he removed his hand to grab some red Jell-O. "And besides, that program you wrote for our computer class last year was totally unreal. I'm sure you can get a great recommendation from Mr. Moyer."

"Yeah, well, it doesn't help that I don't exactly rock the extracurricular arena." I gave an unladylike snort. "It's not like that stuff should even matter. I mean, who cares if you sang in chorus or scored twenty points in some game."

"I know, but it does. Why don't you just join something? What about the newspaper? You like to write."

"No thanks." I shook my head. After throwing an orange and a bottle of water on my tray, I turned and headed to our usual table by the last set of tall windows at the end of the room. We always ate with Abby, Pete, and Celia. Granted, they were really more Jeremy's friends, but they still pretty much accepted me and never brought up anything about my family.

I slid my tray onto the speckled tabletop and swung a

leg over the seat. "Hey guys."

Abby glanced up from a book and finished her last bite of pretzel before answering. "Oh hey, what's up?" Her short black hair had a chunky blue streak woven through on the left side, and her eyes were the coolest color I'd ever seen, a vivid jade green. I envied her quiet confidence. She didn't give a rat's ass what other people thought of her.

Pete and Celia both gave me a distracted wave from across the table. They each held index cards and silently mouthed words between exasperated sighs. They were going to discover the cure for cancer someday, of that I had no doubt. Their combined IQ probably rivaled mine, Jer's, and Abby's put together. They were obviously in the Gold section.

Jeremy twisted the cap open on his bottle of apple juice. "Did any of you guys hear who got tapped today so far?"

I glanced over, one eyebrow arched in surprise. "For the big secret club?"

Whispers flew each year about how only five to ten people were initiated for the Society each October, and pledges were always either juniors or seniors. Members never spoke out to confirm or deny the rumors. They all took some cross-my-heart-and-hope-to-die oath of secrecy.

Secret or not, everyone knew only the best of the best were invited to pledge — the athletes, brainiacs, or the crème de la crème of the beautiful crowd, all with the right address of course. Metaphorically speaking, I was so far away from having the correct zip code that I might as well be in another state.

It wasn't like Jeremy to care about stuff like that.

He nodded. A tiny piece of lettuce stuck to his lip as

he chewed his sandwich. I jerked my head away when he caught me staring at it. *What was wrong with me?* I couldn't help but notice the flash in his eyes before I'd looked away. He hadn't looked annoyed, he'd looked…surprised, but in a good way. I snuck another peek.

"Yeah." He swallowed, and wiped his mouth with the back of his hand. The lettuce disappeared. He offered me a small, private smile. "That starts this week, doesn't it?"

"Uh-huh." I forced myself back to the topic at hand. My eyes roamed the cafeteria, intent on finding their target.

Becky Farron sat alone in the corner, eating a yellow apple while hunched over a book. She wore a button-up white cardigan over her uniform shirt, and looked every bit what she was: sweet and studious. Although not technically a true geek, she was a whiz in chemistry, which didn't exactly endear her to the "it" crowd.

Next, I zeroed in on Patrick Shaw. Every grade had a class clown. We've got Patrick. Right now he stood, one foot propped on the bench at his table, arms gesturing wildly as he entertained the small group seated around him. Although fun, and generally well liked, he was a little too dorky to sit at the "right" lunch table.

Finally, my gaze landed on Zena Patel. She had this exotic beauty that guys tripped all over themselves to be near, while most of the girls at Trinity weren't nearly as entranced. Zena was a born seductress who didn't bow down to Jessica and her mean girl crowd, so even though her father owned his own practice as a renowned surgeon, spitefulness from the golden crew prevented Zena from truly fitting in.

Those three had no idea, but they were instrumental in what I'd planned to get back at Jessica. I pulled myself back to the conversation going on around me, hoping to get some helpful information.

"I know. Most of them apparently aren't talking. The big 'code of silence' or whatever." Abby made air quotes as she said it, then shrugged. "But I did hear someone whispering last period that Kara and Garret each got a note."

She wrinkled her nose, freckles scrunching together on her petite face. "I can't for the life of me figure out why *she'd* get one. I mean, I thought this was supposed to be some big time-honored tradition where they pick students who excel in something. What the heck does Kara excel in?"

Pete snorted, and looked up from the index card he held. "I'm sure plenty of guys on the football team can answer that one."

Everybody snickered. Even though Pete hung with us, the less than A-list crew, he also played on the football team. In reality, although he was a great kicker, he didn't really care about sports. But his dad did, so Pete played to keep him happy.

"I don't get why anyone even cares about some stupid secret society." Celia rolled her dark eyes. "I mean, seriously. What's the point?"

Pete cleared his throat, but didn't respond.

I shrugged. Easy for her to say, with her grades, she'd have plenty of colleges begging her to enroll. She didn't even need all the scholarship money that would undoubtedly be thrown her way. And cliques weren't something she cared about. She just didn't get it.

It didn't matter what anybody said, just about every high schooler craves validation in one way or another, and initiation into the Society screamed, "You matter, you're worthy!"

But the fact remained that most of the students who got asked to rush were complete jerks. Like Jessica. And her boyfriend, Blane.

Regardless of how important Rush week may seem, the following was the one that *really* mattered… Hell week. Each year during Hell week, initiates were instructed to complete certain tasks. Last year, Clay Rygert had to wear a suit and go around to all the houses in town handing out Bible tracts. Someone else had to swim laps in the bay for an hour straight. At night.

If any of the initiates didn't complete every task they'd been assigned, to the satisfaction of the hidden Society monitor watching them, they were out. No second chances. No excuses.

"Sam?"

Jeremy stood next to me, tray in hand. From his questioning look, I could tell it wasn't the first time he'd said my name.

I blinked. "What? Oh, sorry. I guess I wasn't paying attention." Somehow only minutes remained in lunch period. I'd been lost in my own head and hadn't even noticed. Most of my food sat untouched on the tray in front of me. I smiled to hide my embarrassment and jumped up.

"You okay? You've been acting kind of strange today." He waited for me to grab my tray and join him and Abby to walk over to the cafeteria dump station.

Abby glanced over at me curiously from where she stood on the other side of Jeremy.

"Huh? No, I'm fine." I shook my head.

When they didn't look convinced, I tacked on, "Honestly. Just dealing with some junk at home."

Jeremy held my gaze another heartbeat, but I forced myself to look away. We dumped the remains of our lunches in the giant rubber trashcans and deposited our silverware and trays in the appropriate section.

One of the lunch ladies stood behind the metal counter and pulled the items to be washed toward her before twisting to place them in separate racks in a huge dishwasher. Her hair was caught up in a black net, and her face looked tired and wrinkled before its time.

Fear slithered through my veins like a poison. That was what I had to look forward to—years and years of barely being noticed by the thankless rich surrounding me. Or if I *was* noticed, it would be as the butt of some joke.

I used to be happy, maybe not jumping up and down cheerleader happy, but not the shell of a person I'd become. I lifted my chin in resolve. Jessica would have her perfect little existence shattered. Her evil reign was over. Wrongs would be made right—it wouldn't just be the beautiful crowd gaining acceptance. This year's Hell week would be one that went down in the archives at Trinity Academy, I'd see to that.

*M*r. Moyer glanced my way as he walked around the classroom to monitor that we were all actually doing our work, and not hitting up Instagram or Tumblr or whatever. The fact that I'd been rather wildly waving my arm in the air for the past fifteen seconds probably made me a tad difficult to miss.

He sighed. "Yes, Ms. Evans? Did you have a question

about the assignment?"

"No. I was just wondering if I can use the restroom." I offered him my best pleading expression.

"Well, I'm sure you *can*."

I began to get up from my seat in the third row.

He held up a hand, halting me. "However, the more pertinent question would be if you *may* go to the restroom." He arched a bushy eyebrow.

Titters from two seats down on that one.

Jessica smirked at me as she twisted a tube of lip-gloss open.

I shot her a glare that would make lesser mortals shake in their ugly plaid skirts. She didn't even flinch. Instead, she pursed her pouty lips and applied more pink gloss, never breaking eye contact. Then she blew me a kiss. My jaw clenched, and I whipped her the finger with my eyes.

"Ms. Evans?" Mr. Moyer, oblivious to the teen girl drama going down right in front of his face, sounded a bit impatient. Although a decent teacher, Moyer definitely was a stickler for rules and proper language. You'd think the fact that I was acing his class would've earned me some brownie points…no such luck.

I cleared my throat and looked back at him, correcting my previous wording. "*May* I please use the restroom?"

I waited to leave my spot in front of my Mac until he'd granted me the right to go pee.

"Yes, you may." He nodded and turned to head back down the aisle.

I grabbed my messenger bag from the back of my chair and snatched up the big wooden pass marked "Ladies" off the small table next to the classroom door. Nerves caused me to glance around as I stepped into the hallway.

My footsteps echoed in the high, open corridor as I strode toward my destination, and it wasn't the girl's restroom. Empty halls yawned before me. Faint voices carried through as I passed each of the closed doors.

I jumped when a sudden burst of laughter came from room 217. My heartbeat sped up, and my sweaty palms clutched the straps of my bag more firmly against my chest. I swallowed and walked faster. I needed to make it over to the senior hallway before arousing Moyer's suspicion about why I'd been gone so long.

Right after I rounded the bend at the end of the hall, I stopped. The door to Ms. Simms's classroom stood uncharacteristically open. I needed to get to the lockers right across from her room.

Crap.

I slowly backed up a step, and leaned against the wall. Keeping my eyes peeled for anyone that might suddenly come around the corner, I tugged the front of my bag open and reached inside. The whole cloak-and-dagger part of the Society would enable my plan to succeed. A couple hours spent hacking into Jessica's email made it all worthwhile. I'd found it—the holy grail of Society secrets—the names of everyone they planned to tap this year. It was pretty much what I'd expected, with only one surprise. Pete was on the list. I wondered if he'd accept.

My suspicions had been correct, Jessica was in charge. Her emails to Bren had the link given out to each initiate, along with this year's password to access the site. I wasn't going to add my own name to the initiates' list, but I was going to add some other people. Jessica and the other members were in for a surprise.

I wouldn't do it on the Society's real page; they'd notice something like that. So instead, I added a hidden link on their site to a page I'd designed. My picks would access my buried site, get the tasks I'd assigned, and only after that would I add their names to the real list...along with an anonymous note about what I'd done.

And once it was all over, and my initiates completed their tasks, the Society wouldn't be able to revoke their standing without exposing themselves and the fact that an outsider—me—had managed to hack their way in. I was pretty sure Jessica wouldn't want to take that kind of heat.

It'd taken some thinking to decide exactly who to invite to rush. I'd gone through the plan over and over to make sure the people I tapped wouldn't be hurt at all. Only Jessica would reap my own particular version of hell.

Textured paper met my searching hand, and I drew the first note from my bag. I quickly smoothed the tiny wrinkles out the best I could against the wall. With one final, determined glance, I strode across the hall to the long row of yellow lockers numbered 401-435.

When I reached the fifth locker from the left, I allowed my hair to fall forward in an attempt to shield my face. Hopefully no one would recognize me if they happened to look my way. I reached out and pretended to spin the combination lock.

A quick peek assured me I was still in the clear.

I darted my hand out to shove the envelope through the top slat in the locker next to the one I'd been messing with. If anyone saw me, hopefully I'd be identified as screwing with Jessica's locker—totally believable, rather than thinking I might be slipping something into Becky's.

Becky was the kind of girl who'd probably had a lemonade stand as a kid and pulled her teddy bear along behind her in a little red wagon as she'd walked to the library. She volunteered for our school's mentoring program as well as the local animal shelter and deserved to be a member of the Society, especially since I knew things were tough for her at home after her mom died in a car accident two years ago.

Bottom line, Becky was *nice*. But unfortunately for her, average, nice girls were pretty much invisible in high school. The vipers were the ones who got noticed. I'd be willing to bet anything that deep inside Becky prayed to be invited to rush. In fact, I counted on it.

The deed completed, pseudo-invitation delivered, I nonchalantly turned and headed back to Computer Science. I'd handle the other two notes in the morning.

I smiled and hummed a little Violent Femmes as I made my way back to class.

five

She wanted to ask him why they were all strangers who shared the same last name.
—Chimamanda Ngozi Adichie

School finally over, I stumbled wearily up the steps to my aunt's place. The pungent odor of fried liver and onions slammed into my face the second I opened the front door, and my stomach rolled in protest. How in God's name Aunt Lor willingly ate a cow's organ was beyond me.

I covered my nose as I walked closer to the stove, where Aunt Loretta hummed a slightly out of key version of Sinatra. As I approached, still gagging, she turned to face me. She shook her head at my expression.

"So how was school today, Samantha? I thought you'd be staying after for your photography club." Her face wrinkled in an encouraging smile.

I bit my lip. I'd sort of been less than honest with her. I'd figured pretending to join some school club would serve the dual purpose of allowing Aunt Lor to believe I was well-adjusted, while giving me some time away on my own. Win-win. Despite my justifications, lying to her made my stomach twinge.

I smiled weakly. "Nah, not today." I reached over and grabbed a shiny red apple from a wooden bowl on the counter. I rubbed it against my shirt for a few seconds before taking a large bite.

Aunt Loretta paused from her task of stirring and eyeballed me patiently.

I spoke through a mouthful of apple. "We had another history quiz. Freaking teacher is an ass."

"*Samantha*, language." She *tsk-tsked* at me, lips slightly pursed, then reached across the giant green stove to turn the burner to low.

I rolled my eyes a little, but muttered, "Sorry." I leaned my hip against the kitchen table and took another bite, watching my aunt as I chewed. She sprinkled salt and pepper in the cast-iron pan, then covered it to keep warm for later.

When she turned, I knew all was forgiven just by her smile. She took several steps toward me and brushed a stray piece of hair back from my face. "You remind me so much of your father sometimes." The chagrined look that immediately crossed her face told me she regretted the statement as soon as she'd uttered the words.

It didn't matter. My father ruined my life. He was a self-absorbed jerk who didn't care enough about his family to not give in to the lure of quick money. Like we didn't have enough before he went all Wall Street on us.

I jerked my head away from her outstretched hand. "I have homework to do." I pushed away from the table and tossed the half-eaten apple into the trashcan as I escaped to my room.

"Samantha, wait. Please. I just meant—"

"It's fine."

My stomach tightened as I pushed images of my father from my head, images of him shackled, wearing an orange jumpsuit. Older images of him laughing and pushing me on a wooden swing when I was little. I didn't want any memories of him at all.

I locked my bedroom door behind me and crossed to kneel by the bed. My hand snaked under the mattress for the spiral-bound notebook I'd hidden there the night before. When my fingers made contact with the smooth surface, I pulled it out and sat cross-legged on my unmade bed. Resolve built as I stared across the room.

Dark paneling covered the walls. An old poster peeled off the wall in one corner where I'd haphazardly taped it, while index cards with hand-written quotes filled the large bulletin board above my small desk. That was about all I'd done in the form of decorating the tiny space. It wasn't really my home. I no longer had a real home.

I'd barely even known Aunt Loretta before my mother dumped me off, explaining she needed some time for herself. Before that, I'd always gotten the feeling my parents were ashamed to have family living in some trailer park outside of town. Kind of ironic since Aunt Lor had shown me more kindness than either of my parents had in the past several years. And as much as I hated to admit it, that hurt, a lot.

To make things worse, lately I worried about her. Aunt Lor suffered from some weird form of dementia brought on by her thyroid. She'd been given medication to control it, but that only worked if she took it, and sometimes she forgot.

I sighed and slapped the notebook open on my lap to study the words scrawled on the first lined page.

Take her down.
Threaten? HOW??!!!
KEEP IT SECRET!!

My heart rate slowed back to normal as I turned the pages. The knowledge that I held the power to serve my own brand of justice calmed me. The last few pages contained a carefully laid-out plan. I unbuttoned my sweater as my eyes drank in each word. Tomorrow I would deliver the final two notes. After that came the simple matter of instructing my "initiates" to complete my bidding.

My lips curled into a half-smile as I leaned back and held the notebook against my chest, caressing it like a lover. Score one for Team Sam.

six

It's not a terrible thing that we feel fear when faced with the unknown. It is part of being alive, something we all share.
—Pema Chödrön

The next thing I knew, my eyes opened to darkness. I must have fallen asleep. The orange numbers on the alarm clock next to my bed read 7:32. My stomach grumbled about missing dinner, but memory of what was on the menu helped to quiet it.

I slid my legs over the side of the bed, and shifted the notebook to the pile of covers next to me. I cocked my head, listening, except there wasn't anything to hear. No familiar television sounds carried down the hall. The house rang silent. Too silent.

I pushed up from the mattress and walked to my door. As I reached for the knob, guilt engulfed me about how I'd treated Aunt Loretta. I paused, chewing on my dry lip.

The fact that she didn't try to wake me for dinner meant I'd really hurt her feelings. Mealtime was big for her; she always insisted we sit down and eat dinner together. It was her way of trying to make a shitty situation seem more normal.

I sighed and opened the door.

Inky darkness filled the hallway.

"Aunt Loretta?" I called softly, hesitantly.

No response.

I took a few steps and fumbled along the wall for a light switch.

"Aunt Lor?" My voice, a little louder this time, sounded strange in the empty darkness. I swallowed, suddenly nervous.

Prickles of fear raced along my hairline. Some inner voice taunted me, echoing all my worst fears. *Why would she put up with you and stay? No one else cared enough to stay.*

"Aunt Loretta! Are you home?"

I commanded my feet to move. My chin jutted out in resolve as I walked through the thin corridor that led to the living room. I closed my eyes for a few seconds and took a deep breath before making the turn.

Pale artificial light seeped through the slatted blinds above the sofa. She wasn't there.

I pivoted and headed back toward her bedroom. She never went to bed this early, but maybe she wasn't feeling well or something.

The door to her room stood ajar. I reached in and flipped on the bedroom light. She wasn't there either. I looked around, half expecting to see her old round hairbrush gone from the dresser, her closets open and empty.

But everything remained right where it belonged. Her antique brush set next to the bottle of lotion she used each night, the one that smelled faintly of roses. Her faded robe folded neatly at the bottom of the bed, waiting for her to slip into it.

A breath of relief whooshed from my lungs. She hadn't

gotten sick of me and taken off. But then where was she? She never drove at night; it terrified her. Her ritual was dinner, then dishes, then reading or television until bedtime at nine exactly. I could set my watch by her routine.

I turned and jogged back out to the kitchen.

Horrible scenarios stuck in my head like taffy, dark and thick. What if something happened to her? What if she'd gone outside earlier and fallen and had a heart attack or broken something like you heard about all the time in the news?

"Aunt Lor! Where are you?"

I skidded across the beat-up kitchen linoleum and smacked open the screen door to check outside. About fifteen feet away, the bulb atop a metal lamppost cast a lazy circle of light around the dead grass in front of the trailer.

The neighbor's dog yapped at me like crazy. I ran down the porch steps, ignoring him. Aunt Loretta's Buick was parked in the small driveway, so she hadn't gone somewhere. Any tiny hope of her making an emergency run to the market for milk or coffee disappeared at the sight of her empty gray car.

It seemed like I should call someone, but who? The police? An ambulance?

I turned in circles, feeling helpless. There was no one for me to call. I had no other family. I was all alone. My breath came out in choked gasps.

I needed to calm down, to think rationally. I shoved hair back from my face with both hands and closed my eyes, forcing myself to breathe slowly. *In through the nose, out through the mouth. In through the nose, out through the mouth.*

After about ten seconds, my breathing normalized, and

my lungs no longer felt like they weren't getting enough air. My throat burned like it always did when I fought not to cry.

Maybe she'd gone over to the neighbor's for some reason.

I turned and strode over to Martha's bright yellow trailer. My sneakers made smacking sounds on the concrete walkway with each step.

A large wreath made out of large very plastic-y looking flowers covered the center of her door. A light burned in the far left window. I reached out and knocked between an especially obnoxious orange daisy and a hot pink rose.

The noise sent the freaking dog into fits. It bounced around from a thin chain attached to a small stake in the yard. The high-pitched yapping shredded the last of my already frayed nerves.

I knocked again, louder this time, to be heard over the howling. Another light appeared through a window, closer this time. A thin voice called out, "My lands, I'm coming. I'm coming."

I recognized the sound of a chain sliding through a lock before the door opened a few inches. I could barely make out the face squinting through the narrow opening.

"Samantha? My lord, child. What are you doing here at this hour?"

At this hour? It wasn't even eight o'clock at night.

"My aunt. Have you seen my aunt?"

Martha pulled the door open wider and fussed the top of her housecoat together with small, wrinkled fingers. "Loretta? No, I haven't seen her since this morning. Is everything okay?" She stuck her head out the door, turning it left and right like she expected my aunt to pop out of the bushes any second.

"No. Yes." I shook my head. If she hadn't seen Aunt Loretta, I didn't want to waste my time explaining. "I'm sure everything's fine." I turned back down the rose-lined walkway.

"Oh dear. Is there anything I can do?" she called after me. "I hope this isn't one of the things you hear about where hooligans come and snatch you from your home!"

I ignored her, not having the time or patience for her theories on geriatric kidnappings.

Maybe Aunt Lor had left me a note and I'd missed it. I rushed back to the trailer, vaulting the three porch steps in one giant leap. When I entered the kitchen, my eyes roamed over each available surface.

Nothing. There was no note.

I sank into one of the vinyl-padded chairs at the kitchen table, and buried my head in my hands. Now what?

A familiar ringing sounded down the hall. Maybe she was trying to call me. She didn't have a cell phone, thought they were ridiculous, but I raced to my bedroom anyway.

"Hello?" I answered, out of breath and anxious.

"Sam? You okay?"

I exhaled in disappointment.

"Hello? You there?" Jeremy's deep voice held concern.

"Hey, Jer. Sorry, I'm here."

A heartbeat passed before he spoke again. "What's wrong?"

Suddenly exhausted, I sank to the floor next to my bed and leaned my head back against the mattress. I closed my eyes and gripped the phone tighter against my cheek.

"It's my aunt. She's not here. I woke up and she was gone." I whispered the words, afraid if I said them too loud something terrible would happen. I couldn't bear to lose her, too.

I paused, feeling kind of stupid for admitting how worried I was. After all, she was an adult; there was probably no reason to be acting like a scared two-year-old about it.

But knowing that in my head didn't change how I felt in my gut. *What if she'd forgotten to take her meds?*

"I'm sure she's okay."

He meant well. I rubbed my eyes and said nothing.

"You still there?"

"Yeah, I'm here." My voice turned quiet, defeated.

"I'm coming over."

A rustling noise accompanied his quick words and when he next spoke, his voice sounded muffled. "I'll be there in twenty minutes."

I sat up straighter. "Jer, you don't have to."

I heard the jangle of keys and footsteps on hardwood. "Look, I'm sure everything's fine, but I'll stay with you until she gets back."

"Honestly, I'm—"

"Yeah, I know. You're fine. You're always fine." A car door opened and closed. A brief squeak of weight on leather, then the *ding, ding, ding* of Jeremy's fasten seat belt alert carried through the phone.

"Sam, you don't always have to pretend to be so strong, you know."

I didn't know what to say to that.

"I'll be there soon," he promised.

I opened my mouth to argue, but he'd already hung up.

seven

All things appear and disappear because of the concurrence of causes and conditions. Nothing ever exists entirely alone; everything is in relationship to everything else.
—Gautama Buddha

"So do you have any idea at all where she might have gone?" Jeremy sat next to me on the crumbling brick porch step. The pitch-black sky matched my mood perfectly.

I shook my head. "No. Like I said, she never goes out this late." I shivered in the evening air.

Jeremy leaned back a little to face me. "Here." He reached across his chest to pull the gray hoodie up to take it off. For some odd reason, I found myself staring when the movement pulled his T-shirt up as well. His chest and stomach were muscled and still a bit tan, with a smattering of dark hair forming a *T* shape leading toward his...

I jerked my eyes away from where they had no business looking and moved to safer territory. It had to be the stress messing with my head.

His hair was a tousled mess, even more so than usual,

after he finished tugging the fleece over his head. He readjusted his glasses since they'd tilted off to the side of his nose from his undressing. Well, not undressing of course, just taking off a sweatshirt. Which was nothing. Something I'd seen him do a million times over the years.

What in the world was wrong with me? My aunt missing and there I sat acting like it wasn't my *very* familiar best friend sitting next to me, the same one who I'd seen pick his nose as a little kid, burp, fart, and all other types of disgusting actions.

I scooted a few inches away from him, needing some breathing room.

"Don't you want it?"

What?

"Sam?" He eyed me curiously, "I thought you'd want it."

My mouth opened and closed, but nothing came out.

He wrinkled his face in confusion. "Here." He wiggled the sweatshirt at me.

The sweatshirt. Of course he meant the sweatshirt. What else would he mean?

"Oh, uh, yeah, sure…thanks." I smiled weakly and reached out to accept it before pulling it over my head as fast as I could, praying the material and the darkness hid the rising flush in my cheeks.

Sure, I'd noticed girls at school ogling him now and then, but things had never been like that with us. I tried to convince myself they weren't now. Although a tiny rebellious piece of me couldn't help but whisper, *are you sure?*

Lately I'd noticed times his touch lasted just seconds longer than strictly necessary, or caught him studying me when he thought I wasn't looking. I'd blown it off, told myself I was imagining things. But now, I wondered…was I really? Did I want to be imagining things?

As I pulled the welcome softness down around me, it smelled like him, like clean soap and guy magically rolled together. After my head popped through, I caught Jeremy watching me, and the expression on his face made me catch my breath. He blinked, looked down at his shoes, and the moment was gone.

I pushed any unwelcome thoughts of what Jeremy and his stupid sweatshirt smelled like out of my mind. There were much bigger things to worry about at the moment. Like the fact that I had no idea what happened to my aunt. It had to be my anxiety suddenly turning me batshit crazy. I cleared my throat.

"So, what do you think I should do? Should I call the police?" I lifted my head to look him in the eyes.

He shook his head. "I don't think so. Not yet anyway." He shrugged. "To be honest, I don't think they'd even do anything at this point. She hasn't been gone long enough. They'll probably just blow it off like you're overreacting."

My chin jerked up. "I am *not* overreacting, Jeremy!"

"I know, I know. I didn't mean *I* thought you were, I was just saying what the cops would probably say." He reached out and took my hand, weaving our fingers together and setting our joined hands on his jean-clad thigh. "We'll find her, Sam." He squeezed my hand. "I promise."

I closed my eyes until the tears receded. I didn't want him to see me cry…I never let *anyone* see me cry. Hadn't for years.

"C'mere." Jeremy reached out his other arm and wrapped it around my shoulder, pulling me against him. I resisted, not wanting to give in to his kindness. *"C'mere,"* he repeated, a hint of teasing in his voice, not taking my unspoken *no* for an answer.

So I gave in. I let him pull me into his strong warmth, and tucked my head against his shoulder under his chin. It fit perfectly. Like always. Tingles rushed through me at the contact.

He stroked my hair with comforting movements. "Shh," he whispered. "It'll be okay. Everything will be okay. You'll see."

We sat that way, not speaking, for about fifteen minutes. My body finally started to relax, and I allowed myself to believe he might be right. Things would be okay. Aunt Lor would call, or come home soon, and we'd laugh about how worried I'd been for no reason.

Flashing blue and red lights appeared, turning from Sauderton Road into the dirt lane leading to Shady Oak Court. Police lights. There were no sirens, but it didn't matter. I knew it was about my aunt, and that they were there to see me.

I fought the urge to throw up. I stood up on shaky legs as I watched the police car drive closer and closer. Jeremy stood as well, never letting go of my hand. An odd buzzing sounded in my ears, and air fought to fill my lungs.

The cruiser finally halted about ten feet in front of us. The lights still spun circles of *red, blue, red, blue,* around the yard.

All breathing stopped as the car door opened, and a tall officer stepped out of the squad car and removed his hat, asking, "Are you Miss Samantha Evans?"

The buzzing in my ears turned into a dull roar, and I passed out.

"*S*am. *Sam*, can you hear me?" Jeremy's voice sounded far away.

A hand brushed the hair back from my forehead, and when I opened my eyes, Jeremy's face hovered inches from my own. His eyes, a kaleidoscope of green and brown, looked scared, and his throat jerked as he swallowed, watching me intently.

"Thank God. Are you okay?"

Part of me wanted to stay there, not moving, for a few more seconds. Until I remembered.

The police. Aunt Lor.

I jerked up so quickly that I smacked foreheads with him. He tipped over backward and fell off the side of the step.

"I'm sorry. I…" My gaze jerked away from where he'd landed on the ground rubbing his head to the scene to my right.

The police officer stood over by his car, leaning in through the open door and talking on his radio. "Correct. Shady…" He broke off when he saw me striding toward him. "You can cancel that. I'll let you know if we still need you to send one out, but I think we're good here." He bent and returned the radio inside the cruiser.

"Where's my aunt? What's going on?"

"Just please calm down, Ms. Evans."

I didn't give him time to finish. I slapped the hood of the police car. Hard. "Would you please just tell me what's going on?"

He pressed his lips together. "Ms. Evans, I understand you're upset, but I'll have to ask you to please try to control yourself."

"Control myself? *Control myself?*" I shook. "You're standing there like a giant goon not telling me anything!" I waved wildly and took a step closer to him.

Firm arms wrapped around me from behind.

"Sam, it's okay. Calm down." Jeremy's voice worked its way into my addled brain...quiet, soothing.

I froze. My body sagged in Jeremy's arms as I gave up the fight.

The cop adjusted his belt, and motioned with his head toward the steps. "Would you like to sit down and we can talk?"

I nodded, suddenly unable to form a simple, *yes.*

Jeremy rubbed his hands along my upper arms briefly, leaning in to whisper, "C'mon." He reached down and took my trembling hand to lead me to the steps once more.

Once Jeremy and I were seated, the policeman knelt down to our eye level.

"My name is Officer Daniels. I'm with the county sheriff's office. We were called about two hours ago by a woman a few streets over."

My heartbeat accelerated. He must have seen the fear in my eyes, because he held up a hand as though to stop my thoughts from racing into the terrifying unknown.

"Your aunt is fine."

The tightness in my chest let up some. "I don't understand. Where is she? Why were you called then?"

Officer Daniels rocked on his heels and glanced briefly at Jeremy.

I whipped my head toward Jeremy in confusion before zooming back in on the policeman. "Would you please just tell me what's going on?" I repeated in a whisper.

"Your aunt was found wandering around in the caller's yard. She seemed confused and wasn't immediately able to give her name, or tell us where she lived."

The blood drained from my face. "That's impossible."

Jeremy squeezed my hand gently.

Officer Daniels shook his head. "I'm sorry. We had her transported to the Good Samaritan Hospital for evaluation."

"She's…she's in the hospital?" I couldn't completely process what he was saying. "Is she okay?"

"I can't answer that." He shook his head again. "I can tell you that after she arrived in the emergency room, she seemed to come around. She was more cognizant and able to tell the doctors who she was. And she was worried about you." His eyes gentled. "She was adamant that she needed to come home to be here with you, but the doctors felt it would be better for her to stay overnight for observation."

"But why can't she come home if she's okay now? Why didn't she call me?" I threw questions at him like bricks.

"The last I heard, she was still in the ER getting some testing done. We let her know we'd come by and make sure you knew what was happening." He winced and rubbed his knee before standing up. "Do you have somewhere you can go for the night so you aren't alone?"

I couldn't even think straight. Go for the night? What if Aunt Lor wasn't all right? What if taking care of me had made her sick?

He stood patiently, waiting for me to answer.

When I said nothing, Jeremy spoke up. "She can stay with me tonight. With my family."

Officer Daniels seemed relieved. He tapped his hat against his leg. "Okay then. If there's anything else I can do, call the station." He adjusted his hat back into position on his head.

I nodded dumbly.

Jeremy obviously felt the need to extend pleasant courtesies. "Thank you, officer."

Daniels nodded briefly, and headed toward his car.

Crickets chirped around us like it was any other night. Didn't they realize everything was different now? For some reason, it was even more difficult than the day my mother left. "She'll be fine, Sam. I know it." Jeremy's voice broke the silence.

I didn't answer him.

"You can come stay at my house tonight. I'm sure my parents won't mind."

When I still said nothing, he stood and tugged my arm gently, pulling me up next to him. "Let's get your stuff."

He led me inside, not saying anything more, somehow understanding I wasn't ready to talk.

I walked through the living room and turned down the narrow hall to my room. As I passed Aunt Lor's bedroom, I paused. Tears threatened, but I pushed them down and kept going. Once I reached my bedroom, I dug in the bottom of my closet for an old duffel bag and threw some clothes inside, not caring what I grabbed.

Jeremy sat on my bed, watching me for a few minutes.

"Can I help?" he asked.

"No. Thanks, I'm fine." Nothing could have been further from the truth. I zipped up the bag and looked around. The notebook I'd fallen asleep holding earlier lay on the bed next to him. I walked over and grabbed it. I couldn't even think about the plan right now, but I didn't want to just leave it out in the open.

He eyed it curiously. "What's that?"

"Nothing. Poetry," I lied. I grabbed my backpack from the floor and shoved it inside.

"Okay." He looked around the room. "Well, you ready to go?"

I nodded.

He stood and walked over to me. "Here, let me take that." He reached for my duffel bag. My first instinct was to refuse, to tell him I could carry it myself, but I could see he wanted to help. "Thanks." I handed it over, smiling halfheartedly.

We headed out of the room together.

"Do you think they'll let me see her?" I asked quietly.

"I don't know. Visiting hours might be over by now. But we can call and check."

I nodded again and followed him out the front door. I'd never appreciated the little home Aunt Loretta had made for me more than I did as the door clicked shut firmly behind us.

eight

Remember all the times we had together?
What happened to best friends forever?
—Unknown

"Y ou sure your parents don't mind me staying here tonight? I'm fine staying at my own place." I wasn't but couldn't bring myself to admit it.

"For the last time, it's fine; you shouldn't be alone right now. Besides, Mom and Dad kind of think of you as family anyway."

He threw a heavy sleeping bag on the hardwood floor next to his bed and unrolled it. "And besides, you used to sleep over all the time."

Yeah. When we were in grade school.

But in reality, his parents wouldn't care; they were pretty laid back. I shuffled my feet and glanced around before settling on the edge of his bed.

Jeremy's room fit him. A wild mash-up of IKEA and Comic-Con. Movie posters covered the hunter green walls. A curved black lamp sat on top of his wide computer desk, which held books stacked in one corner and a TARDIS on the other. Jeremy made it easy to bust on his geekiness, considering his one-sided bromance with *Doctor Who*.

It seemed kind of crappy kicking him out of his
but no way would we share it. Obviously. Because that wou..
be weird. I pushed down the curiosity of what it would be
like to fall asleep next to him.

"So…" I chewed on my lip and nodded my head for
absolutely no reason. "I can take the floor. Really, I don't
want to put you out."

He rolled his eyes. "Don't be stupid. I'm not going to let
you sleep on the floor." He laughed and plopped down next
to me on his double bed. I inched away the tiniest amount,
hyperaware of how close he was. He eyeballed me but said
nothing. Restless, I flopped backward and clasped my hands
behind my head as I stared at his ceiling. A few seconds
later, he followed suit.

"I'm sorry we couldn't go see your aunt," he whispered.
He turned to face me, so close that his warm breath caressed
my cheek along with his words. "But we'll definitely go
tomorrow after school when the hospital has visiting hours
again."

A single tear escaped. I angled my face farther away
from him so he couldn't see my body's betrayal of my hard-
fought stoic front. My strategy to appear invincible didn't
work. He inched a little closer, and I sensed him looking
down at me, even though I'd merely felt the bed shift when
he'd propped up a little on his elbow.

With achingly slow movements, he brushed away one of
the tears I tried to hide. I rolled farther away from his touch,
turned to face the wall, and said nothing in reply. After all,
what was there to say?

Jeremy exhaled behind me. Probably frustrated that
I wouldn't open up and do the expected sharing of my

feelings bit. Especially given we could usually tell each other anything. But I couldn't...my feelings were too raw, and to be honest, I didn't want to face them.

After about ten minutes, his breathing became deeper, more regular. I peeked over and saw his face inches from my own. He'd removed his glasses. His eyes were closed, long dark lashes fanning his olive complexion. I studied him, and fought the urge to stroke his hair back where it fell into his eyes. Growing up, why hadn't I ever really noticed how good-looking Jeremy was?

Probably because for years, before I'd moved in with Aunt Loretta, he'd just been the boy down the street who I'd known forever. He'd been this combination of best friend slash brother to me for so long, it hadn't even occurred to me to look at him any other way. Until lately, when I constantly caught myself staring at him a little too long or wondered what he really thought of me.

My mind flashed back to a much younger Jeremy, when we were about seven years old. I smiled, remembering. Even back then, he'd had the most gorgeous eyes I'd ever seen and a heart to go with them. He'd stood before me in my backyard, one hand clasped shyly behind his back, shifting his weight from one leg to the other. One knee sticking out of his denim shorts sported a large scab, a badge of honor from rolling it on his bike the week before.

"Here." He'd pushed a handful of flowers, mostly pretty weeds really, toward me with a bashful smile. I'd reached out to accept his gift, the first I'd ever received from a boy. Then, he'd leaned in, and plopped a quick, awkward kiss on my lips. I remembered my heart jolting, my eyes widening, before he'd turned and raced down the street, waving goodbye, his crooked grin wide.

He was part of every good thing that had ever happened to me. Unlike so many other people I knew, the years hadn't pulled us apart. He'd sometimes come over and we'd watch Jeopardy together. He usually beat me in calling out the answers. I'd made it a rule never to play Trivial Pursuit with him after being soundly trounced no less than a dozen times in a row. So we played chess instead. We were about fifty-fifty for that one.

I'd go to his house for dinner at least once a week; sometimes we'd even cook together. Jeremy was an amazing cook, always trying new recipes. I'd told him more than once that he should think about going to culinary school somewhere after we graduated. I kind of hoped he'd go the Culinary Academy in New York if he did…so we could at least still be in the same state after graduation.

I remembered a food fight we'd had about a year ago in his kitchen. Pasta had ended up clinging to the cabinets. His mother hadn't been nearly as amused as we were when she'd walked in and found us, sauce and noodles everywhere. I chuckled a little at the memory.

His eyes opened. I immediately looked away, feeling stupid to be caught checking him out.

"What are you doing?" His voice held that raspy, sleepy quality.

"What? Nothing." I jumped up. In my hurry, I reached out both hands to push myself off the bed, and one of them made contact with Jeremy's thigh. His *upper* thigh. He glanced down to where my hand had just been then looked up at me.

The need to bolt out of the door became overpowering. I

bit my lip and swallowed. He didn't blink, but instead stared at me so intently, it was like he was trying to read my soul. I cleared my throat.

"Ah…sorry about that."

His lips twitched. "Not a problem."

Omigod. I wanted to crawl under his bed and hide.

"I didn't do it on purpose."

The lip twitching turned into a full-on grin. "Sam, if you wanted to share the bed, all you had to do was ask."

I stared.

He laughed. "Oh, come on. I'm just teasing you." He poked me in the arm.

I smiled weakly.

Still embarrassed, I cleared my throat and walked over to where I'd thrown my duffel. "I have homework to do." I opened the bag and pulled things out, rooting for my English book. Not like I'd really be able to concentrate on *Hamlet*, but Jeremy didn't have to know that.

I grabbed the dog-eared paperback and sat down at his desk. It helped that I could no longer see him. Hopefully by tomorrow all of the stupid would be gone from my system, and Jeremy and I would be back to business as usual. Best friends. Nothing more.

After a few minutes of pretending to read, I relaxed enough to start comprehending the words on the page in front of me. I rested my head against my hand as I absorbed the flow and imagery of the prose. The old-fashioned language was beautiful in its oddity. I wished I were like that.

The bed squeaked, and rustling pages carried my way. I read quietly a few more minutes.

"What the hell is this?" His shocked voice startled me.

I glanced over my shoulder.

Jeremy sat up straight on the bed, my spiral notebook open on his lap. I spun around and jumped up so quickly that I tripped on the chair legs and almost went flying. I dove toward him.

"What do you think you're doing? That's private!" I reached over to grab the notebook away from him, but he moved faster.

He strode over to his bedroom door and shut it, then turned back to me, holding the notebook out like it was something dirty.

"It was on the bed. I thought it was your poetry, which you always let me read." He shook his head, face still in shock. "Sam, what is this?"

I knew I wouldn't be able to wrestle the notebook from him without making noise that might attract his parents' attention. So instead I sat on the bed, arms crossed in front of me, glaring. I didn't say a word. I didn't owe him an explanation, and obviously he wouldn't understand given his horrified reaction.

He wagged the notebook at me. "Are you seriously planning to do this?" He took a step toward me. "Please tell me you aren't."

I closed my eyes for a moment, trying to decide how much to tell him. I hadn't wanted him to be involved. When I opened my eyes, he stood stock-still a few feet away from me. The notebook was lowered now, resting against his thigh. I raised my eyes to meet his. Instead of the judgment I thought I'd seen moments ago, I saw concern.

I sighed. "It's nothing. Please give it back." My hand reached out, and my eyes begged him to do it. Instead, he rolled it in half and stuck it behind his back into the waistband of his jeans.

"Not until you tell me what's going on." His jaw set, and I recognized the look in his eyes. Jeremy could be stubborn when he wanted.

"Fine. I'll tell you."

He raised an eyebrow, waiting. He was smart enough not to move closer, probably figuring I'd have no qualms about going for the notebook, down his pants or not.

I exhaled a deep breath. "I'm sick of it, Jer. I'm sick of how Jessica *constantly* feels the need to humiliate me in public. It's always something." I paused.

He watched me, listening, not saying a word.

I shook my head. "You don't know what it's like. I mean, ever since my dad went to prison, it's been hell at school every single day. It's like she forgets that *she* was the one who eavesdropped on my dad's phone calls to report back to her father, and helped *put* my dad there. Do you know she never once even apologized? We were supposed to be *best friends* and she did that to me. Did that to my family!"

I brushed an angry tear away.

His expression softened a little, but he still didn't make a move toward me.

"She won't let it go. I mean, I get that she blames my dad for her parents' divorce, but that wasn't my fault. And at least she still gets to see both of her parents. They're both still in town." I paused. "It's like it's her life's goal to make sure I know I don't belong. To make sure everyone knows I'm trash. That I'm nothing but the daughter of some convict."

My voice got louder. "But you know what? *I know that.* I *live* it. I've lost everything that matters."

He never broke eye contact, and when he answered, his voice was gentle. "You haven't lost me."

But I didn't want gentle. I didn't want soothing. I needed him angry *for* me…to agree with me. I jumped up and stalked toward him. His hands moved behind his back as though to block any sudden movements on my part. But by now, I didn't care about the stupid notebook.

"No, you're right. I didn't lose you, and I'm grateful for that." My face twisted, and my eyebrows narrowed. "But how does that help me with all the rest of the crap I have to face every day, huh?" I poked him in the chest, hard.

"How does that stop Jessica from painting bars on my locker, and making freaking signs with my face on them and hanging her clever artwork all over the school, or from her and her minions calling me names constantly?" My voice heated as I stood inches away from him, feet planted in a wide stance. "It *doesn't*, Jeremy."

My hands clenched at my sides, and the familiar burn of bitterness and anger began to pump through my veins, fueling me. I hated that I was launching it at Jeremy, but it felt like I was breaking inside…and needed to let everything out before I burned up into nothing.

"Sam, you just have to—"

"If you tell me I just have to ignore her, I swear to God I'll scream."

His mouth snapped closed.

"I've tried ignoring her. I've tried being nice to her. I've tried telling her off." I shoved the hair back from my forehead in frustration. "Don't you get it? Nothing I do changes anything. *Nothing*." I spit out. I turned and stepped away before whirling back to face him.

"But that?" I pointed behind his back. "*That* will change things. It'll make her pay for all the shitty things she's done to me."

I looked directly at him, my gaze pleading for him to understand. "And not just to me. Think of everyone else she treats this way. For once, Jess will know what it's like to be on the other end. To not be the one in charge." My heart thundered in my chest.

He shook his head. "But Jesus, Sam, I only got through the first couple of pages, and some of the stuff you wrote in there that you plan to do next week…"

He paused, and his face hardened a bit as he held up a hand. "No, wait, I stand corrected. That you plan to have *other people* do to get some stupid revenge on Jessica." He stepped toward me. "Don't you get it? If you do this, you're no better than she is."

For a second I wondered if maybe he was right. Then I remembered the note I'd already placed in Becky's locker, and knew it was too late to stop now even if I wanted to. But more than that, I knew that people like Becky and Zena and even Patrick deserved a chance for all the Society offered too. Even if Jessica and her crew didn't agree.

Righteous anger flared. "So what? Why do I always have to take the high road?"

He stepped closer, reaching out to touch my sleeve. "Because it's who you are. You *are* better than this, I know it. Because I know *you*."

I yanked away. "That's where you're wrong." I shook my head. "No, Jer. I'm not. Like it or not, this is *exactly* who I am."

"But some of this, my God…this isn't put-a-picture-on-

Instagram crap. This is…"

"I'm aware of what it is, Jeremy."

His face fell and he shook his head in protest, but I ignored him.

Part of me wished I were brave enough to speak the words I really wanted to say…to beg him to understand, to plead with him to stand by me. To not leave like everyone else in my life. But I'm not brave, and I didn't do any of that.

He reached behind his back to pull the notebook out of his waistband and held it tight by his side. His eyes never left mine.

"And what about the people you're using?" He pinched the bridge of his nose, his voice tired.

"I'm not using anyone!"

He shook his head. "Yeah, you are. You're using them as pawns to get your revenge."

"And I'm helping each of them in the process," I argued. "And besides, it isn't like anyone is going to get hurt. So I mess with Jessica and some of the others in the Society a little. I'd say that's a small price to pay for showing them that they can't just steamroll over everyone and call all the shots. It's not fair."

"And what if it doesn't all go down the way you hope? What if they do all of that, and the Society still doesn't let them in?"

"They will."

"And if they don't? Becky, Zena, Patrick. How do you justify hurting *them*?"

I snatched the notebook from him. "There are always casualties in war." I refused to let anyone, even him, see any sign of weakness, of the doubts racing through me.

"Sam, you could get in trouble if you get caught doing this. You have to realize that."

"I covered my tracks; I'm not going to get caught. Sometimes you have to be willing to stand up and do what's right, even if the methods aren't perfect."

He nodded. "Sure. Of course. That makes sense." He paused, eyebrows furrowed in concentration. "I get it now."

"Really?" Hope built that he was on my side after all.

"*No!* Not really!" he shouted and shook his head. "Are you fucking *insane*?"

"Why'd you want me to tell you about it if this was gonna be your reaction?"

He sat, silent a moment, gazing deep into my eyes before slowly answering. "For the same reason why you decided to tell me." He stopped and bit his lip. "You knew what I'd say. Because deep down somewhere, you *know* this is wrong."

"No, Jer. I don't. It just makes you feel better to think that I do." I shrugged my shoulders.

He stared at me; his eyes seemed to be searching my own. Apparently he didn't find whatever it was he was looking for, because after about a minute, everything shifted. His gaze roamed over me like I'd suddenly morphed into a stranger. It killed me inside.

"So are you going to try to stop me? Are you going to tell them?"

He shook his head. "No. Because I know even if I did, you'd just try to do something else." He stared at the wall for a minute before turning back to face me. "Please just tell me you'll reconsider."

"I can't. I already gave out the notes." Well, one note anyway, but he didn't have to know that. "And besides, I think if you stop to think about it, you'll see what I'm doing is right."

His face twisted and his eyes narrowed. "Fine. Don't come crying to me when this all blows up in your face. I'm going for a walk. Don't wait up. I'll see you in the morning."

"Jeremy." I touched his hand. "I don't want us to fight."

But I could see he'd given up on me. His shoulders slumped in defeat, and pain shone in his eyes.

He turned to leave.

"Jeremy, wait, please." I reached out to stop him, but this time he yanked free of my touch. He held up a hand in warning without turning back to look at me.

"Don't. Just don't, Sam. I can't talk to you right now."

His back straightened, rigid, as he walked out, slamming the door closed behind him. The one person I'd always counted on had left me too. And somehow, I'd never felt more alone in my life.

nine

*The doors we open and close each day
decide the lives we live.
—Flora Whittemore*

I woke up to the sound of Jeremy opening his closet door.

After waiting several hours for him to stop being mad and return, I'd ended up falling asleep in my clothes on top of the covers. Either he hadn't come back until morning, or it'd been awfully late. Either way, it was clear he felt no burning desire to speak to me or try to make up.

Fine, if that's how it had to be, then so be it. I pushed down the hurt and stood up, not saying a word. I grabbed my school uniform from the bag on the floor and headed into his bathroom to change.

I didn't bother with a shower. I'd do that after school at the trailer. Even if Aunt Lor needed to stay in the hospital another day or two, I refused to spend another night at his house. After I threw on clean clothes and brushed my teeth, I walked back into his room. He sat on his bed, bent over, tying his shoes.

My stomach churned as I made my way over to my bag

to stuff yesterday's wrinkled clothing inside. I zipped it up and slung it over my shoulder, along with my book bag. Their combined weight was nothing compared to the weight I carried inside about arguing with Jeremy.

He sat unmoving on his bed, head bowed. I paused at the bedroom door, hand wrapped around the smooth knob. *Please say something. Please tell me we're okay.* Seconds seemed like hours.

"Don't do it. Please. This isn't you. I don't want anything to happen to you when this goes bad." His voice was so low I barely heard him.

I turned back to face him. He still stared at the floor, shoulders bent forward. When I didn't answer right away, he finally looked up. I met his gaze, and a piece of me broke inside. I wished I could say his words were enough to make me rethink everything…that seeing him look at me with such caring and confusion changed my mind about the whole plan. But it didn't.

I knew the second he realized it too. He simply turned his head away. I turned and walked out the door, headed to school. As much as it killed me, I understood. Most times I couldn't stand to look at me either. But I had work to do. There were only three more school days left in pledge week, and I still had two more notes to deliver. Each of my initiates needed to have them before Hell week began.

The entire time I walked the eight blocks to Trinity, I kept trying to convince myself, *there are always casualties in war.* Only when it came to me and Jer, that mantra wasn't much comfort. Actually, the stupid line wasn't any comfort at all.

I'd delivered the last two notes during lunch period. Both Zena and Patrick were the proud new owners of an invitation to rush the Musterian Society, or at least my version of the Society.

As luck would have it, I'd been walking down the hall at the end of the day when Patrick found his note. He'd pulled it out of his locker, a huge smile plastered all over his face, and did some awkward dance that'd involved a bunch of hip thrusting and fist-pumping.

Safe bet he was happy to be asked. Good. That meant he'd be willing to do whatever it took to make it through Hell week, and my plan required exactly that sort of commitment and drive.

"Can I help you?"

The chipper voice of the barista in front of me broke my musings. She smiled way too happily for someone wearing flair.

I glanced up at the board above her head out of habit, although my order never varied. I always went for boring; it was cheaper. "Coffee, black."

"Would you like that tall, grande, or venti?" She presented me with her toothy grin.

I sighed. "Large." The pretentious names for coffee sizes annoyed me. Like calling it *venti* made it any fancier than what it was.

She rang in my order and took my money. I stepped aside to wait for my daily dose of caffeine and rolled my eyes as she smiled broadly at the next customer. "Hey, Mike, the usual?"

A bored looking guy behind the counter handed me my coffee, and I wandered over to a small table and sat down. Lately, this place provided more than my much-craved hit of caffeine; it also provided internet service that couldn't be traced back to me. Gotta love free wifi.

I pulled a small netbook out of my bag and signed in. Unfortunately, the MacBook my parents bought me as a junior high graduation gift died about six months ago, and since I couldn't afford to replace it, the cheap netbook had to do.

I logged into the brains behind my entire plan, the website I'd set up to provide each of my initiates with instructions on tasks I'd assign to them. The notes I'd given out each contained separate usernames and passwords to access the site. Of course, the notes also stressed that if any of the information were to be leaked, the guilty party was automatically out of consideration for the Society.

The website loaded, revealing a skull and crossbones logo for the landing page, and I smiled. I found the image to be a nice touch. With my own login information, I could access data showing who'd logged in and when. I could also change what each person saw on their screen when they accessed their personal page on the site.

I sipped my coffee and began typing, programming each of the initiate's first two tasks. They would only see one day's at a time, and the first one wouldn't show on their end until Saturday, which would give them time to make any necessary arrangements to complete their directive.

I scanned over what I'd just typed on each of their pages. Zena's instructions for her first task had been clear, and I'd made sure to throw some flattery in for extra incentive and ego boosting.

Do you have what it takes to be one of us? Prove it. Your task this week is to get Blane Reichert to choose you over his current girlfriend. It won't be easy, but we've had our eye on you for a while and think you may be just the kind of intelligent, powerful woman we're looking for. The kind who knows how to do what it takes to get the job done. Use your feminine wiles…flatter and tease. By the way, we want to see it all happen. So think classes and lunch, to start. ;-)

I hoped Zena had the guts to go through with it. The idea had sprung up thanks to remembering something Jer had mentioned to me a couple weeks ago. He'd told me that he'd noticed Blane talking to Zena whenever Jessica wasn't around, and that Zena—for some reason that I couldn't figure out for the life of me—actually seemed to like him too.

We'd laughed about it at the time, joking about how Jessica would go off her rocker if Blane actually had the balls to dump her. But now, Zena's lack of taste in guys would be to my advantage. If she succeeded, Monday's task would lead smoothly into the one where the shit would really hit the fan, Tuesday's task.

You've lured him in, and now's the time to take things to the next level. We know Blane has been checking you out… now be brave and show him it's mutual. Ask him to meet you down by the bleachers during lunch on Tuesday and rock his world with five minutes of kissing. Do you have what it takes to make a guy weak in the knees? Prove it. xoxo

What made Tuesday's plan epic was where Patrick came in. He'd be there with Jessica to capture the moment in all of its face-sucking glory. Of course, he wouldn't realize that

Zena was also on a task. I'd tried to make his sound like he was meant to immortalize whatever poor souls happened to stumble down to the popular make-out spot.

We all know students love to sneak out over lunch and head down to the football field to duck under the bleachers for a little romance. What better moment to capture for posterity? Your task is to convince Jessica that this is the place to capture real student memories. Use your pull on the yearbook staff to get our fearless editor to realize real life is what should be captured. Wait for any young lovers to appear. Who is this week's "It couple?" Kisses!

Just as I'd finished reading over Patrick's info, the hairs on the back of my neck tingled, that weird prickly sensation you get when you know someone is watching you, and has been for a while.

I glanced up, slowly lowering the lid of my flame red Asus, and looked around. I half-expected to see Jeremy, with his disapproving stare aimed my way, but he wasn't there.

An old couple sat a few tables away, pointing at some newspapers and nodding to each other. They weren't the least bit interested in me. I continued to scan the small coffee shop. Some business-type dude sat one table over, tie flung over the shoulder of his dress shirt, while he scarfed down a sandwich and muttered into his Bluetooth. Not him either. I twisted in my seat to check behind me.

Piercing green eyes stared straight at me. My hand slipped a little on the computer lid. He didn't look away, or even bother pretending not to stare. I looked around to see if maybe he was watching someone else and I was just imagining things. When I turned back, he still looked right at me. Then he winked, complete with a slight smile on his full lips.

My heart rate sped up and I tried to act nonchalant—like hot guys stared and winked at me all the time.

He looked just a little older than me, maybe eighteen or nineteen. A black fitted T-shirt practically invited drooling over his chest and arms. Thick, dark hair, long enough to make most mothers nervous, and a corded necklace with some silver symbol I didn't recognize completed his badass look.

I swallowed.

He tilted his coffee cup in my direction and raised an eyebrow.

Who was he? I'd never seen him before in my life. I'd remember if I had.

I wasn't used to the attention, so I busied myself stuffing my netbook back in my bag. In my hurry, I knocked over my tall paper cup, splashing the few remaining sips of coffee all over the table. *Damn it.*

Warmth crept up my neck and into my face, causing my cheeks to feel like I'd spent too much time in the sun. A metal dispenser rested in the middle of the table, so I grabbed a handful of napkins and wiped up my mess. Of course I'd do that while some strange, gorgeous guy sat ten feet away from me. I prayed he'd gotten bored and was no longer paying attention so he hadn't seen my latest graceful move.

"Can I help?" He materialized next to me.

Cripes, talk about tall.

I closed my eyes for a second in mortification before responding. "Nope, I'm good. Thanks." Wild horses couldn't drag my eyes to meet his. I wiped longer than necessary, waiting for him to take the hint and walk away. Images of the whole Chase debacle that Jessica had orchestrated flashed in my mind. Paranoia that she'd somehow planted some hot stranger to talk to me so I'd make a fool of myself kicked in…I told myself I was being ridiculous.

He didn't leave.

Dark jeans leading to black biker boots met my downward gaze.

It finally reached the point where continuing to scrub nonexistent coffee would just make me look mental. My stomach, all tight and fluttery, reminded me of the time I'd ridden the Steel Force rollercoaster one too many times.

Screw it.

I jerked my head up to face him head on. "Did you want something?"

His eyebrows rose at my abrupt tone.

I shook my head and grabbed my bag, ready to walk away, until his hand shot out to stop me. I tensed, and looked down to where his fingers—his skin a delicious shade of light mocha—grasped my forearm and slowly raised my eyes to meet his once again.

He dropped his hold and raised both hands in mock surrender. He smiled, revealing toothpaste-commercial-worthy white teeth. One was just a little crooked in the front.

"Whoa. Sorry, I was only going to introduce myself."

It was my turn to raise an eyebrow. "And what makes you think I care who you are?" I tucked a stray piece of hair behind my ear, trying to act like I meant it. I wondered if my actions were fooling either of us. I was being a bit of a bitch for no reason, and I knew it. But paranoia was putting me on the defensive.

He smiled again. A knowing smile.

Self-conscious, I cleared my throat and stood still, waiting. When he didn't say anything more, I asked, "Well? Is this like Rumpelstiltskin? Am I supposed to guess?"

After a heartbeat, he held out his hand. "The name's Ransom."

When he touched my hand, small unexpected tingles shot through me. I yanked away and shoved my hands in my pockets.

"So, do I get yours?" He looked at me, one eyebrow raised in question.

"My what?"

He gave a small laugh. "Um…your name?"

I tilted my head and examined him, then shook my head. "I don't think so. After all, what fun would it be if I made it too easy on you?" I couldn't help my grin. Damn him.

His eyes lit up in what seemed to be admiration. Definite interest.

He nodded. "Fair enough. But you should know, I don't give up quite that easily."

"I wouldn't imagine you did."

He laughed and turned to retrieve something from the extra seat at his table. When he lifted it up, I had to laugh too. A black motorcycle helmet. Of course Ransom rode a bike. He must have noticed my expression, because he asked, "What?"

I shook my head. "Nothing. It doesn't matter." Time to go. I offered him what I hoped was a mysterious smile and turned away, headed to the door.

I'd only taken three steps when his husky voice followed me.

"I'll be seeing you."

Part of me hoped he was right, but I didn't look back, or answer. I just waved my hand and left the coffee shop. Regardless of how hot Ransom—if that was even his real name—was, I had other things to concentrate on that had nothing to do with a bad boy on a bike.

ten

Sometimes, good people make bad choices. It doesn't mean they're bad people, it means they're human.
—Unknown

"Oh my God! You're home!" I launched at my aunt the minute I stepped in the kitchen. Relief washed over me like a much welcomed spring rain.

Aunt Loretta patted my back when I hugged her tighter than I ever had before. "My goodness, Samantha. It's like you haven't seen me in a week." Her tone sounded pleased.

I pulled back a little to look at her.

She appeared the same as always, with her bright blue eyes, so like my own, twinkling. Her gray hair was pulled up in a neat twist. But when I peered closer, her face looked paler than usual, and gray smudges shadowed her eyes.

"You look tired. Are you sure you're okay? What did the doctor say?" I led her over to the sofa where we both sat down. I didn't let go of her hand.

She patted mine with her soft wrinkled fingers. "I'm sure, child. I just had a little spell, nothing to worry about."

"What do you mean *a spell*?"

She shook her head. "Nothing. The heat probably got

to me."

I stared at her. She was lying. "Aunt Lor, it's October. I doubt it was the heat. Now would you please tell me what the hospital said?" A thought suddenly occurred to me. "And how'd you get home, anyway?"

"Oh, Martha gave me a ride. I called her a few hours ago, and she had some errands to run, so she zipped by and picked me up. No bother."

It didn't take a rocket scientist to see my aunt was trying to convince herself more than me; she hated asking for help. Must be a family trait.

I offered her a gentle smile. "Can I get you anything? What about some tea?"

"That would be nice, dear. Thank you." *Pat, pat, pat* on my hand again.

"Why don't you go in your room and lie down? I'll bring you the tea when it's ready."

The fact that it was only a little after six at night and she agreed concerned me even more. She crept down the hallway, using an outstretched thin arm to guide her way.

I refused to consider the reality that something could happen to her…that she wouldn't live forever. Instead, I got up to brew her some of her favorite chamomile tea with honey and decided to also make her some buttered toast. Maybe food would help. I tried to convince myself that it would.

After I'd delivered Aunt Loretta's tea and toast, along with firm instructions to eat every bite, I made my way to my room. I wasn't hungry, but I'd grabbed some trail mix since I knew I'd pay for it later with a migraine if I didn't eat anything. A million thoughts whirled around in my head as I munched on my own snack. I just wanted to talk to someone. *Needed* to talk to someone or I'd crack.

I pulled my cell phone out of my bag and automatically searched for Jeremy's name in the contact list. Just as I was about to press the button to call him and tell him that Aunt Lor was home, it hit me. I couldn't. We weren't talking.

I halfheartedly scrolled through the rest of my contacts. There weren't very many.

Even though we weren't that close, I briefly considered calling Abby. But if Jeremy told her about the plan, she'd be upset with me too. I sighed and dropped my phone next to me on the twin bed.

Since I'd gone to the library to hide out from Jeremy instead of eating lunch in the cafeteria, I hadn't been able to get a feel for whether or not the others knew. Even though Jeremy was mad at me, I didn't think he'd blab to anyone, but I couldn't be sure. And he'd ignored me in all of our classes, which hurt way more than I cared to admit.

On the other hand, his attitude also ticked me off. He should support me, period. It's not like I was asking *him* to do anything. And to act like doing the whole thing made me some awful person was ridiculous and unfair. Jessica deserved everything I'd planned for her...and then some. And besides that, I was actually helping three other people. With what I was doing, I would change their lives forever—for the better.

I jumped off the bed to get a shower. Maybe it would help me relax. A quick glance around my room revealed that I was running out of clean clothes. Random piles of dirty laundry were piled all over. Aunt Loretta yelled at me all the time to throw my stuff in the hamper or she wasn't washing it for me. She always said she refused to come in and pick it up if I chose to live like a slob.

I wrinkled my nose. Hopefully I still had some clean pajamas at least. A hesitant sniff confirmed the long sleeve sleep tee hanging off my bedpost was still wearable. Maybe not springtime fresh, but it didn't reek.

The hot water felt wonderful against my skin a few minutes later. As I lathered shampoo into my hair, the sweet pea scent combined with the steam helped soothe my frazzled nerves and the dull throbbing in my temples. I hummed, rinsing the lather out, and poked at the iridescent bubbles with my toes as they swirled in a lazy circle toward the drain.

My aunt wanted me to keep my showers to a reasonable time limit, but I didn't rush this time. The heat massaging my bare skin relaxed me, more than I'd been in a long time. Only after the water began to turn cold did I turn it off and reluctantly wrap an oversize pink bath towel around my shivering body.

I missed the days of showering as long as I liked, or soaking in the giant tub with jets massaging my skin in my own bathroom with the heated floor at my old house.

Dried off, I slipped into my sleep top and ran a comb through my hair. As calming as the shower had been, it was still way too early for bed. I didn't feel like watching television and for once didn't have any homework.

I wandered back into my room and sat on my bed, looking around for something to do. There was nothing. I plopped backward and stared at the ceiling. Counting tiles bored me after about thirty. I groaned and rolled over.

The clock showed that it was only seven thirty. Seventeen years old, the supposed prime of my life, and I sat home alone, bored, with no one to talk to. Other kids my age were all busy hanging out with friends, partying, or making out with their boyfriends. Hell, even being in some after school club was starting to sound good. Better than counting freaking ceiling tiles anyway.

I jumped up and walked over to my dresser to search for a clean pair of jeans. I shimmied into them and rooted for a hoodie to throw on over my long T-shirt. I wasn't going for any fashion awards. After slipping my feet into a pair of sneakers, sans socks, I quickly twisted my damp hair into a messy bun and shoved my phone into my back pocket.

I poked my head into my aunt's room as I walked past. "Aunt Lor? You awake?" I stage whispered. She lay still on her side, turned away from me. "Aunt Lor?" I called just a little louder this time. She didn't stir.

I stepped into her room, taking care not to make noise and disturb her once I realized she was fast asleep. She probably needed her rest. Her favorite afghan was folded at the foot of her bed, so I reached out and opened it up, then gently pulled it over her. I smoothed it across her thin shoulders before leaning down and brushing a kiss against her cheek. "Sleep well," I whispered.

In case she woke up while I was gone, I wrote a note and propped it against the coffeemaker on the kitchen counter.

Went for a walk, might go to the park for a little. I won't be late. Love you, S.

I grabbed the spare house key from a glass dish on the counter and slipped outside. The early evening air was cool but not uncomfortable. Headlights from the occasional car broke the twilight darkness ahead of me. An owl hooted somewhere in the distance, and crickets sang to each other. My footsteps made muffled crunching sounds against the uneven blacktop. I had no specific destination in mind; I'd just needed to get out.

After walking about twenty minutes, more buildings and houses began to pop up. My old house was only about five blocks north, over on Cherry Blossom Drive. I purposely walked in a different direction.

Lights from the coffee shop I'd been in earlier came into view. My steps slowed, and without thinking, I searched for familiar dark hair.

He wasn't there. Not like I'd really expected him to show up again the same day, right when I just happened to stroll into town.

I grabbed a coffee and left. I kept walking, but paused outside an old bookstore to check out the displayed titles. It'd been a while since I'd read for pleasure. I used to do it all the time. I'd just leaned in closer to the glass, trying to read the fancy script written on a small book resting against a pedestal, when rumbling sounded from down the street, getting closer.

A single approaching headlight reflected in the window in front of me for a couple of seconds then turned off a few feet from where I stood, frozen. Really, what were the chances? I wasn't sure if I wanted it to be him or not. Maybe a little of both.

"Hey, mystery girl."

I'd recognize that husky drawl anywhere. I reflexively swallowed then licked the dryness away from my lips. It felt ridiculous that the voice of some guy I just met could transform my insides to mush. It crossed my mind for about a millisecond to ignore him and walk away.

Then it hit that he didn't know me…didn't know my family's disreputable past. I could be anyone I wanted with him, and it wouldn't matter. So instead of doing my usual introverted disappearing act, I turned and faced him.

Ransom pulled his helmet off with one smooth motion. His hair fell almost to his shoulders in a completely sexy mess. He smiled. "I wasn't sure it was you." He raised his eyebrows and glanced at the cup in my hand. "You must really like coffee."

I laughed. "You have no idea."

"I was hoping maybe we'd bump into each other again, I just didn't expect it to be so soon."

I willed myself to relax, to be a normal seventeen-year-old girl. Flirty, fun. I smiled back at him. "Well, then I guess it's your lucky night because here I am."

Wait…that came out wrong. I hoped he didn't think I meant *lucky night*. Like, he was going to get lucky. I was so not good at flirting.

Thankfully, he didn't seem to take it like I was one step shy of charging him by the hour. He grinned again. "Are you going to keep me guessing, or do I get your name this time?"

I took a few steps toward him. "And why should I tell you?"

He cocked his head, studying me. "You don't have to. Just thought it would be nice to know your name before I take you for a ride."

My eyes widened, and my eyebrows shot up somewhere in the middle of my head.

"Well? You in?"

He held the helmet out toward me. His expression held teasing, along with something more. A challenge. I lifted my chin and walked up next to where he straddled the bike.

"You don't think I will."

One eyebrow rose. "Prove me wrong."

That's all it took. I reached up and pulled my hair free from its bun and shook my head, allowing the still damp waves of my hair to cascade over my shoulders and down my back. I slipped the hair tie around my wrist. Ransom watched each movement with appreciation.

I snatched the helmet from his hand and shoved it over my head. It fit a little loose, but didn't wobble too much. The tinted visor was raised, so I caught the pleased expression that crossed his face.

I was done playing everything so safe in my life, watching everyone around me have fun and live their lives. Besides, Jeremy wasn't speaking to me, so it wasn't like *that* had a chance in hell of going anywhere…so why not do something just for me?

When he didn't move, I asked, "Well, are we doing this or not?"

He grinned, the streetlights glinting off his teeth. He moved forward slightly, and motioned for me to slide on behind him. I slung a leg over the leather seat and immediately realized how close I'd have to sit to him to keep from falling off the back. I gulped.

He grabbed each of my thighs and pulled me even closer. Heat filled me as I came into direct contact with his body. I was completely pressed against him.

"Now wrap your arms around me."

"What?"

"No time to be shy now, Princess, unless you want to fall off. Put your arms around me." He shifted and reached around to take each of my hands, and placed them against his flat stomach.

Wow. The boy had some abs. I forced the thought from my mind, telling myself it was more important to concentrate on not flying off and getting killed.

He must have read my mind, because he shot me a knowing smile. "You'll want to keep that closed, or you'll end up eating bugs." He pointed to the visor.

"What are you going to wear?" I looked around for an extra helmet.

"Don't worry, I'm fine." He pulled out a pair of sunglasses from the pocket of his leather jacket and slipped them on.

"Sunglasses? It's night."

"Yeah, but they help with the wind hitting my eyes, and keep things from flying in." He revved the idling engine with one swift twist of his hand. The rumble ran through the seat and up my body. I fought to pay attention to what he was saying.

"Oh, that makes sense, I guess." *I'm so lame.*

"Have you ever ridden before?"

Embarrassed, I shook my head.

"Okay, real quick, the most basic rule...once we get going, it's important not to move around too much, so stay close to me." He tightened his hold on my clasped hands around his middle before continuing. "The other thing, even if you're tempted to lean the opposite way when we go around curves, don't. That could make the bike lose balance. So, just lean *with* me into the turns."

"Got it." My heart thundered in my chest. From fear of riding on what my aunt called a deathtrap with some guy I barely knew, or excitement for the same reason, I wasn't quite sure.

"I won't be able to hear you well once we really get going, so if you need me to stop, just tap my leg twice." His voice rose over the whine of the bike. I nodded to show I understood. He reached back, and snapped my visor closed. "There ya go."

He revved the engine again and stretched his leg back to raise the kickstand with his foot. "You ready?"

I loosened my death grip long enough to give him a thumbs-up. He grinned and did the same. "Okay, Princess, hold on tight."

The warning wasn't needed. I was holding on so tight I might crush one of his ribs. I took a deep breath as he looked over his left shoulder to check for traffic.

And suddenly we were pulling out. I involuntarily jerked back slightly, and he reached down to rest his hand against my clasped fingers for a few seconds.

"Just relax. Enjoy the ride," he called over the rushing wind and throaty whine of the bike.

After a minute or two, I felt it—this amazing rush from the speed, the sense of freedom, totally exhilarating and so different from anything I'd ever experienced before that I couldn't help but grin like crazy behind the visor. I gave in to the delicious sensation. Racing through the night with Ransom felt exciting and dangerous. I loved it.

Once we passed through the town limits, the road

became darker; only the moon and the thin beam of his headlight pierced the darkness. The wind whistled against my helmet, and it seemed like we were the only people who existed.

The heat from his body warmed me where I pressed against him, and the chill from the night air rushing past us didn't even bother me. For the first time in a very long time, I felt truly alive.

eleven

Sometimes good things fall apart so
better things can fall together.
—Marilyn Monroe

I rolled out of my bed before the alarm even had a chance to go off.

The muted voice of Ellen DeGeneres carried through my plywood bedroom door. That was a good sign. It meant Aunt Loretta must be up, curlers in her hair, wrapped up in her faded housecoat as she cozied up to yet another taped episode of her favorite daytime show. Maybe the toast and a good night's rest really *had* done the trick and she felt better.

I raised my arms above my head to stretch for a minute in anticipation of the day ahead. Only two more days of pledge week, and then the real fun began. Plus, Ransom said he'd call me after school. I grinned, thinking about him.

He'd dropped me off at the end of the lane after the motorcycle ride. I hadn't let him drive me all the way home since I didn't want to take the chance of Aunt Lor seeing me getting off some strange guy's bike. She'd flip.

After getting dressed, I headed to the kitchen to grab

something to eat and check to see how she was feeling.

She sat in her chair, holding a cup of most likely lukewarm black coffee. When she saw me, she called out, "Good morning, sweetie," without tearing her eyes away from the screen of the small television set a few feet away from her familiar position.

"Good morning." A gentle smile crossed my face. The kitchen-slash-living room areas were on opposite ends of the same room, with only a small divider going a few feet up the wall on the left side to separate them, so I could see from where I stood that Aunt Lor seemed to be back to her normal habits. I was relieved.

I walked over to the counter and poured myself a cup of coffee. Taking a sip, I grimaced at the stale, bitter taste and wandered over to grab a Pop-Tart from an open box sitting on the table. As I tore open the shiny silver foil with my teeth, I joined her in the living room for our morning ritual of TV time.

Plopped on the edge of the small flowered sofa, I began to nibble on my frosted strawberry pastry.

Aunt Loretta looked over. Her wide blue eyes wrinkled into a smile. "How did you sleep, honey?"

I returned her smile. "Good, thanks. But more importantly, how'd *you* sleep? Are you feeling any better today?"

"Oh, I slept very well, thank you. And I told you, there's no reason to worry about me, I'm fine."

I watched her eyes carefully as she answered, trying to gauge if she was telling the truth. She set down her coffee cup on the side table. "Samantha, stop your worrying. Everything is right as rain."

A cliché wasn't bolstering my confidence level, but I let it slide. If she said she was okay, I guess I had to believe her. It's not like she'd ever lied to me before.

"I thought I heard you come in late last night. Were you out with Jeremy?"

Oh crap. "Um…No."

It probably wasn't a good idea to let on where I'd really been. Or whom I'd been with. "I ah…went for a walk into town and met up with some friends."

"I hope you didn't walk home alone that late!"

"No, I didn't. A friend gave me a ride." That much was true at least.

I decided to revisit the subject of my driver's license. I hated always having to beg for rides and not having the freedom to go somewhere when I wanted to. And while her old Buick was no eye-catcher…it had four wheels.

"Do you think since it's senior year I could finally go get my license? You wouldn't have to worry about me getting rides that way."

She shook her head immediately. "Samantha, you know my decision on this. You driving is an expense we don't need right now."

"I could get a part-time job. I'd pay for the insurance and gas and whatever."

"No. You are not getting a job. You need to focus on your schoolwork so you can get into a good college."

Translated, she knew I'd need scholarship money to pay for school and didn't want to risk my grades taking a nosedive.

"Will you at least think about it if I promise to keep my grades up?"

She sighed. "I'll think about it." She suddenly looked confused. "Why are you in school clothes on a Saturday?"

I cocked my head and studied her. "Aunt Lor, today's Thursday, not Saturday."

Her eyes clouded for a moment, and she reached over to busy herself with the lace doily on the small table next to her.

"Oh, of course." She shook her head and smiled brightly. "Silly me. Must be all that sleep. My brain isn't working right yet." She tried to laugh off her mistake.

My doubts from earlier stormed back, but I didn't want to push it. It seemed pretty clear she didn't want to talk about it yet. I decided to play along, nodding and smiling weakly.

It was almost time for me to leave, so I stood up and went to the kitchen to rinse my coffee cup. After setting it upside down on the towel next to the sink, I grabbed my book bag and called, "I'm heading out! I love you!" I paused.

Her familiar response came immediately. "Have a good day at school, sweetheart. I love you too!" It was the same thing she said to me each morning on my way out the door. The ritual made me feel safe. I refused to give in to the fear that something might be seriously wrong with her health, that some unknown enemy could destroy the only family I had left.

"Please be sure to put on your safety glasses before beginning the experiment," Mr. Wellers droned.

I reached over to grab a pair of goggles and smacked hands with Jeremy.

"Sorry," he muttered and snatched his hand back like he'd touched something gross.

It was the first word he'd spoken to me all period, even though we were lab partners. The first word he'd said to me in almost two days actually.

"No problem," I said.

It should be interesting, getting through our lab without speaking. Maybe we could pass notes or use sign language or something.

After I slapped on my glasses, I shifted on my stool and glanced across the workspace. Jeremy sat across the lab counter, looking anywhere but at me.

I sighed and reached over to turn on the Bunsen burner and watched as the white-blue flame shot up. I pulled the ring stand closer. "Can you please pass me the first test tube?"

He handed it to me, not saying a word. When our fingers touched, he finally looked up. "Thanks," I said.

"Yep."

I tucked a flyaway piece of hair behind my ear and tried to think of something to say. I cleared my throat, which I hoped he'd interpret as me wanting to talk. He ignored my less than subtle hint.

"I like your shirt," I said.

I like your shirt? Seriously, that was the best I could come up with? It was pathetic; we wore uniforms for crissakes.

My stupidity must have worked. He actually half-smiled. Relief zoomed through me. Maybe he wasn't still angry. I missed talking to him so much that the past two days seemed more like weeks.

I placed the tube in the ring stand next to the burner to

heat up. While I watched to make sure it didn't get too hot and explode, I tried to figure out what to say next. Perhaps an especially witty, "Nice pants."

He beat me to it.

"How's your aunt? Did you go see her?"

"She's actually home." I smiled.

"That's great!" His eyes warmed, and I could tell he meant it.

"Yeah, it is." I frowned then, remembering the morning. "But I'm worried about her."

He reached over to turn the flame down slightly. "What do you mean? What's wrong with her?"

I twisted the end of my long braid between my fingers. "That's just it. I don't know."

He looked at me, brows furrowed.

"She went to bed really early last night, and then this morning, she thought it was Saturday."

Jeremy moved the ring stand away from the heat, studied the tube a moment, and scribbled something in our lab book. When that was done, he placed his pen down and gave me his full attention. "Well, that doesn't necessarily mean anything bad. I mean, I forget what day it is all the time."

"I get that, Jer, but this is different, this is…" I trailed off, not knowing how to explain it. "Never mind, you're probably right." I found it easier to simply agree with him.

It felt like we were strangers making polite conversation. And it sucked.

I tried to think of a new topic, but the only other news I thought of related to my plan, and the guy I'd met yesterday. The first was obviously off the table for discussion, and the second...for some reason it seemed awkward to bring up Ransom.

The silence stretched between us like old gum you don't want anymore and decide to play with instead. Thankfully, only five minutes remained in the class period. We worked together to clean up our lab space and filled in the rest of the questions on the worksheet. The only words spoken pertained directly to the assignment. When the bell rang, I smiled weakly and told him I'd see him later.

He nodded. "Later," he echoed. His tone sounded as confused as my own, like neither of us quite knew how to make things right between us again.

I'd gotten a pass to go down to the computer lab during final homeroom, so I headed in that direction. I wanted to make sure that everything was ready to go on the website for next week, and that I hadn't missed anything.

Minutes after slipping into the seat in front of a computer in the back of the room, I was satisfied. Everything was good to go on my site. Curiosity prompted me to log back in to Jessica's email. I didn't care about any of the emails I sorted through from her friends, or about her orders from Amazon and Victoria's Secret, so I ignored those. I only had eyes for the ones with the familiar subject line of "THE SOCIETY." I rolled my eyes, thinking they could at least make the attempt to be a little stealthy. Not super secure for a supposedly secret society.

The first email I clicked on listed some tasks they were planning for the initiates during Hell week. I clenched my teeth when I read that they were instructing someone to dine and ditch at a pizza place in town, and another to steal a bra from Wal-Mart. Really? They'd stooped to petty theft to join their hallowed organization? It just infuriated me more, and made me feel even better about what I was doing. If anyone should be ashamed, it should be *them*.

I logged out of Jessica's email, cleared the history and temp files, and stood up seconds before the bell rang. I couldn't wait to bring them down.

All great changes are preceded by chaos.
—Deepak Chopra

I walked down the school steps after the final dismissal bell. My bus was in the second round to arrive, so I generally waited around for about five minutes until it got there. I didn't mind too much since most of the upperclassmen drove, and didn't hang out at the bus landing, which meant no Jessica and her crew. It was usually me and a bunch of freshman and sophomores, and we pretty much ignored each other.

"Sam!" Jeremy's voice carried over the dull roar of just released underclassman.

Surprised, I turned to see him jogging down the steps toward me. He waved. I slowly waved back, confused to see him. He was one of the kids who drove to school, and they usually went out the side door since it was closer to the student parking lot.

He reached me and played with the strap of the navy gym bag he rotated back and forth in his hands, not saying anything.

"Hey." I finally offered.

"Look, I just wanted to say…" He shoved his glasses up a little. "I guess I wanted to say that I hate how things are between us lately." He looked right at me.

"Me too." I smiled at him.

"Do you wanna hang out later?" He shrugged, causing his backpack to slip down his shoulder a little.

I beamed. "That would be—"

A familiar rumble filled the air around us.

My eyes widened, and I turned to look behind me.

Oh my God. It was Ransom, pulling right up to the curb in front of the school. Still straddling the bike, he lifted off his helmet and shook out his hair before tucking the helmet in the crook of his arm against his thigh.

A rush of excitement raced through me.

Several girls around us clearly had the same reaction. There were stares and immediate huddles with lots of whispers, lip biting, and hair tossing action. I couldn't help but stare myself.

"Do you know him?"

I whipped my head back. I'd forgotten Jeremy stood two feet away. It felt like I'd just been caught stealing a cookie when I'd thought no one was watching. I opened my mouth to answer, then immediately closed it again.

He raised his eyebrows and looked back over to where Ransom now stood next to his bike.

"Who is he?" Jeremy looked confused, and something else. *Jealous?*

"What?"

Jeremy cleared his throat. "I was wondering who he is, since he seems to know you considering he hasn't torn his eyes off you since he pulled up."

I immediately felt flattered. First, that it was obvious that Ransom came to the school to see me. And second, that Jeremy seemed to be taking a very keen interest in exactly who Ransom was to me.

"Oh, he's…a friend."

"A friend?"

"Yeah, a friend." I crossed my arms in front of my chest.

"Well does your friend have a name?"

I paused. "His name's Ransom."

Jeremy snorted. "*Ransom? Ransom what?*"

I looked at him, brows furrowed. "What's with all the questions all of a sudden? What does it matter?"

He shrugged, and his eyes showed hurt. "It doesn't. Sorry. I was only curious since I've never heard you mention him before."

"Jeremy, it's not like I tell you every little thing about my life."

A shadow crossed his face. "Yeah, so I learned recently. Read it in a notebook."

"Oh my God, do you seriously have to bring that up again?" I narrowed my eyes and sighed.

"You better go, I think your friend *Ransom's* waiting for you."

I stared at him. "What's your problem?"

He opened his mouth and closed it a second later. Charged silence stretched between us for a few seconds. He shook his head. "Never mind. I guess we'll get together some other time. See you later. Have fun." His voice was tight. He stared at me for a few more seconds and then turned and walked away.

Un-freaking-real.

Ransom waited next to his bike, long legs crossed in front of him as he leaned against the seat. As I walked toward him, a slow grin slid across his face.

When I was within touching distance, he smiled again and the air between us turned electric. He made me feel desired, which was new to me. Definitely a heady sensation.

"I saw you talking to your friend, and I didn't want to interrupt. Wanna go for a ride?"

Like I'd say no.

Ransom stepped closer, and my breath caught. He slipped the helmet over my head and leaned in to tighten the strap under my chin. His hair smelled like fresh air and freedom.

"What about my back pack?" I suddenly felt every inch the schoolgirl.

"Got it covered." He reached out and took my bag, then crossed to the back of his bike. He hooked the straps over the top of the low silver bar behind the seat, and pulled on them a few times to make sure they'd stay.

"Ready?"

I nodded and stepped closer, then stopped. I was wearing a skirt. How the heck was I supposed to crawl on there in a skirt? He eyed me, obviously not getting my predicament.

My cheeks flushed. "I don't know if I can ride wearing this." I pointed down.

"Why not?"

My eyes widened. "Because it's a skirt."

He eyed my legs…slowly. Then he nodded with a grin. "I can see that."

My cheeks were on fire. "How am I supposed to get on?"

"You swing your leg over. Like this." He hopped on

the bike and twisted to face me, still smiling. "Come on, Princess."

"I'm not a princess," I muttered.

When I continued to shift back and forth on my feet, he laughed. "I'll turn around. I won't even look."

I glanced over my shoulder. Huddles of underclass females watched with blatant interest. I stepped over to the bike and placed my right hand on Ransom's shoulder for leverage.

Even in my uniform, swinging my leg over his Triumph felt almost familiar. I fought to tamp down my satisfied grin at the knowledge that every girl on the bus landing was busy staring at us, mouths agape.

Ransom laughed and turned his head to look me. "See? I knew you could do it."

It felt somehow taboo to be in my school uniform straddling a motorcycle behind a guy I barely knew. A hot guy. I tugged at the hem of my skirt, trying to cover some of my exposed skin. Ransom's eyes followed my hands.

His lips curved into a half-smile, but he said nothing.

I didn't wait for him to tell me to move closer or to hold on. I scooted up tight against his back, and wrapped my arms around his waist. Like before, my body tingled at the contact.

Seconds later, he turned the key, and the familiar rumble filled the air. The vibration of the bike ran through me. The feeling, coupled with being pressed so tight against him, made me think all kinds of wicked thoughts. Thank God he couldn't read my mind, or I'd die of embarrassment.

"Oh! By the way!" I called out over the whine of the bike.

He turned to look at me again, one eyebrow raised.

"It's Samantha. Well, Sam."

He grinned, a totally heart-stopping grin. "Pleasure to meet you, Samantha."

I couldn't help but laugh.

We took off. All thoughts, wicked or otherwise, left my head. Instead, I became aware only of sensation. Heat. Movement. The feel of his back pressed against my chest. My legs wrapped around his thighs, his taut stomach under my clasped fingers. I didn't want the ride to end.

thirteen

Life is always at some turning point.
—Irwin Edman

"So was that your boyfriend?"

Ransom's question came out of nowhere. We'd stopped at an old baseball field on the edge of town to stretch and grab something to drink after riding about an hour. I paused from sliding a dollar bill into the Coke machine and looked over my shoulder at him. "Who?"

"The guy talking to you when I picked you up." He took a long swallow of his own soda, watching me over the tilted can.

I pressed the plastic button and waited for my Diet Coke to drop out. "No, he's just a friend." I bent to retrieve my soda and pulled back the tab.

Ransom raised an eyebrow. "And does *he* know that?"

I shrugged. "Well, yeah. We've been best friends since we were kids. That's all."

It felt weird answering those kinds of questions about Jeremy. Almost like a betrayal. And a tiny voice in my head whispered, *are you sure that's all you are?* I was confused. Things had never really gone anywhere with Jeremy in that way. And now I had Ransom standing in front of me, showing an interest in me, and offering an escape from my everyday life.

He nodded, still eyeing me over his Coke.

I walked over to the timeworn wooden bleachers and sat down. I set my soda next to me and wrapped my arms around myself. The sun was warm for mid-October, but I still wished for something heavier than my oxford shirt and thin cardigan. When we rode, the rushing air took no prisoners, and I still had the goose bumps to prove it.

Ransom followed and swung his leg over the bench below, straddling it to face me. He wore the same black boots and leather jacket as the last time, but his shirt looked different, one of those woven Henley jerseys. Jeremy wore them sometimes too.

It seemed odd to find similarities between the two of them; they were so completely different. Jeremy was sweet and safe. Ransom was…I wasn't sure yet how to describe him, but I knew safe and sweet definitely weren't two of the first adjectives that would spring to mind.

Ransom nudged the side of my sneaker with his big black boot. I nudged back.

"So how'd you know where I went to school?" I reached for my can to take a small sip.

He leaned back on the bench. "Not that hard to figure out. You told me you went to some fancy private school right outside town. Trinity's the only one in Cloverfield."

Oh, duh.

"I was surprised to see you." *Understatement.*

He shaded his eyes from the late afternoon sun and looked at me. "Why?"

"I don't know. I didn't expect you to show up at my school like that."

"Did it bother you?"

"No, no, I didn't mean that. I was happy to see you. I just…" I shrugged, feeling stupid. "I didn't expect to see you," I repeated, lamely. I tightened my arms across my chest, more from feeling awkward than to block any chill in the air.

He studied me a moment longer. "You don't really open up around people, do you?"

I shoved my foot back and forth restlessly. "I don't know." I looked at him. "Well, I don't see you sharing any deep, dark secrets about yourself either."

He hopped up to sit next to me. "So you're curious about my deep dark secrets?" A slow grin appeared. "What do you want to know? Ask me anything, I'm an open book."

Where to begin?

"Okay. Is Ransom your real name?"

He ran his hand through his thick hair and laughed. Watching him made me wonder what it would feel like to do the same thing. To touch his hair, run my fingers through it.

"I tell you that you can ask me anything, and *that's* what you come up with?" He teased.

I felt dumb. Girls he was used to hanging out with probably would've come up with something much more interesting, something edgier and seductive. Not *Is that your real name?* No wonder I'd never had a boyfriend.

"It's a valid question."

"Well, to answer your very valid question, yeah, it is." He nodded. "Ransom Levi Morgan. I don't know, my parents were hippies I guess." He ran his hand through his hair again, messing it up. He did that a lot. "So now it's my turn."

I tilted my head.

"We'll take turns asking each other questions. Sound fair?"

Not really since I wasn't sure how much I wanted to share with him, and who knew the kinds of stuff he'd ask. I wrinkled my nose. "What if you ask something I don't want to answer?"

He shrugged. "Don't answer. It's not like I'm gonna ask for state secrets."

"Okay." My stomach twisted a little. What if he asked about my family?

He shifted a little closer. "Is that guy really just a friend?"

I gave an exasperated sigh that was all for show. "Yes. I already told you that." But inside I did a happy dance that he bothered to check.

My turn. "How old are you?"

"Eighteen. I'll be nineteen in two months."

So I'd pegged his age correctly.

His eyes studied my reaction. I made sure not to give one.

"How old are you?" He asked.

"Seventeen."

"Does it bother you that I'm a little older than you?"

"No. Why would it bother me?" I made sure to sound casual, a woman of the world. What a laugh. The only time I'd ever dated a guy was if you counted going to the eighth grade formal with Bobby Peterson, which totally *didn't* count since we'd only gone together since Jessica was going with Bobby's best friend, and she'd kind of forced the whole double-date thing.

It'd been clear Bobby had about as much interest in being there with me as I had in spending the evening with him. The few times we'd actually danced, I'd had to breathe through my mouth the whole time so I didn't pass out from his armpit smell.

After that, any chance of a normal dating life had pretty much gone down the tubes, thanks to my family's fall from grace.

Ransom moved even closer to me on the bench, jolting any thoughts of Bobby Peterson from my head.

"I don't know," he said, voice low. His deep eyes drew me in, like a black hole I might never resurface from. "I guess since we've been hanging out more, I was just trying to get a read on how you felt. And…" He paused, staring at me.

And…what? My mouth went dry and I tried desperately to guess what he'd say next, what I wanted him to say. I licked my lips while I watched him watch me, then immediately regretted it. Talk about the world's most blatant come-on gesture.

His lips curled up in a seductive half smile. "And I like you. And I think we might have something here."

He placed his hand on my knee where the skirt didn't quite cover my bare skin. I tried to remember if I'd shaved my legs, and prayed they weren't stubbly where he touched me. I wavered between the thrill of having his hand on my leg, and freaking out that it was there. I told myself to calm down and act like a normal person.

"Like what?" I finally croaked. I now had the Sahara in my mouth. I wanted a drink so badly, needed to wash away the desert, but didn't want to move.

"I don't know," he said. "I'd like to keep getting to know

you better. What do *you* want it to be?"

What did I want? I had no idea. I didn't know what I was supposed to say or do. Part of me wanted him to keep looking at me the way he was right then, like I was a delicious sundae and he couldn't wait to take a bite.

But the other part of me was freaking out. I was seventeen, and I'd never even kissed a guy. Not really. I pushed away the memory of Jeremy kissing me when we were seven. It was a pretty safe bet Ransom had kissed plenty of girls. More than kissed. So I did the only logical thing I could think of in that situation. I changed the subject.

"Do you live around here?" I glanced around the baseball field like I expected his house to magically appear somewhere between second and third base. A second later, I wanted to slap myself. What if he thought I was fishing for an invitation?

"I have a place over on Warren Street."

The west side of town. West side mainly consisted of tiny houses and a couple of warehouses converted into apartment buildings.

"You live alone? Not with your parents?" Sure, he was older, but not that much. I didn't think he'd have his own place.

He moved his hand when he shifted a little to take another swig of his soda then shrugged. "Yeah. I left home when I was sixteen. Been on my own ever since."

I nodded. I kinda knew how that went, not having your parents around. "Do you still see them?"

"Nope. Don't really see the point. They have their lives, I have mine." His voice turned bitter.

"I know how that goes. I live with my aunt, my dad's

older sister."

"Where are your folks?" His one eyebrow rose with the dreaded question.

I stalled. "That's a story for another time."

He didn't push. We talked for a while. General, getting to know you stuff. About an hour later, I rubbed my hands over my arms. The goose bumps fought to break through the thin material of my sweater. He must have noticed because he stood up and reached his hand out to help me to my feet.

"Such a gentleman," I teased.

"Hardly." He chuckled. "C'mon, we'll get going." He waved his outstretched hand toward me again.

After a second, I took it and allowed him to lead me down the bleachers. His palm felt slightly rough, different than Jeremy's did when he'd held my hand.

Stop thinking about Jeremy! I scolded myself.

He released my hand as soon as we reached the grass, and we walked side by side in silence to his motorcycle.

"So why did you say that?" I asked.

"Say what?"

"When I said about you being such a gentleman, you said *hardly*."

He paused a moment, looking at the ground before meeting my gaze. "Trust me, Samantha, I'm not your knight in shining armor. I'm not looking to be that for anyone right now."

Then almost as if to belie his words, he spoke again.

"Here." He shrugged out of his jacket and stood behind me, holding it open. I smiled and slipped my arms into its welcomed warmth. It smelled of leather with a hint of smoke. Weird. I'd never seen him with a cigarette.

"Thanks."

"No problem." He grinned. "It's big on you."

I wagged my arms and giggled. "Just a little."

"Hey, it's early yet. Do you want to come see where I live? We can order a pizza. I'm starving."

What if ordering pizza was code for having sex? I bit my lip and stopped wiggling my arms.

He caught my hesitation. "Hey, it's cool. No big deal."

"No, it's not that I don't want to, it's just…"

I felt dumb admitting I was nervous to go there alone with him. Plus, Aunt Loretta would probably be wondering where I was. I remembered an appointment card I'd noticed that morning on the fridge that I'd wanted to talk to her about. "I should probably get home."

He nodded. "Sure. Maybe another time."

I offered a smile. "I'd like that."

Ransom jerked his head toward the bike. "C'mon. I'll get you home."

*W*ithout me saying a word, Ransom somehow knew to drop me off at the end of the long dirt driveway. I hopped off the bike and tried to unhook my backpack from the silver bars. He crossed over to help, our fingers tangling together as he worked to get it loose. I cleared my throat and pulled away, letting him get it.

"Here you go." He'd worked it free and handed the bag to me.

"Thanks." I traded him his jacket for my bag, then slid it over my shoulder, not sure what else to say.

He hopped back on his bike, still watching me. "So how about this weekend?"

"This weekend?"

"Do you want to come over and hang out? Order that pizza?"

Part of me was intrigued by him, but part of me was still trying to figure him out. And besides, it was nice to have someone to talk to who didn't know my history, and who didn't make me feel judged. Before I could question my true motivations, I blurted out, "How about Saturday? About three?" I waited for him to scoff at getting together in the afternoon, but he didn't.

"Sounds good. Pick you up here?"

"How about I just come over? Is that okay?"

He nodded and smiled again. "Sure thing, Princess. I got your number, I'll text you the address."

"Okay. I'll see you Saturday."

He gave me a little salute against the side of his helmet and revved the engine before taking off down the dirt lane.

Guess I had a date.

When spider webs unite, they can tie up a lion.
—Ethiopian Proverb

unt Lor's car was gone. I again remembered the small card on the fridge, her appointment that afternoon. My gut twisted with worry.

I needed to do something normal to keep me from pacing the kitchen while I waited for her to get back. Food. I'd make dinner for her. I opened the refrigerator. It looked pretty grim—a half jug of milk, some eggs, and a few condiments. I studied the shelves like a meal might suddenly materialize. No such luck.

Sighing, I swung open the freezer door and shut it almost immediately. I didn't quite trust my culinary abilities far enough to make anything that required thawing first. There had to be something in the cupboards I could handle.

A quick check revealed a box of Tuna Helper. That I could do. I grabbed a nearby can of tuna. After reading the directions on the back of the box, I measured out the ingredients and popped the covered dish in the microwave. Twenty-seven minutes and we'd be good to go. It could just stay covered until she got home, and we'd eat together.

I changed out of my uniform and threw on sweats and

an old, baggy T-shirt. My lack of clothing choices reminded me that I needed to do some laundry. I scooped up a huge armful and stuffed it in a basket. It barely made a dent in the pile of dirty clothing left on the floor. I carried the basket out to the kitchen where an apartment sized washer/dryer combo hid behind folding doors. I threw a load in the washer, tossed in a cup of detergent, and turned it on. Then I headed back to my room to get to work on details of my plan for the tasks to be completed later in the week.

My notebook was once again hidden under my mattress; I slid it out and opened it. The second page revealed which initiate was scheduled for a task on each given day.

> Monday – Zena
> Tuesday – Zena and Patrick
> Wednesday – Becky, Zena, Patrick

I turned the page and read over the detailed outline that laid out what I'd planned for each of them to do for the first three days of Hell week, the ones I'd already updated on the website. After thinking for a few minutes, I wrote out the tasks for the rest of the days, all the way through the weekend. I added notes in careful script:

> Thursday – Becky
> Friday – Patrick and Becky
> Saturday – Becky and Patrick
> Sunday – Zena

Zena shouldn't have any problems with her task on day one. She certainly had what it took to complete her role looks-wise, and her attraction to Blane should make it one she'd actually enjoy on top of it.

Tuesday's tasks were a little trickier. It was a two-man job, although neither Zena nor Patrick would know what the other was up to. Still pretty foolproof.

I grinned in anticipation. Oh, would that one make Jessica freak out. It was so beautiful in its underhandedness, I almost wanted to frame my words. I carefully reviewed the plan one last time, knowing I couldn't leave room for error. A delicious shiver ran through me just thinking of Jessica's response when it all went down.

*M*y phone beeped late that night, almost eleven. I couldn't sleep, so I heard it right away. It was probably Ransom, texting his address like he'd promised.

I reached out and checked the screen. Not Ransom after all. Instead, Jeremy's photo beamed up at me from my phone. Unexpected guilt tickled when I saw his face after I'd been expecting to hear from Ransom. I bit my lip and swiped to read his text.

Hey.

I rolled over onto my side and answered him, *Hey you. What's up?*

I'm sorry about acting like a jerk earlier.

I typed back, *It's okay. You didn't really anyway.*

My guilt intensified reading his words after spending the afternoon with Ransom. I tried to tell myself I had no reason to feel bad, that there was nothing going on between Jeremy and me. It's not like Jeremy had ever asked me out or anything.

My phone dinged again. *So, you okay?*

I'm fine, why?

It took longer for his response to come through this

time. *I don't know. I saw you leave with that guy and just wanted to make sure everything was okay.*

So that's why he'd messaged me. He wanted to find out more about Ransom. I wasn't getting into that discussion; it seemed rude to talk about another guy with him.

Everything's good, but thanks. Right after I pressed send, I typed another message. *I'm tired. See you in school tomorrow?*

I wasn't really sleepy, but for some reason, it felt like an iron fist was squeezing my stomach tight, and I didn't know what to say to him.

Okay. I'll see you then. Good night, Sam.

Good night.

I punched my pillows a few times and attempted to get comfortable. I tried to soothe myself with thoughts of the plan, but dregs of remorse floated up and kept interrupting me. This wasn't the person I'd aspired to be years ago... someone who plotted and planned to bring another person down.

The niggling thought that doing the whole thing made me as bad as Jessica kept tiptoeing in. Maybe Jeremy was right. Did wanting to get even with Jessica for the years of bullying make me an awful person? Worries slithered through my brain like poisonous snakes. No wonder Satan preferred the form—they were evil and hard to keep at bay.

fifteen

They say curiosity killed the cat. Probably
for a damn good reason.
—Samantha Evans

The homes around me all looked like they could use a fresh coat of paint. Or a wrecking ball. I hadn't been to this section of town in years. It was more the fringes of town, like the ratty tufts of material at the end of a scarf that people usually plucked off.

I slowed my pace and glanced around. Some of the buildings didn't have numbers, so I hoped I could find Ransom's place. From the looks of it, most of the houses on the street had been long since sectioned off into apartments.

A sharp gust of wind blew, and I shoved my hands in the pockets of my down vest. I'd thrown it on over my sweater since the thermometer hanging outside read forty-two degrees, and I hadn't wanted to freeze on my walk.

Walking sucked. So did depending on other people to get me where I needed to go. It wasn't like I could ask Jeremy to drive me to Ransom's apartment. Slightly awkward.

Anyway, Jeremy and I hadn't talked Friday in school after all.

He'd texted me in the morning to let me know he was

home sick but told me to have a good day. And he'd sent a smiley face. Hopefully that meant he was over being angry with me for what was about to go down next week.

Another glance and I decided it looked like the right place. I stood in front of a tan duplex. The numbers were missing on the one side, but the left side read 314. Ransom's text said he lived in 316-B, so I assumed he was on the right half.

No one else was out on the street. No kids played, although there weren't really any front yards to play in anyway. Some kind of mechanical, whining noise carried from somewhere nearby. A leaf blower maybe? But there were no trees in sight to even scatter leaves.

I tightened my fists in my pockets and took a deep breath for courage. It's not like I had anything to be scared of, I'd spent plenty of time with him before; he wasn't a stranger anymore. But I wasn't naive. I was going to his house. Alone.

Still stalling, I pulled out a ChapStick and ran some cherry balm over my lips. I tossed my hair back and walked up the wooden steps. He'd said to go in and up the stairs to his door.

I hesitantly pushed the front door open and quietly called out, "Hello?" No answer.

A narrow foyer led to another door to my immediate right. A flight of carpeted stairs in front of me rose to what I assumed was Ransom's apartment. I stepped inside the landing. It smelled like burnt food and must. I twitched my nose but kept going.

The railing was smooth from years of use. I tried not to make any excess noise as I climbed the stairs, although I had no idea why I felt the need to walk so quietly. When I got closer to the top, music carried through a closed door off to the right—some classic rock song that I recognized, but couldn't name.

Before I could chicken out, I knocked on the door. Three quick raps. I unzipped my coat, then rezipped it while I waited for him to answer. Except he didn't. Right when I'd decided to leave, the door swung open.

Ransom stood before me, sexy as sin in a white T-shirt and a pair of dark-washed, low riding jeans. No boots this time. No shoes at all, in fact. He was barefoot.

I swallowed.

"Hey! I wasn't sure if I heard a knock. I thought maybe you changed your mind and weren't coming." He smiled, and his eyes lit up. He motioned me inside.

I stepped forward, smiling back nervously. He looked good. Too good. And I was in his apartment, alone, with him.

"Um...sorry. It took me longer to walk here than I expected. I don't have my license yet, but I'm getting it soon." I was babbling but couldn't quite help the rush of words.

He shut the door behind us. "No problem."

We were in his living room. Somehow the smallish space seemed even smaller with him standing so close. I could practically feel the heat from his body next to me.

A fish flopped in my stomach as I looked around. A sofa faced a large flat screen television. The TV seemed out of place with the rest of the furniture. The only other pieces were a low coffee table and a dinged up end table. There were no pictures on the walls.

"Well, come on in and sit down. Do you want something to drink?"

I noticed a bottle of beer on the table next to the sofa. "Uh, sure, thanks." I wandered over and perched on the edge of the worn out couch.

He returned from the adjoining kitchen a minute later with a can of soda and a beer. "I didn't know what you'd want." He set them both on the table in front of me and sat down next to me.

I didn't want to look like a child, so I said, "Beer's fine, thanks."

He grinned and reached over to twist the top off the bottle then handed it to me before leaning back. "I feel bad that you walked all this way. I would have gladly picked you up."

He picked up his own beer. His long fingers curled around the dark bottle. "So, did you have any problems finding the place?"

I shook my head and took a sip. I rarely drank, didn't really like the taste of beer, but I managed a smile after I swallowed. Being so close to him was wreaking havoc on my nerves. I wanted him to move closer, I wanted him to stay where he was. I took another drink, bigger this time.

"You look great. I like your hair down like that."

A blush skittered up my neck and filled my cheeks. "Thanks."

"Do you want to take your coat off? It's pretty warm in here."

"Oh, um...sure." I set my drink down and slipped my arms out of the vest, then wondered what to do with it.

"Here." He took it from me and tossed it over the arm of the sofa. His fingers were warm when they grazed mine during the exchange.

He offered an understanding smile. "Sam, I can tell you're nervous, but you don't have to be." He gave a small shrug. "Look, we can do whatever you want. Movie? Food? Talk? Charades?" He smiled wider this time.

He had tiny dimples I hadn't noticed before. I relaxed a little.

"Food sounds good. I'm starving," I said. I immediately wondered if I was supposed to admit that to him, or pretend like other girls I knew that I never ate. And if I did, it was only things like kale or cucumbers. I decided if I was going to do this, try to hang out with him, he might as well know I had a healthy appetite, one that didn't involve only eating rabbit food.

He reached into his pocket and pulled out a phone. While he placed the order for a large pizza, I tucked my legs beneath me and glanced around some more, sipping my beer. The taste didn't seem as horrible now after a few large swallows.

After he finished the call, he set the phone down and looked at me. "So, tell me more about you."

"What do you want to know?" I tucked a piece of hair behind my ear.

"Anything. Everything."

I laughed and curled my toes inside my shoes. "I'm not all that exciting."

He shook his head. "It doesn't have to be exciting. I just want to know you better." He twisted to face me, and leaned forward a little. "Tell me whatever you want to."

So I did. Somehow, amidst a second beer, I found myself telling him about how I came to live with my aunt and about all the crap at school. The fact that I felt free to share that much with him surprised me. But he was a great listener. It felt good. I relaxed a little more into the sofa.

A knock sounded on the door.

Ransom jumped up. "Must be the pizza. Hang on."

He paid the driver and carried a large box back into the room.

"C'mon, let's eat." He motioned me to the floor, where he'd set the box and some napkins he'd grabbed from the kitchen.

I slid from the couch to join him. It smelled great. After talking for so long, my nerves finally settled enough that I could take a large bite.

"Mmm…this is really good." I spoke through a mouthful of tangy sauce and melted cheese.

"I know. They make the best pizza in the neighborhood. I usually order from them at least twice a week."

He licked some sauce from his lips, and I tried not to stare.

"So, you were telling me about this Jessica girl."

Somehow, I had the feeling that Ransom wouldn't judge me, that he'd understand what I was doing.

"I came up with this plan," I began.

He arched an eyebrow and grinned. "Sounds devious."

"Oh, it is." I gave a fake evil laugh, and he laughed with me.

I told him everything about my strategy to get back at Jessica. And he told me I was brilliant.

"I know, right?" I beamed. By now the pizza box sat empty between us on the floor. "I mean, it's so perfect!"

He nodded. "Remind me never to get on your bad side."

"Oh I will!" I winked. It felt good to joke and tease with

him, to know someone else *got it.*

He even offered some suggestions that I could do during Hell week with the initiates. Being able to share the whole thing with someone, someone who understood what I was doing, and why I was doing it, was like a weight lifted off my shoulders.

I suddenly became aware that Ransom had stilled and was staring at me, at my mouth, staring in a way that screamed, *I want to kiss you right now, this second.* My heart raced, and my breathing quickened. He still didn't move toward me, and I wondered briefly if I had the guts to lean in and kiss *him.*

His eyes rose to meet mine. As I gazed at him, completely unable to move, I noticed his jaw twitched the tiniest bit, and I heard him swallow.

His eyes moved closer and closer to mine. It was like everything was moving in slow motion. Like we were swimming underwater toward each other—all speckles of light and movement and lungs tightening in need of air.

I wasn't even sure I was still breathing until the second he was a fraction of an inch away, and I felt myself gasp.

Then his eyes closed, lashes fanning against his bronzed skin. I must have done the same because the next thing I knew fireworks exploded through me as his lips moved on mine.

His kiss started soft, for just the briefest seconds, but quickly turned hungry. My mouth seemed to know what to do because it opened and welcomed him in. His hands were in my hair, on my cheeks, my neck. I wanted to taste him over and over. Sparks raced through my body and pooled in my stomach. Every place he touched electrified me.

I wanted more, more of him, more of the sensation. I learned what it felt like to run my fingers through his thick hair. It was even better than my fantasies. Somewhere I heard deep moans and didn't know if they came from my throat or his. But it didn't matter. We fell back on the floor, side by side, never coming up for air.

His hand moved down from my head to my lower back, pulling me tighter against him. I'd never imagined...couldn't have imagined...what it would feel like to be so desired. So wanted. I reveled in the sensation. Someone wanted *me* that fiercely. The knowledge emboldened me, made me feel powerful for the first time in my life.

He breathed my name against my neck as his lips trailed a path down my collarbone. My head tilted back. I couldn't think, I just felt. His rough palm grazed my hip, fingers splayed under the hem of my thin sweater.

It became harder to concentrate on enjoying his kisses when his hand moved across my rib cage. Although it felt amazing, I'd never done anything like this with a guy and nerves were getting the better of me. I tried to relax and just let it happen.

"God, you feel so good." His mouth moved from my lips down my neck again. His lips slid down the V of my sweater, and he pushed one side away with his mouth, his tongue flicking patterns as he went.

"Ransom, wait, stop." I pushed against him to sit up, pulling my sweater back into place. Unexpectedly, tears threatened.

He sat up, hair mussed, and licked the edge of his bottom lip. "What's wrong?"

"I can't. I'm sorry...if I lead you on." I pushed my hair

out of my face with a shaking hand. "But I'm not ready for this."

He didn't say anything for about five seconds; he just sucked air in slowly and ran his fingers through his hair, messing it up more. His knee bent in front of him, his other leg still tangled against mine.

He shook his head. "Don't apologize. I should be the one apologizing. I pushed too far, too fast. I'm sorry."

Relief washed through me that I wasn't going to have to make some awkward escape, or worse, have to try to fight him off if he didn't take no for an answer.

My eyes must have shown him what I was thinking, because he sighed and reached for my hand. "Did you really think I was going to try to make you do something you didn't want to do?"

When I didn't answer, he pulled his hand away. "Jesus, Sam, what do you take me for? I'm sorry. I shouldn't have gone as far as I did, I should have stopped sooner." He drew in a long slow breath and looked down. "I like you, and it felt good. But that's no excuse."

I reached out and took his hand. "I like you too." I took a deep breath. "And it felt good to me too."

He looked up.

"But." I shrugged. "This is all I can offer right now. I'm not ready for…"

"Sex," he said bluntly.

"Anything more than this."

His dimples peeked out. "I'm not going to lie and say I'm not kind of disappointed." When my eyes widened, he hurried on. "Hey, I'm a guy. But," he stressed, "I'm not going to push anything either. I told you, I like you, and I meant it."

I weaved my fingers through his, a warm glow building inside. *He liked me.*

He bit his full lower lip. "I don't want to ruin the one possible good thing I have going in my life right now." He leaned in to kiss me.

But I wasn't ready to pick up where we'd left off, so I pulled away.

He sighed. "Maybe we should get you back home." When I looked at him, he quickly added, "Next time, I'll take you out somewhere on a real date. If I didn't already blow it that is."

"You didn't blow it," I said softly.

"Good." He smiled.

He helped me up, and I walked over to grab my coat.

"Why don't you let me give you a ride?" he asked. "It's getting cold out. You're going to freeze walking all the way home."

I laughed. "I'm pretty sure it's just as cold on your motorcycle."

His eyebrows furrowed. "I meant in my car."

"You have a car?" My eyes widened.

He snorted. "Um…yeah. How do you think I get around in winter?"

I shrugged one shoulder and zipped my jacket. "I don't know. Taxi?"

He cracked up. "Yeah, because I can afford that." He walked over to the closet and grabbed a black hoodie to pull over his head. "Give me a minute to grab my shoes."

"You really don't have to drive me, I'm fine."

"Samantha, I'm not taking no for an answer. So shut that sexy mouth of yours and give me one minute to get my shoes on."

I shut my mouth, but still smiled.

He tapped me on the nose as he passed me to grab a pair of sneakers at the end of the couch.

After he turned off the stereo, he picked up the empty pizza box and beer bottles and carried them into the kitchen. On this way back out, he asked, "Do you need to use the bathroom or anything before we head out?"

Even though I did need to go, there was no way I was peeing down the hall from him. I shook my head.

"You ready?" He walked closer to where I stood, waiting.

"Yep, whenever you are."

"There's just one more thing I have to do quick before we leave."

I looked around. "What?"

"This." And he leaned in and kissed me gently on the lips. No pressure, no hands, just a feather-soft touch that lasted several delicious seconds.

When he was done, I slowly opened my eyes. "What was that for?"

"Because I wanted to kiss you the way I should have kissed you the first time." He took my hand and nodded toward the door. "Come on, Princess, your carriage awaits."

sixteen

To exact revenge for yourself or your friends is not only a right, it's an absolute duty.
—Stieg Larsson

*H*ell Week.

It'd finally arrived. I shoved my coat on the hook in my locker and peeked around after hurrying into school. For once, I'd actually wanted to get there early.

Zena strolled down the hall, and based on her outfit, she was all set to do her first task. Holy crap, did she take her role to heart. I pressed my lips together to keep from smiling—or worse yet, cackling with glee.

She walked past me without a single glance and sashayed straight toward Blane, who stood rooting around in his locker.

Blane Reichert, quarterback golden boy and boyfriend to Jessica.

Zena's oxford shirt was unbuttoned halfway down her chest, and she sported a black lace push-up cami underneath. Her uniform tie hung right in the center of her rather impressive cleavage. She must have rolled the waist of her skirt, because it fell a solid four or five inches above her knees. Tall black boots completed the student-vamp look. Zena was gorgeous on a bad day, but looking all sexed up like that? Poor Blane didn't stand a chance.

I opened a book and held it in front of me as I leaned against my locker, pretending to page through it as I observed my handiwork. Seemed she took the bait. And from the looks of her, if she didn't get hauled to the principal's office first, she was following my suggestion to do whatever it took to lure poor little Blane right in. I once again thanked the heavens for Zena's poor taste in men.

She sidled up next to him, and leaned provocatively against the locker next to his. One arm stretched above her head, and her hip jutted out as she twirled a strand of her long, dark hair. Blane glanced up then did a double take. His chest puffed out like a rooster as he tossed her a smug grin.

Oh yeah, it'd work. Thank God his locker stood close enough to mine that I could eavesdrop without being obvious.

"Hi, Blane," Zena purred.

Okay, maybe not the most original opening, but with that outfit I'd let it slide.

Blane's eyes were still double their normal size, and kept zooming in on Zena's chest. "Hey," he stuttered. I had to cover my mouth and fake a cough so they didn't hear me snort.

"I wanted to tell you how much I loved watching you in the game last Friday." She leaned in just enough. "You looked so hot in that uniform. Your big…" She ran her fingers down his chest. "Muscles."

He gave a cocky grin and actually flexed. "You like that, huh?"

"Oh, you have no idea how much I like that." She squeezed his tricep. Part of me felt amused, but a bigger part of me wanted to hurl.

I willed her to keep it short, keep him wanting. She must have received my psychic message because she trailed her fingers down his arm and started to turn away from him. Right before she gave him the full back view, she used a throaty voice to instruct him to, "Don't be a stranger," and winked.

Just then, Jessica turned the corner and caught Blane ogling Zena as she slinked away.

Oh. My. God. Talk about sheer perfection. I couldn't have scripted it better myself.

"Excuse me?" Jessica slapped him on the arm, eyes blazing.

"Ow! What the hell, Jessica?" He came out of his stupor and stared at her, his big, dumb mouth agape.

"What the hell was *that*?" Her eyebrow rose, and her perfectly glossed lips pursed in disgust.

"What was what?" He slammed his locker closed. "Christ. Are you on the rag or something?"

Her eyes widened into saucers. She leaned in and poked him in the chest. Good to know it wasn't just me on the receiving end of that trademark move.

"If you think you can check out other girls, think again. I can have any guy I want with the snap of my fingers." She exhibited her guy-fetching snap. "And I'm not about to put up with my boyfriend panting after trash like *that*." She jerked her head in Zena's retreating direction.

I'd become so enthralled with the scene unfolding in front of me that I'd forgotten to be discreet.

"And what are *you* looking at, freak?" She stared straight at me, glittering eyes daring me to say a word.

It amazed me how little her taunts bothered me now that I knew what was in store for her. So instead of my normal blushing and stammering, I offered a sweet smile in return.

Her mouth snapped closed, and she grabbed Blane's hand to yank him down the hall. I could tell he was still getting chewed out the whole way by how her head bobbed up and down and her hand gestured wildly. Little did she know, but her going into all out bitch mode had only helped my cause.

I hadn't been sure Zena would do it, but obviously she also had enough issues with Jessica and her crew that she felt no qualms stealing Jessica's douche boyfriend out from under her turned-up nose.

The bell rang, and I rushed to make it to English Lit before the teacher marked me late. I thought of the passage from *Hamlet* that'd stood out for me the night before as I'd read the assignment for class.

O wicked wit and gifts, that have the power so to seduce!

Ms. Sheppard would be so proud of me, proving Shakespeare was still relevant even today. I grinned and slipped through the classroom door. I couldn't wait for lunch. It was going to be epic.

*J*eremy waited at my locker when I went to drop off my books before lunch. I approached, trying to read his expression. I figured he'd try to make a last ditch effort to stop me.

"Hey," I said, cautiously.

He grinned. "Hey yourself."

Okay, nice surprise. I'd been expecting furrowed brows or his judgy face.

I slipped next to him and opened my locker.

"What are you doing Saturday night?" he asked.

I turned from trying to wedge my thick history book onto the shelf between all my other books and junk. "I'm not entirely sure yet. Why? What's up?"

"Because we're going to a party Pete's having at his house." He waved a fluorescent orange piece of paper my way.

"Pete's having a party?" Pete never had parties. He didn't even go to parties. The image of his name on the list in Jessica's email flashed before me. Could it have something to do with that?

I took the paper and scanned it. *Dress up and party on— It's a Masquerade Party this Saturday night!*

A light went on in my head. This party could so work with my plan. I could weave in some of the ideas Ransom had given me and have my initiates do them Saturday night.

"Okay, sure!"

He eyed me skeptically. "*Sure?*"

"Um, yeah. Sure, I'll go." I smiled and closed my locker door.

We headed toward the cafeteria. Jeremy still looked at me like he expected me to sprout a second head any second.

"Why are you looking at me like that?" I asked.

"I'm surprised. I thought I'd have to twist your arm to agree to go." His eyebrows raised above his glasses.

I shoulder bumped him. "Don't be dumb. Why wouldn't I go with you?"

He cocked his head and gave me a meaningful look. "I'm not sure where to even begin answering that one."

We rounded a table of football players throwing food at each other. I didn't see Blane. I hoped he and Jessica hadn't snuck out for lunch together. That'd put a kink in things. I turned my attention back to Jeremy as we slipped into the line for our trays.

"What's that supposed to mean?" I asked him.

"Seriously?"

"Uh...yeah." I grabbed a salad and a roll. Jeremy went with the plate of unidentifiable meat and a blob of instant mashed potatoes. You'd think for what they charged in tuition, we'd be eating lobster.

We rounded to the dessert station, where I snagged two slices of cherry pie and put one on each of our trays. After we both pressed our finger to the scanner to pay, we headed to our usual spot.

He slowed down as we approached the table. I turned to face him. "What's going on, Jer?"

He looked like he wanted to say something but changed his mind. He shook his head. "Nothing, forget it."

I sighed. "Okay."

We slid into our seats. I sat across from Abby, and Jeremy took the spot right next to her. I noticed he didn't sit next to me, even though there was plenty of room.

"You guys are all coming, right?" Pete looked up from his tray.

"What brought this on? Since when are you the party master?" Abby teased.

Pete shook his head. "Blame her." He pointed to Celia. She grinned and clapped her hands.

"It's going to be awesome. Everyone has to come in costume. His dad even agreed to book a band," she gushed. Celia was easily the most social of all of us.

"Dude!" Jeremy high fived him. "Welcome to the land of the socially aware."

Abby elbowed Jeremy. "Oh, like you're one to talk. Mister party out among the masses himself." She smiled at him, a flirty smile.

He grinned back. "Hey, I know how to socialize."

My fork paused on its way to my mouth, momentarily forgotten as I observed the exchange. What the hell was that? Abby and Jeremy? Since when had they become so buddy-buddy? I bit down on my cucumber slice so hard that I managed to get my tongue along with it. I ignored the pain and kept watching them.

Their heads tilted together as Abby whispered something in his ear, and he laughed like it was the funniest thing in the world. I stabbed a cherry tomato.

Pete told us all about the party, while Celia kept jumping in. Abby turned to Jeremy and asked, "So, what are you going as?"

"I'm not sure yet. I'll have to think about it." His fingers wrapped around his bottle of juice. He always drank juice with lunch; he was lactose intolerant. I wondered if Abby knew that about him.

She smiled and played with her hair. "Well, I think I'm going to go as Cat Woman."

I wrinkled my nose. "Cat Woman?" My words came out harsher than I'd planned.

Everybody at the table turned to look at me.

Abby frowned. "What's wrong with Cat Woman?"

Nothing, except the fact she'd be running around in a tight body suit, probably trying to get her claws in *my* best friend.

"Nothing," I muttered. I shut the lid of my half-eaten salad. "I just figured you'd want to wear something with a little more class." Yikes. Did I just say that out loud?

The shocked expressions on everyone around me confirmed that I had.

"Geez, Sam. Why don't you tell us what you really think?" Jeremy's look was a mixture of surprise and reproach.

Abby squirmed on the bench next to him, playing with the spoon in her yogurt, not saying a word. Or looking at me. She usually wasn't one to take crap…it must be the fact that she knew how close Jeremy and I were that kept her from telling me to shove it. Correction…how close we were until our fight, anyway.

"Well, I think you'll look great," Celia said, leaning in to smile at Abby. Ever the peacekeeper.

Jeremy shook his head and started to eat again. An awkward silence descended upon the table like a storm cloud.

"You *asshole*!" Jessica's familiar high-pitched squeal pierced the air. We all looked over. She stood, shaking a phone inches from Blane's face. "What the hell is this?"

I lifted my chin, trying to see over the students at the table between the show and me.

"Jessica, would you calm down?" Blane reached up for the phone. "My God, you're making a scene."

"I am *not* making a scene!" she hissed.

She was, actually. The entire cafeteria had gone silent. Everyone watched in rapt attention to see how it would play out, although I was probably more interested than anybody. I kinda wished I had some popcorn.

What in the world had Zena done? Sexted him? And how had Jessica discovered it? Then again, she probably had Blane by the short and curlies and monitored his every move. Stupid boy.

Jeremy caught my eye. He stared at me with something close to disgust. I straightened my shoulders and looked away. Abby could probably do a better job of living up to his standards anyway. I fought the emptiness that swirled through me at the realization.

Jessica continued to rant. Blane finally had enough of being embarrassed in front of his jock friends. He stood up and grabbed the phone. "It was just a freaking picture! Give it a rest!" he shouted.

Whoops. Guess that answered that question.

They'd finally gained the attention of Mr. Peltz, the assistant to the dean of students, who also served as lunch monitor. He strode toward their table, expression tight. His horrendous striped tie flapped a little as he marched toward Jessica and Blane.

Whispers all around the cafeteria rose to epic levels. Everyone busied themselves trying to guess just what, or who, they'd been fighting over. Jessica stood still, hands clenched at her sides. Her chin quivered, but she didn't say anything else.

"What is the meaning of this?" Mr. Peltz grabbed Blane's elbow and attempted to turn him around. Blane shook his arm free.

"Nothing. A misunderstanding," he muttered, not even bothering to look at Peltz.

Jessica looked ready to explode. Her eyes bulged, and I swore a faint green mist rose from her head.

"Ms. Wainright?" Peltz swiveled his head to include her. She refused to say a word.

"I want to see both of you in my office, immediately following lunch. Is that understood?"

They both nodded with stiff jerks of their heads.

"Fine. And one more outburst like this and you will both find yourself with detention." His voice rose. "Anyone else who behaves like that will get the same."

Ripples of laughter crossed the cafeteria. Even normally stoic Pete tried not to laugh at Peltz's round, red face as he thundered.

I spotted Zena at a small table in the corner. She had a phone in her hand and a very pleased look on her face. Score two for team Sam.

seventeen

Survival is a game with a chance;
revenge is a calculated plan of action.
—Ace Hood

J essica wasn't in school. She was probably shoe shopping to salve her wounded pride after the spectacle in the lunchroom yesterday. Although I welcomed the reprieve from her normal verbal smackdowns at my locker, I needed her here.

Perfect. Just freaking perfect.

I slammed my locker and tried to figure out what to do. The first part of the plan went to Zena. She would have to do some lead-in work before the second part of the plan. Part two included both Zena and Patrick, and those tasks required Jessica's presence. I needed to make some adjustments, pronto. I tapped my fingers against the strap of my bag, thinking.

Hopefully Patrick had the common sense to check the website to see what he was supposed to do considering his target wasn't around. I clenched my hands into fists, feeling my plan start to crumble around me.

I took a deep breath. It was still doable.

Mr. Moyer had prep period right after morning

homeroom. Most of the teachers stayed in their classrooms in case a student needed help or had a question. Not Moyer. Jeremy and I had seen him leaving the school several times during first period, and joked that he was probably sneaking out to blaze up. So instead of heading to my own homeroom, I hurried over to Room 318, the computer lab. Moyer's room.

He looked surprised to see me rush in, out of breath, messy ponytail flying behind me.

I held my hand over my chest to calm my racing heart. It didn't entirely work. I felt kind of gross considering the pseudo sucking up I was about to do.

"Mr. Moyer! I'm so glad I caught you."

His bushy unibrow rose. It looked like a fat caterpillar crawling across his forehead. "Yes, Ms. Evans? Can I help you with something?"

I turned on my best wide-eyed innocent look and stepped into the classroom. Several students looked up in curiosity. I ignored them.

"See, the thing is, I saw someone sideswipe your car when they drove past it this morning." I made sure to adopt a concerned tone, and bit my lip hoping to look nervous about relaying the information.

Moyer's eyes widened, and the fat caterpillar jiggled some more.

"I couldn't see who was driving, but I felt it was the right thing to do to come and tell you." I clasped my hands in front of me and shuffled my feet a little.

Now the caterpillar was halfway up his forehead. He stood. "They hit my car?"

Everyone knew his car was his baby. A vintage Jaguar convertible, he'd actually been seen wiping it down with a soft cloth after rainstorms.

I nodded, frowning.

He faced the class, mouth twisted in a grimace. "Attention." He briskly clapped his hands twice to be heard over the chatter. "Class, please excuse me. I have a personal matter that needs my immediate attention. Homeroom is over in a few minutes, so be on your best behavior until the bell rings and you move to your first period class."

A few kids nodded while the rest looked bored.

Moyer turned to me again. "Was it damaged badly? Could you tell?" He'd already begun slipping into the long, gray overcoat he'd grabbed from a hook next to the classroom door.

I shook my head, my expression sad. "I'm sorry, I couldn't see. It was on the opposite side from where I was standing."

It worked; he was leaving to check for damage. That would give me maybe five minutes. Of course, he'd probably wonder what was up once he got out to the lot to see there wasn't so much as a scratch on his precious Jag. I decided to cover my bases so he wouldn't become suspicious.

"I heard a loud noise when they drove by your car. Like I said, I couldn't actually see from where I was at, so maybe it was only them running over something. But I'd feel terrible if they really did something awful to your car and I didn't say anything."

He nodded. "Thank you, Samantha. I greatly appreciate it." He turned to head out. I had to keep him there until the bell rang.

"Wait!" I called.

"Yes?" He pulled at the sleeve of his jacket and looked impatient.

"I had a quick question about the assignment from yesterday."

He didn't bother to try to hide his annoyance. "Can't this wait until class?"

I glanced at the clock. Two minutes until the bell. I needed the room empty for what I was about to do.

"It's just…I wanted to make sure I copied down the correct coding that we need done for class today."

He glanced at his watch, then out the window toward the teacher's lot. Finally, he sighed and strode over to his desk. I followed. He shuffled through a folder, and pulled out a sheet of paper.

"Here's a copy of the assignment."

I took it from him. "Oh, thank you so much, Mr. Moyer. I really appreciate this," I gushed and glanced over his head to the clock.

"Yes, yes. That's fine. You're welcome. Now, if you'll excuse me." He brushed past me and hurried out the classroom door.

I held my breath and waited. Less than fifteen seconds later, the bell rang, dismissing students from homeroom. I pretended to busy myself studying the assignment sheet, trying to look like I was supposed to still be there.

When the last student filed out, I hurried over to the door and shut it, then as an added precaution, I flicked off the lights so no one would come in. I made my way as fast as I could over to a computer. My fingers clicked on the keys in record time. When the familiar skull and crossbones logo appeared, I logged in as administrator and adjusted the task for Patrick for today. Done, I logged back out, and made a point to clear the internet cache, including all temporary files.

I bent to grab my books from where I'd set them on the floor and stood up. The clock showed only three minutes had passed. I would be okay. Just as I walked by the wide set of windows, Mr. Moyer appeared marching toward the school. I knelt down, hands pressed flat against the floor, pulse racing. I scuttled as fast as I could to the door, afraid to stand up again in case he'd look in the window.

Wait. So what if he saw me? I could say I'd been waiting to see if he needed a description of the car. Play stupid. After all, I had no idea his car wasn't really hit. At least that's what I'd tell him if he saw me leaving his room.

The tardy bell rang for first period. Crap. I had to get to class; I didn't want to draw any more attention to myself. I flipped the lights back on.

The coast was clear as I opened the door and slipped into the hallway. The dominoes were all lined up. Now it was only a matter of hours until the first one tipped and they all fell down in the precise pattern I'd designed.

eighteen

I'm a bad girl because I like to tease. I know I've got sex appeal in my deck of cards.
—Katy Perry

Seniors had the option to eat outside or leave campus for lunch. I watched as Blane shut his locker and headed toward the exit doors. I followed behind, far enough back that my stalking wasn't obvious.

We rounded the end of the school building, and he headed down the grassy bank that led to the football field. He looked left and right a few times.

I made sure to stay pretty far back, and I'd thrown a baseball cap on to try to hide my face. I clamored down the grassy rise once he hit the bottom and turned right where he'd gone left.

The metal stadium bleachers sat empty this time of day. Most of the kids that went out for lunch had vehicles, and they ran to Panera or McDonalds. I'd counted on the privacy.

I snuck around the far side of the bleachers and crouched down to the right of the ticket booth. The cold air made me wish I'd grabbed a jacket. My ponytail whipped against my face from the wind, and I shoved it back impatiently.

Dark storm clouds rolled across the gray sky. Shadows

played peekaboo on the gravel in front of me as I waited, holding my breath. I stuck my head around the side of the narrow booth and jerked back a little when Blane came into view. I recognized his red letterman's jacket, although I couldn't see his face.

He walked under the first set of risers and stopped. I panned the area. Where the heck was Zena? If she didn't show up, Patrick wouldn't be able to complete his task. And he *needed* to do this one.

I cursed softly under my breath when Blane began to walk away back in the direction of the school. He'd only taken about five steps when a second figure appeared over the rise. Zena. I recognized her long hair blowing around her head even from this distance. Blane clearly noticed her too, because he stopped dead in his tracks.

When she caught up to him, the two of them walked together back over to the bleachers. I wanted to creep closer but didn't dare. I held my breath, waiting. They ducked underneath.

A minute later Zena leaned in toward him.

The two figures morphed into one giant shape. It looked like quite the make-out session based on how long they pressed together.

A flash appeared in the waning light from about twenty yards away, from the direction of the concession stand. Then another.

Blane jumped back from Zena and looked around. She reached out an arm to draw him back in. He apparently didn't argue since just seconds later they were smashed up against each other once again.

Another flash.

They didn't seem to notice or care anymore.

I no longer felt the sharp gravel against my knee as I knelt down, observing. I pushed up from the ground and pressed against the side of the wooden booth, waiting it out. A quick glance at my watch showed there were two more minutes to go. I kind of felt bad for Zena. I couldn't imagine having Blane's tongue down my throat for five whole minutes, but she obviously held no such issue with it based on her hands running through his hair.

And it appeared Patrick had done his new job as well. Since Jessica wasn't in school to witness it, then we could still get the proof to show her.

I rested my head against the wall, closed my eyes, and breathed in deep. The chill no longer bothered me; it invigorated me. By this time tomorrow Jessica's love life would be over.

"*W*ant a ride home?"

Jeremy materialized next to me as I made my way down the wide front steps of the school at the end of the day.

I stopped abruptly. We rarely went home together anymore. Not since April when he'd gotten an afterschool job at the art supply store in town.

"Don't you have work?"

He shook his head. "Things have been kind of slow since that Michaels opened up out on the highway. They just cut my hours."

I frowned. "That sucks."

"Yeah." He kicked a loose stone. "Anyway, I was wondering if we could talk. We haven't been doing too much of that lately."

I took a step toward him. "I'd like that. Thanks."

His hair blew into his eyes as he looked at me. He didn't say anything, but a hint of his familiar smile peeked through. He jerked his head in the direction of the student lot and began to walk. I fell into step beside him, shoving my hands in the pockets of my jacket to keep them warm. Towering oak trees lined the pathway, probably planted a century ago. Colored leaves drifted in lazy patterns toward the ground around us.

We reached his Acura, and he pressed a button on his key fob. After the familiar *beep-beep*, I grabbed the passenger door handle and climbed in, tossing my bag at my feet.

Once he'd started the car, he turned on the heat. I held my hands toward the vents.

"Um…so how do you think we did on our lab today?"

"Sam, I didn't ask you to ride with me so we could talk about our schoolwork."

I figured as much. I looked at my lap then him.

"What did you want to talk about?"

He sighed. "I don't know."

I studied my clasped hands, afraid that whatever I said would only make things worse.

"Look, I'm really sorry about how I've been jumping down your throat. You're my best friend, and that was wrong." He looked right at me as he apologized.

"I'm sorry too. I hate fighting with you, Jer." I meant every word.

"It's just… I'm worried about you, that's all. I just don't

see how any good can come from all of this."

"Jeremy—"

"No, wait. Let me finish." He reached over and touched my hand. "I want to be there for you, and support you. I hope you know that. But…"

"But you can't." I looked down. He had a paper cut on his thumb. I tried to concentrate on that, instead of what he was saying. I couldn't even imagine it might mean that the relationship we shared was coming to an end.

Where does friendship draw the line? Apparently for Jeremy, it was in a spiral notebook.

He squeezed my hands. The motion, the feel of his hand, I'd recognize it in my sleep. Then again, maybe dreams were the only place I still deserved his touch, his caring. In dreams, maybe I hadn't turned in to some hateful monster. The one even I didn't like very much a lot of the time, but couldn't control. Sometimes being out of control was easier.

I looked up. "I get it, Jer," I said softly.

"I'm sorry." He stroked my thumb. "I really do care about you, you know."

I believed him. More than anyone, I trusted Jeremy. I knew when he said something, he meant it. But more than words, I knew it from his actions through the years. I hoped he knew how much he meant to me, too. Even now.

We sat, not speaking, another minute or two, and then he pulled his hand away to shift the car into Drive.

I missed his touch immediately. I missed my friend.

But it was too late to turn back now, and maybe both of us knew it. As much as I didn't want to admit it, too much had changed.

After Jeremy dropped me off, I sat outside on the front

porch steps. I didn't feel like going inside yet. A part of me just wanted to leave town, to run away somewhere no one knew me. To start over.

Tears rolled down my cheeks. I didn't care, didn't even bother to brush them away. Martha's dog barked like crazy as usual, but for once it didn't annoy me. I actually appreciated the normalcy of the loud yaps.

When had my life spun so far out of control? That day in the courtroom? The day I first heard my parents arguing about what my father had done? When my mother dropped me off at Aunt Loretta's promising to be back soon? The day Jessica ended our friendship? When had I stopped believing I mattered?

I had no idea.

I tucked my chin farther down into the collar of my jacket, closed my eyes, and imagined a completely different life for myself, one where I didn't feel less than everyone around me every day, or have to wish I had parents who wanted me. *Really* wanted me, and loved me.

One where I was happy.

The door to the trailer squeaked open behind me. I didn't turn around. I wasn't ready to face reality yet.

"Samantha? Why are you sitting outside in this cold?"

I tried to hold on to my fantasy life in my mind; I wasn't willing to let go just yet.

"Samantha? What's wrong? Come inside before you catch a chill."

I sighed. "I'll be right in, I promise."

Aunt Loretta didn't immediately go back inside. I'd expected that. I knew what I'd see if I turned around, concern filling her face, her thin arm holding the aluminum door with the chipped paint open as she watched me.

I squeezed my eyes closed even tighter for a few seconds, but I'd learned three years ago that people like me don't get their wishes. So instead of making one, I opened my eyes, stood up, and turned around. Seeing Aunt Lor's face riddled with caring and concern, just as I knew it would be, made me grateful for the one piece of my life that was constant, that was good.

And right now, that just might have to be enough.

Even if you fall on your face, you're
still moving forward.
—Victor Kiam

y face stared back at me from a postage-stamp-sized square on my brand-new driver's license. I looked like someone had shone a spotlight directly in my eyes before the bored-looking guy behind the counter at the DMV snapped the photo. Huge bug-eyes made me look perpetually startled. Not my best look, but at least I was legal to drive.

Aunt Loretta stood by me as I collected my license, and leaned over to give me hug. "I'm so proud of you, sweetie. I knew you'd do just fine."

I didn't know about *just fine*. Parallel parking wasn't my strong suit, and I had a feeling the test instructor took pity and passed me despite my many attempts to get between the bright orange cones.

"Thanks." I smiled, and I felt a rush of pride as I slipped the laminated card into my wallet.

Aunt Loretta had seemed to sense my mood earlier, and suggested heading over to the DMV after dinner. Maybe my promises to keep my grades up last time we'd talked had convinced her to change her mind. Or maybe she realized that with her health deteriorating, she couldn't always do all of the running that needed to be done, trips to the store or whatever. Knowing that I could drive myself places and not be dependent on her or Jeremy, or even Ransom, definitely boosted my bum mood.

I wiggled the keys in the air. "So this means I get to drive home, right?" It felt so nice to see her feeling okay, the Aunt Lor I used to know. I wanted to hold tight to each moment, and pretend the other times were a bad dream.

Her eyes twinkled. "It certainly does."

"Yes!" I pumped a fist in the air and ran over to the car. Aunt Lor followed me at a slower pace. When she caught up with me standing beside the old Buick, I opened the passenger door for her with a flourish. "Your chariot awaits, madam."

She tittered at my theatrics.

My euphoria dimmed just a bit once seated inside the car. The driving instructor was cake compared to Aunt Loretta's watchful eye.

"Make sure you don't drive too fast," she instructed me.

"Got it." I put the key in the ignition and turned the engine on.

"And don't forget to use your turn signals."

"I won't." I pressed down on the brake and shifted the car into reverse.

"Not too fast now!"

"I know," I said through gritted teeth. I checked the rearview mirror and backed out at a snail's pace to mollify my aunt.

"Make sure—"

I braked to a stop before I even left the parking space and faced her. "Aunt Lor, seriously. Stop. Please. You're making me nervous."

She sat quiet the rest of the way home after that. We made it in one piece, and I pulled in front of the trailer, grinning like a hyena.

"Ta-da! Home again, home again, jiggety-jig," I sang.

She looked over at me, and smiled gently. "I'm proud of you."

I smiled back. "Thanks. Come on, we deserve some ice cream."

For once, I didn't feel like the weight of the world rested on my shoulders. I just felt happy. Just as we had settled in to watch some TV with our dishes of mint chocolate chip set before us on the scarred coffee table, my phone rang. I glanced down.

"Uh, I'll be right back." I hurried halfway down the hall toward my bedroom before answering. "Hello?"

"Hey, beautiful." Ransom's husky drawl filled my ear.

I shut my bedroom door behind me and crossed the room to plop down on my unmade bed.

"Hey." I smiled against the phone.

"I was wondering what you're doing this weekend. Thought maybe you'd want to come over."

I plucked at my bedspread. "I don't know." Did I really want to open myself up? Was I brave enough to do that? Jeremy's face flashed before me, unbidden.

"What can I do to convince you?"

I leaned back into my pillow, deciding I deserved to be happy. "How about we go out instead?"

"Sure, we could, but I thought it would be more romantic to stay in." He paused. "I'll light some candles, put on some music…"

When I didn't respond, he switched gears.

"But hey, if you want to go out, we can do that too."

"I'm going to a party Saturday night. Why don't you go with me?"

I wanted to take back the words as soon as I uttered them. Where had *that* come from? And how would Jeremy and the others feel about me asking Ransom to go with me to Pete's party?

"A party's always good. Sure, count me in."

I couldn't deny the flutter of relief when he accepted, even though I was wary of how my friends might react when I showed up at Pete's with Ransom next to me. Guilt niggled; I didn't want to hurt Jeremy any more than I already had.

I pushed it down. Jeremy had made his choice clear. And it wasn't me.

"Okay. I'll give you a call later this week once I find out the details, okay?" I left out mentioning that it was a costume party. I figured I'd throw that in when I called him later.

"Sounds good," he said.

I was still kind of surprised that he'd agreed to go. "Thanks again for being cool about it."

"No problem." When he didn't say anything more, I bit my lip and wondered again if I'd made a mistake asking him to a high school party.

"Well, I guess I'll talk to you later then," I said, trying to think of a way to prolong our conversation. He didn't give me the time.

"Good night, Princess." And he hung up.

I sighed and stuck my tongue out at the phone. But at least now I'd have someone with me Saturday so I didn't feel like the odd man out. Abby would probably be all over Jeremy in her catsuit, and I certainly wouldn't be hanging out with the football players or cheerleaders. Hopefully Pete would think to invite some other kids, ones that didn't go all gaga for the Friday night lights.

Even though I'd asked Ransom to the party, I wasn't sure I wanted him to actually *go*. As much as I liked hanging out with him, I'd begun to question my reasoning for doing so. How much was real interest in *him*, and how much of it was to play someone I wasn't? I wasn't sure.

I glanced at the time. Almost eight. I really needed to get caught up on homework; I'd been pushing off a report for English and had fallen so far behind on reading for history that I wasn't even sure what chapter we were on. I couldn't believe how much I'd allowed the whole plan thing to mess with my grades.

Disgusted with myself, I jutted my chin out and resolved to change that, starting tonight. I wasn't about to lose my shot at a scholarship. Even getting back at Jessica wasn't worth that price. Besides, there wasn't anything left for me to do. It was out of my hands now. My website had the tasks for each of the initiates already posted under their respective log-ins for the rest of Hell week. Tomorrow's tasks would be another two-parter, Becky and Patrick, along with the second part of what Patrick started today.

I'd flung my book bag on the kitchen floor when we'd come home. I got up with a groan and headed out to get it. Looked like my first night as a newly licensed driver would be spent at my desk cramming. Fun times.

I'd just begun reading a chapter on American foreign policy when my phone rang. To my surprise, Celia's number was displayed on the screen.

My brows knotted together as I answered. She barely gave me a chance to say hello before she began commanding me to get down to the school. Now.

"Whoa, hold on. What for?" I tried to get a word in edgewise.

"It's Pete. I have no idea what's going on, but we all have to get down there to stop him."

I had a feeling what might be going on, and was surprised that Pete hadn't told Celia about being invited to rush. I was surprised that Pete was even going along with it. Maybe top grades weren't enough to make you feel secure in getting into the college of your dreams. Maybe he felt he had to.

"So are you coming?" Her voice snapped me back to the situation at hand.

"Did you call Jeremy and Abby?" Celia calling me rather than Jeremy was a vivid reminder of where things stood with Jeremy and me, and broke me inside.

"Yes, of course I did. But the more of us there, the better. Look, I have to go, he's…" Muted shouts and laughter carried through the line.

What in the world?

"I gotta go. Just get here." She disconnected the call.

I stood up and grabbed a hoodie. So much for American foreign policy.

twenty

*A difficult task can be done immediately. An
impossible task requires a bit more time.*
—George Santayana

I pulled into the student parking lot and looked around, trying to figure out where I was supposed to go now. Aunt Lor hadn't been thrilled with me going out this late, but I'd covered up by telling her I just had to go drop some class notes off at Celia's, because she'd forgotten her book. She seemed to buy my lie.

I hopped out of the car and walked toward the school. The windows were all dark, and I didn't see anyone moving inside or on the steps leading to the entrance. It flitted through my mind that maybe it was some kind of trick getting me to come here. But that didn't make sense, so I pushed the thought away, telling myself not to be stupid.

As I reached the rise overlooking the football field, flashes of light caught my attention. I squinted, trying to see better.

Down on the field, yellow-white dots danced in the air around the fifty yard line. Flashlights. I walked closer to the edge of the twenty foot rise of grass which lead down to the football field, and stared. My eyes had adjusted to the darkness, but they couldn't quite believe what they were seeing.

Two people—their build suggested they were guys— were throwing pieces of wood in a pile in the center of the field. It looked like they were building a bonfire. I cursed myself for not having the foresight to bring a flashlight too, and made my way down the slope to get closer.

"What are you doing? Pete, stop and think about this. If you get caught, you could get suspended." I recognized Celia's frantic voice as coming from the shadowy figure that stepped towards the two guys. I could now make out that the one closest to her was Pete.

"Celia, just go home, please. I have to do this, and now isn't the time to talk about it."

"What the hell is she doing here anyway?" I knew that voice too. Andrew Reichert. He played with Pete on the football team, and was in a few of my classes. I'd always thought him to be a bit of an ass. Like his cousin, Blane.

A hand touched my shoulder. I screamed and whirled around, nearly punching the person in the face as I flung my arms out wildly in front of me.

"Sam! It's me!"

My heart rate slowed back down at the sight of Jeremy standing about six inches away. His hair was tousled, like he may have been lying down before Celia commanded us all to show up to help with Pete. He took a step closer and reached out, almost like he was going to take my hand, but then drew back, seeming to think better of it. I stamped down my disappointment.

"Sorry if I scared you. I saw you headed down here and

followed you," he said.

I shook my head. "It's okay. What's going on?" I jerked my chin toward the field. "Celia didn't say much when she called, just to get here ASAP."

He shrugged. "Your guess is as good as mine."

My relief to see Jeremy was short lived, because seconds later, Abby appeared too.

She glanced from me to Jeremy. "Hey." It was clear her greeting wasn't meant for me.

"Hey," Jeremy replied, and an awkward silence fell.

Jeremy broke the silence first. "Well, let's go see what they're up to."

I nodded and we all headed toward the group on the field. By now, someone had lit the small pile of branches on fire. Smoke carried through the night sky, and the smell reminded me of the fireplace in our living room my family had growing up. Crackles and pops sounded as tiny sparks danced in the inky darkness.

Celia spotted us and marched over. "Tell him this is stupid," she demanded.

Pete and Andrew stood next to the fire and began to take off their clothing. My eyes widened as Pete tossed his T-shirt into the flames. Andrew tugged off his sweatpants and they went in as well.

Jeremy whistled, while Abby snorted. I stood there, mouth agape, trying to figure out what the hell was going on. Celia yelled again for Pete to knock it off and put his damn clothes back on.

It didn't work. Within minutes, they were both stripped down to their boxers. Glow-in-the-dark paint lined their chests, forming squiggles and broad stripes.

I looked to Jeremy. His shocked expression mirrored my own.

Celia pointed and stamped her foot. "Do something," she snapped at Jeremy. "He won't listen to me."

Jeremy shrugged. "What do you want me to do?"

She crossed her arms in front of her chest and stared in stony silence for a few minutes before speaking again. "This is crazy. I was over at his house, and about an hour ago he got a text from someone. The next thing I know, he says he has to leave. Said he had something important to do and that *he* was going to pick him up." She jerked her head toward Andrew. "So Andrew shows up with tubes of glow-in-the-dark paint and they disappear into the bathroom for like five minutes, and then they take off. He tells me he'll be back soon."

She frowned. "I wasn't just going to wait at Pete's house by myself, so I left too. I was driving behind them and got curious when they turned into the school, so I followed them down here to see this." She rolled her eyes.

I shook my head, trying not to laugh as the guys began dancing in weird, jerky motions circling the fire, ignoring us. Their knees drew up and down, some insane march, and they flailed their arms around.

Why would the Society have them do something like this here, at night, when no one was around to see it? The answer slammed in to me. Because someone *was* there to see it. As with all of the other Hell week tasks, someone from the Society was sure to be hidden somewhere close by, observing them to be sure their task was completed. They probably weren't thrilled that we'd stumbled upon it too, and were trying to stop it.

I peeked left and right, but saw no one in the shadows beneath the bleachers. They were well hidden. I had to fight the urge to wave anyway.

"Pete, you look like an idiot and if anyone catches you here…" She yelled again.

"Celia, I know it's a kind of weird, but it's not like they're hurting anything." Jeremy tried to calm Celia down when it became obvious that neither painted dancing guy was going to acknowledge us.

She stared at him. "He's playing Lord of the Flies in his underwear on school grounds. If he gets caught — "

"How's he gonna get caught?" Jeremy interrupted her.

Whoops and cheers drew our attention back to the crazy scene unfolding ten yards away.

"I…I don't know. But why is he even doing it?"

Jeremy just shrugged again.

I had a good idea, but it wasn't my secret to share, so I said nothing. I wondered if Jeremy had his suspicions too. Probably.

We stood in a huddle, shivering and watching while the guys ignored us and danced for about twenty more minutes. Finally, as the small fire began to dwindle down, Pete grabbed a nearby jug of water he'd obviously brought with him and threw it over the remaining embers, drowning them.

The four of us looked at one another, trying to figure out what would happen next. The guys had thrown their clothing in the fire, and I didn't see any bags or extra clothes lying on the ground.

Pete and Andrew gave each other high fives, and before we could say a word, ran toward the main road, not the student lot. I stared. Clearly their task wasn't over.

No way. I had to hide a chuckle.

We all took off chasing them. Celia obviously wanted Pete to stop, based on her shouts. I think the rest of us just wanted to see what was going to happen next.

"Come on, get in my car, we can head them off," Jeremy called. We veered to the right, where Jeremy's car sat parked, and piled in.

"Hurry up!" Celia instructed.

Somehow, Abby and I landed in the backseat together. We studiously ignored each other.

Jeremy ripped away from the curb, and we all rolled down our windows. It only took a couple of minutes to catch up to them. Thank God we were on a street with only a few houses. Pete and Andrew zigzagged back and forth on the road with their chests and backs glowing from the paint. They looked like two inebriated fireflies.

"Pete, would you get in the damn car?" Celia shouted. Pete turned around and waved, but kept going.

I couldn't help but giggle.

"It's not funny," Celia protested, but I could see a grin threatening to break through. Maybe she'd realized it wasn't that big of a deal. Stupid? Sure. Dangerous? Other than the world seeing Pete's skivvies, not really.

A moment later, we were all suddenly laughing, we couldn't help it. Jeremy beeped his horn and leaned out of his window a little bit to yell, "Go Titans!" Abby and I leaned out our windows and began whistling and cheering too.

Our noise must have attracted the attention of whoever lived in the house on the left hand side of the street because the front door opened, and an older man stood silhouetted by the warm light behind him. Pete and Andrew dove into the thick bushes at the side of the road. I winced. That'd leave a mark.

Jeremy slowed to a crawl. I twisted my neck to watch the man at the door as we drove past. He shook his head and went back inside, most likely used to the mayhem this time of year.

We waited a minute to see if Pete and Andrew would climb back out of the brush, but they didn't emerge. Maybe they'd cut through the woods and headed back to the school.

"Probably some dumb football thing. Who knows?" Jeremy glanced at Celia before meeting my gaze in the rearview mirror. I again wondered if he too suspected the real reason for Pete's antics.

She nodded. "You're probably right." It was clear Celia was oblivious, which kind of surprised me given how smart she was. I guess we all sometimes miss what's right in front of us.

I leaned forward and put my arm around her. "C'mon, why don't we all go grab a pizza or something, and by the time we're done eating, I bet Pete will be headed to your house." I smiled. "And besides, you always say Pete needs to come out of his shell a little."

She snorted. "I'd say after tonight that won't be a problem."

We all laughed.

I remembered how the firelight had danced on Pete's bare chest, and although he'd whooped along with Andrew, he'd looked less than into the whole thing. I again puzzled over why someone like Pete, who seemed to have everything going for him, would even want to be a part of the Society.

But I guess needing to feel like you belong, needing to have that safety net for the future, entraps all of us.

"I just hope the school doesn't figure out it was him. I don't want him to get in any trouble." She worried aloud.

"Everything will be fine," I assured her again as we hung a left to head to grab some food.

*D*ays later I thought back to that evening, of all it foreshadowed. Too bad I sucked at telling the future. Except it wasn't Pete's life that would be screwed up...it was my own.

twenty-one

What is to give light must endure burning.
—Viktor E. Frankl

Students hovered throughout the hallway in small groups the next morning, whispering and pointing, and for once, not at me.

Blown-up shots of Blane and Zena caught in a rather heated kiss were taped all along the rows of red lockers in the senior hallway. The fact that I didn't hear screaming and fighting led me to believe that Jessica and the man of the hour hadn't arrived yet.

I casually strolled to my locker and feigned surprise. "I didn't know Jessica and Blane broke up," I said to Bren, who stood about three feet away with two other cheerleaders.

"Shut up." She shot me a dirty look and turned away, tearing down several of the posters closest to her.

Not like it would make much of a difference. The damage was already done.

The whispered buzzing grew louder for about thirty seconds then turned to dead silence. The Queen had arrived.

I recognized the tap of heels that only Jessica bothered to wear with our fugly uniforms. I peeked out from behind my locker door. She strolled arm in arm with Blane, and I knew the minute she realized something was up, because the *tap-tap* of her heels slowed.

No one said a word. Some kids looked down, suddenly very interested in studying their shoes.

"Bren, Jaz, what's going on?" Her gaze drew to the papers plastered just feet away. She broke free of Blane and speed-walked to the first set of lockers.

Jessica ripped one of the pictures down and tore it in half. Her head snapped back around to Blane. I hadn't realized skin could turn that exact shade of purple.

She rushed toward the other lockers that held pictures, ripping them down one after the other.

Blane stepped toward her. "Jess, I can explain."

Jessica wheeled around and slapped him across the face. The posters she'd gathered dropped and flew everywhere with the quick movement of her attack.

Blane's cheek turned fiery red. His eyes bulged.

Gasps and muffled laughter filled the hallway.

Her eyes roamed the crowd, probably looking for Zena, maybe planning to smack her too. Jessica's gaze stopped when she reached me. I stared right back, refusing to be intimidated. Her ice blue eyes narrowed the slightest bit before she turned and stalked off.

The laughter that filled the hallway was no longer muffled. Everybody had something to say about the high drama scene they'd just witnessed. It definitely ranked up there as one of the better ones so far this year. A few guys even slapped Blane on the back and cheered him on.

I wanted to be thrilled that all went according to plan, but something I'd seen in Jessica's eyes made me nervous.

It almost seemed as if she knew I was behind it, like she blamed me.

The memory of Jessica telling me how my father had cheated with her mother and broken up their family flashed in my mind like a neon sign. It made me feel shitty for what I'd done. I hadn't really thought about that, about how it would bring back very real, painful memories for her when I'd orchestrated the whole thing.

I reminded myself that she deserved it.

They always say *Hell hath no fury like a woman scorned.* Jessica had not only been scorned, she'd been publicly humiliated, and somehow I didn't think she'd take it lying down.

"Our President being elected is not a current event, Ms. Shayne."

Mr. Cooper stood behind the wooden podium he always used for lectures. His wire-framed glasses tipped down his nose as he shook his head in exasperation.

I wasn't sure how Beth Shayne got in my section. The saddest part about it was, she'd been dead serious, even though Cooper had clearly specified we were to select a topic that had occurred in the past month.

Beth raised her hand. Again. "But, doesn't like the fact that he's still, you know, president make it current?"

Cooper was spared having to explain the concept of a month and how many days that meant by a horrendous mechanical shrieking noise. I winced, and several kids around me covered their ears. Mr. Cooper even dropped the long wooden pointer he loved to use and had to bend to retrieve it in a hurry.

The fire alarm sounded again.

Students all looked at each other, trying to figure out if this was practice. Usually we knew if there was going to be a fire drill. Someone in the office always leaked it.

"Class! Class!" Cooper rapped the pointer against the blackboard with three strong *whacks*. "Please line up in an orderly fashion against the wall. We will exit through the doors off the practice gymnasium, just like we went over the first day of classes." Eyes wide, he kept looking back and forth between the hallway and the windows. Shouts came from down the hall that led to the west wing of the school, yelling about smoke.

Kids finally got the message that it wasn't a drill and began to move. Desks scraped against the wooden floor as students stood up in a hurry. Cell phones were whipped out left and right, and just about everyone typed frantically as they shoved to get out the door.

So much for Cooper's orderly fashion.

I tried to see over the shoulder of the guy in front of me, but couldn't. Of course I'd be behind Jacob, the center on the basketball team. I looked around for Jeremy. His assigned seat fell three rows over on the far side of the classroom, and I'd lost him once we got in the hallway.

A deafening explosion sounded. I jumped and screamed.

Students poured out of classrooms, all yelling and pushing while teachers tried to get us to calm down and walk single file. Acrid smoke filled my nostrils the farther we walked. A grayish cast took over the air around us, but I couldn't see any flames. Some teachers tried to direct their class to turn around and go the opposite way, while teachers at the far end of the hall continued to send their students in our direction.

"Turn around! Go the other way!" Mr. Cliffton, the gym teacher, waved what looked like a tube sock above his head as he buried his face in the crook of his other arm.

Claustrophobia set in. Too many people closed in, pushing and shoving from either side of me. The smoke got thicker, and it became more difficult to breathe. No one seemed to know for sure where to go.

One girl, about fourteen, slipped in the open classroom door of the Home Economics room. She crouched against the wall under the chalkboard, hands over her head, rocking back and forth, sobbing.

"Out! You need to go out the exit by the junior hallway!" someone shouted.

The alarm continued to wail.

I looked around again, frantic. "Jeremy!" I yelled. *Where was he?*

Everyone screamed for their friends as we hurried, trying to get back the way we'd just come from. Sirens sounded in the distance.

Why weren't sprinklers coming on? Shouldn't there be sprinklers?

One teacher dashed by with a red fire extinguisher.

A hand grabbed my shoulder.

I whipped around and almost burst into tears when I saw Jeremy. His glasses hung crooked on his nose as if someone ran into him. He didn't seem to notice. He took my hand, and we fell in with the tide of students pushing toward the EXIT sign off the end of the junior hallway. We finally made it through the door and ran across the grass to the student parking lot. My eyes burned and my heart raced.

Students huddled together. Some cried, others talked in loud voices to be heard above the sirens and the alarm that still shrieked. Teachers hurried around with clipboards attempting to take head counts.

Flames shot from the far side of the building, coming from the practice gym doors—the ones we were originally trying to get to. A high buzzing sound mixed with cracking, like thousands of tiny bees fighting to escape the heat. Glass exploded out from the tall window next to the door, making everyone jump and scream louder.

One guy stumbled across the lot, holding his hand to his forehead while blood dripped down his arm.

I began to shake, violent tremors wracking my body. Jeremy put both of his arms around me and held me close.

"It's okay. We're out. It's okay," he whispered in my hair, trying to calm and reassure me.

But it wasn't okay.

It was as far from okay as you could get. Because I was petrified that the fire that had gotten so out of hand was all my fault.

Nothing like this was supposed to happen.

I'd been clear on my instructions. Becky was supposed to sneak into the girls' locker room during gym class and swipe the cheerleaders' uniforms. I knew they'd all worn them since it was picture day for all of the school clubs.

I'd justified the theft with the rationalization that it

wasn't as if the cheerleaders would be naked; they had their gym clothes after all. They could simply wear those for their pictures.

After she grabbed them, the directions told Becky to take the uniforms out back and throw them in the giant green Dumpster outside the practice gym doors. Students used the practice gym for PE, while the newer, larger gym was used for basketball games and other indoor sporting events.

Patrick had been instructed to grab the uniforms out of the Dumpster, take them to the bonfire Friday night, and bury them in the tall logs used to make the fire. That part had actually been another one of Ransom's suggestions. Patrick wasn't supposed to burn them himself in the Dumpster during school hours. Even I wasn't that dumb. But the location of the fire couldn't be a coincidence.

What the hell had he done? Why hadn't Patrick followed the task's instructions? How could he have been so stupid?

Some students still huddled in groups of two or three, whispering or crying. Everyone looked dazed. We'd been dismissed and told to go home. Most kids had already been picked up. Fire trucks and police cars still filled the lot around the gym. A paramedic bandaged a girl's arm a few yards away. When she glanced up and caught my eye, I gasped. It was the young girl I'd seen crying huddled by the desk in the empty classroom.

Even though our eyes met, I knew she didn't really see me. Hers were wide, blank. I stood, immobile, staring. She looked broken. I did that to her, and I didn't even know her name.

I hunched over, and dry heaves wracked my body.

Jeremy rubbed my back in slow circles until I could stand upright again. "Sam, let's go. Come on, I'll give you a ride." His voice cut through the haze of my shock and guilt.

I turned to face him, not able to speak.

"C'mon," he repeated, tugging at my sleeve.

I followed, mute.

All of my posturing about blaming Patrick meant nothing. It all came down to me. What I'd done. It had all started with my stupid instructions, even if he hadn't followed them correctly. A tear slipped down my cheek.

I didn't speak as Jeremy drove. Homes sped past my window, a blur of color and shapes. As I pressed the palm of my hand against the passenger side window, the glass cooled my hot skin. I welcomed the feeling. It was solid. Strong. Real.

Not like me.

I rested my forehead next to my hand and closed my eyes. Tears slipped down my cheeks. Even pressed smack against the window, no one really saw me. And it was better that way. Right now, if I'd caused what just happened, I didn't even want to face myself.

twenty-two

Getting over a painful experience is much like
crossing monkey bars. You have to let go at
some point in order to move forward.
—*C.S. Lewis*

*T*hey'd shut down school Thursday to investigate the fire. Every time the house phone rang, my heart leapt into my mouth, sure it would be the police calling to tell me they'd discovered what I'd done, but it was always just someone for Aunt Loretta.

We'd just sat down to sandwiches for lunch when I saw it.

Aunt Lor had the television on like usual, and a bright red banner flashed across, reading, *Special News Report.* An image of our school filled the screen. A reporter stood in a blue suit, her blond hair pinned tight in a bun, gesturing behind her. My stomach lurched, and I whirled around to face my aunt. She leaned closer to the small television set, watching intently.

"Maybe we should turn it off," I said, praying she'd do it.

She waved her hand over her shoulder in my direction. "Shh, I want to hear this. Maybe they have some news about what happened."

That was exactly what worried me.

Aunt Lor reached out to turn up the volume.

"I'm standing in front of Trinity Academy, an area private school, where fire broke out yesterday while classes were in session."

The screen filled with images of smoke billowing out the tall school windows on the far west side of campus, of fire trucks racing into the lot, and firemen rushing toward the building while carrying thick white hoses.

I stared. I hadn't realized there'd been camera crews there. Then again, I hadn't really been in the right frame of mind to notice. The announcer's voice could still be heard over the pre-recorded videotape. "Officials have determined that the blaze originated here." The announcer was back, pointing toward the charred brick wall next to the practice gymnasium doors.

I wanted to puke.

"It seems there was a buildup of gas from a faulty pipe that ran below this section of the two-hundred year old building. Officials speculate that a tossed cigarette ignited the fumes, causing the explosion that rocked this school, which resulted in an undisclosed amount of damage, mainly due to smoke in the sub-level and a broken fifteen-foot-high window on this side of the school. As you can see, the exterior of this section also sustained smoke and fire damage.

Officials also report that today, the school brought in experts to replace the pipe as well as the window and to assess if the school is safe for students and faculty to return."

My mouth dropped open. *A gas leak?* So it had nothing to do with me, with Patrick?

"Viewers may remember the deadly explosion that

took place in East Harlem in early 2014, killing seven and wounding over sixty people in a similar situation."

The screen now switched to some old news clip, showing buildings with giant flames bursting from shattered windows, people screaming, rubble everywhere.

I gasped.

"School officials have not responded to our requests for an interview. We are told that there were no fatalities, although several students and faculty were injured in Wednesday's blast; none are reported as life-threatening. We are also told that despite the damage, the situation could have been much worse than it was. Thanks to quick response times by several local fire crews, the fire was able to be contained and extinguished. Although the school will need to shut down this section of the campus for repairs and continued safety assessment, classes will resume tomorrow at Trinity Academy in Cloverfield."

When the report ended and a commercial took its place, Aunt Lor turned the volume back down and turned to me, eyes wide. "Oh my gracious. Samantha, did you hear that?"

I nodded, still mute and in shock.

She stood up and came over to hug me. "I'm so thankful it wasn't any worse and that you're safe. If anything had happened to you…" She sniffled.

I reached around to hug her back. "But it wasn't worse, and I'm fine."

She patted my shoulders and nodded. "That's because the good Lord had His hand on you. I just know it."

I doubted that was true. I was pretty sure the good Lord had better people to watch over than me. Heck, he might have even been aiming for me with the explosion.

I couldn't wrap my head around the news report. So the fire really wasn't my fault? Patrick hadn't started it? I was dying to question him, but knew I couldn't, not without giving away my identity. And I couldn't risk doing that. I exhaled a long, slow breath and thanked my lucky stars.

Aunt Loretta sat back down across from me and picked up her turkey sandwich. I reached out and picked up my own as well and took a large bite. It tasted like a reprieve.

twenty-three

But the fever's gonna catch you when the bitch gets back.
—*Elton John*

"Samantha, wake up! Why aren't you getting dressed?"

My aunt's voice crashed through a rather odd, yet enjoyable dream involving Jake Gyllenhaal, a motorcycle, and mint chocolate chip ice cream. The pleasurable visions dissipated with the light of a new day. Before that dream, I'd suffered through nightmares of Jessica taunting me and kept waking up every twenty minutes or so. I was still bone-tired.

"Ugh. What?" I shoved my pillow over my head and tried my best to bring back Jake and the motorcycle. Instead, I kept seeing flashes of Jessica, cackling at me.

All the bad feelings I had toward Jessica grew again, especially now that I knew the fire wasn't my fault. After all, nothing I'd planned or assigned was the least bit dangerous. Well, not really. A part of me argued that I should shut the plan down, quit while I was still ahead and stop stressing myself out. But the renewed desire to get back at Jessica squashed any rational decision making.

My aunt should've made me stick with the therapist I'd

blown off after those four sessions. Maybe then I wouldn't be such a train wreck.

"Out of bed, young lady!"

"It's not time to get up. My alarm didn't even go off yet." I burrowed deeper under my comforter.

"Samantha!" The blanket disappeared in one swift jerk. "Your bus will be here in less than ten minutes."

What? I sprang up and looked at my clock.

"That can't be right, it didn't go off! I know I set it!" Or did I? I couldn't remember. Damn it!

I leapt from bed, frantic. "I need a uniform. Where's my uniform?" God, my room was a mess.

The fact that Aunt Lor still seemed her normal self struck me out of nowhere. She'd been good the last few days. The realization washed over me in a wave of relief, but only for a moment. How long until one of the episodes happened again?

I stopped and stared at her like I hadn't seen her for a year before crossing over and hugging her tight.

Aunt Loretta looked confused by my affection but patted my back anyway.

"I love you, you know," I whispered into her gray hair.

"I love you too, child, but you're going to be late. Now get moving before you miss your bus."

She shook her head and left the room, leaving me to find my uniform myself. Familiar plaid peeked out from under a pile of wadded up shirts. I grabbed the skirt, along with one of my tops, which I frantically turned right side out. So what if I'd worn it before; now was not the time to be overly conscientious about a little thing like ketchup stains.

I ripped my nightshirt over my head and threw on the

uniform in record time. My book bag lay on the floor by my dresser. I snatched it up, along with a tie dangling off the edge of the bureau. I couldn't be late, not today.

I tore out of my room, headed to the bathroom to brush my teeth and throw my hair back in a quick pony. Good enough.

Aunt Lor handed me a cereal bar as I rushed by, praying the bus hadn't already hit my stop.

"Have a good day, sweetie. I love you!" she called after me. I waved as I flew out the door.

The large yellow bus rumbled up the drive as I hurried, out of breath, to my pick-up point.

I stumbled, panting, into my regular seat in the back. I bit into my breakfast bar, choking a bit as I caught my breath. I closed my eyes and chewed.

Things weren't great, but they were looking up. Aunt Lor seemed to be doing better, and tomorrow was Pete's party where I'd see Ransom again. Plus, today's tasks were going to be epic.

Things with Jeremy and me hadn't really improved like I thought they would after he gave me the ride home. We'd talked on the phone last night, and he had asked me once again if I was still going through with my "little revenge scheme." His words, not mine. I'd changed the subject.

Our call had ended abruptly after he'd brought up Ransom, asking me if I was seeing him. I hadn't known exactly what to say, and Jeremy got upset and hung up on me. I planned to talk to him today, try to sort things out between us. I couldn't stand him being mad at me.

I stuffed my wrapper into my book bag. I wasn't stopping the plan. Wednesday was an unfortunate accident that the news made clear I was in no way responsible for, and it didn't change anything. It didn't take away the years of torment at Jessica's hands, or what she'd done to my family. Thursday's task had been cancelled, obviously, but that was okay.

For once, I was looking forward to the school's obsession with all things football. We had a pep rally last period, and I couldn't imagine that even with the fire, the school would cancel it. If anything, they'd either hold it in the main gym or down on the field. I was going to love it. A certain cheerleader and football player? Not so much.

twenty-four

Luck is a very fine wire between survival and disaster, and not many people can keep their balance on it.
—*Hunter S. Thompson*

The hands of the clock moved at a slug's pace during calculus, my last class of the day before study hall in ninth period homeroom. I tapped a pen on my open textbook, not paying attention to whatever Ms. Mills was droning on about in the front of the room.

As expected, this morning in homeroom, they'd made the announcement that due to the fire damage in the practice gymnasium, the pep rally would be held in the main gym this afternoon. Students were also advised that the west wing of the school would be closed off for renovations until further notice. Not a huge deal, since it was the oldest part of the school, it was really only the practice gym, the shop, and the home ec room down there anyway.

Thank goodness they hadn't cancelled, or I would have had to scramble for new tasks to assign.

Would Patrick and Becky do it?

I'd find out next period.

After what seemed to be an eternity, the bell rang,

signaling the end of class. I dropped my pen and had to retrieve it from where it rolled under the desk next to mine before shoving my calculus book and unused notebook into my bag to head out. Once again, I'd missed the assignment, since I hadn't been paying attention.

Jeremy didn't wait for me before leaving the room. He didn't even look my way.

I pushed through the throng of students headed down the hall. It was a rare day for me to be excited for final homeroom, since I shared it with Jessica and several of her cheerleader drones. But today, the thought of seeing her filled me with anticipation instead of a dull dread. Let the games begin.

Students jostled and took their seats as I walked into the room. Mr. Jacobs sat at his desk buried in a newspaper. He was cool about letting us talk during study hall as long as we didn't get too loud. Probably more so it didn't disturb his reading rather than concern over breaking school rules.

I slid into my fifth row desk and glanced around the classroom. Jessica sat two rows over in the front, plucking at her sweater like it made her sick. The fact that all of the cheerleaders had to wear their old uniforms, instead of their fancy new ones that were lost in the fire, probably didn't help her attitude any. She'd be looking even more nauseated by end of day.

The bell rang, and Mr. Jacobs glanced up. "Okay, class. Everyone take your seats. Don't forget there's a pep rally today. We'll be heading over to the gymnasium in about ten minutes. Remember, it is now being held in the *main* gym, not the practice gym. Please do not go in that area of the school. Also, please make sure you don't leave anything on your desks when we leave. Take it with you." His teacher duty done, he stuck his nose back in the *Wall Street Journal*.

I glanced at the door. *Where was she?* Just as I began to worry that she'd chickened out, Becky's familiar face popped in the door. Her mouth twisted in a nervous smile.

"Excuse me, Mr. Jacobs. I have brownies for the cheerleaders." She licked her lips and swallowed visibly. Her gaze bounced around the room, everywhere but at the four girls from the cheer squad that shared homeroom with me. "Um…the student council made them."

Jacobs waved her into the room.

Most of the guys in class started clamoring for a treat. Becky's hands shook holding the tray, and her eyes widened. "Sorry boys, these are specifically for the cheerleaders." She held the serving plate above her head as she wedged around some guys begging for free food.

"They can have mine," Jaz said, sounding bored. "I don't eat sugar."

"Oh, these aren't made with sugar. They're actually healthy." Becky circled the room, handing an individually-wrapped brownie to each girl on the cheer squad.

When she got to Jessica, I held my breath. She had to take one. Jessica glanced up and looked like she was about to refuse. The breath whooshed out of me when she finally said, "What the hell," and reached out to take a brownie off the tray.

Becky stopped her. "Oh no! Here, take this one. I decorated it especially for you. Since you're the captain."

Jessica looked pleased at the special treatment. She grinned broadly and tossed her golden mane. "So what's it made of if there's no sugar?" she asked, one eyebrow raised.

"Oh! It's a recipe my mom uses. It has quinoa and almond milk. Plus she adds a little pumpkin puree to add some extra flavor." Becky's shaky smile didn't quite meet her eyes.

Oh yeah, she went through with it, but she needed to calm down before her nerves gave her away. I silently willed her to relax.

"Well, whatever." Jessica didn't even bother with a thank you. She peeled the plastic wrap from her large brownie and broke a piece off to pop in her mouth. After chewing a few seconds, she nodded her head grudgingly. "Not bad." Despite her lame praises, she scarfed the rest down in record time, probably because she never allowed herself to eat in front of Blane, and he wasn't there to see her eat like a normal human. Then again, Blane was most likely out of the picture, period.

Becky slipped out of the classroom.

I smiled behind my book. The fun would begin in about thirty minutes, right in the middle of the pep rally. To quote the rah-rah crew, it would be A-W-E-S-O-M-E.

No way did I want to show up on Queenie's radar, so I made sure to keep my face hidden behind my oversized science text, pretending to study. By all appearances, kinetic-molecular theories held me thoroughly engrossed.

About ten minutes later, Jacobs rattled his paper before setting it down on his huge oak desk at the front of the room. He glanced at the round clock next to the top of the doorway. It read two fifteen.

"All right, ladies and gentleman. It's time to head over to the gymnasium. Please be sure to gather all of your belongings to take with you. You'll be dismissed from the rally to go to your lockers, so you won't be able to come back and get anything you left behind." He paused. "And remember, you're heading to the main gymnasium, do not go to the practice gym." His brow furrowed.

The cheerleaders and football players were excused first. The rest of us lowly mortals formed a single-file line waiting for permission to head to the gym for another half hour of rousing displays of school spirit. At least today I'd be entertained for once during the assembly.

As I walked from the room, I noticed Jana's brownie left behind unopened on her desk. Guess she was serious about not eating anything she considered junk food.

No one else remained in the classroom, so I snagged it and shoved it in the bottom of my large book bag.

Seated in the gym a few minutes later, I looked around to find Jeremy. We always sat together, but he wasn't waiting at our regular spot at the bottom of the second section of risers. Two guys stepped over me, pushing and shoving each other until the second one almost landed on my lap in the process.

"Whoa, sorry." He smiled and laughed a little. I recognized him as one of the people who'd stood in the hall and laughed at Jessica's convict drawing on my locker. The ironic part was that I don't think he recognized me. To him, I'd just been an easy target to join in with the crowd and mock.

I rolled my eyes. His friendly expression turned to mild annoyance. "Whatever, sweetheart. It was an accident."

His friend looked back. "Come on, Seth. Ignore her."

Seth glanced my way again and shrugged. "Sorry," he muttered again before following his buddy.

I turned away and spotted a familiar head a few rows down and to the left. I reached over, grabbed my bag, and jumped up to move toward him.

"Jeremy!" I called. He didn't acknowledge that he heard me.

"Jer!" I yelled again, a little louder this time.

He finally turned to face me, his expression not nearly as welcoming as I'd hoped for.

I offered an unsure smile and waved.

Instead of waving back, he turned and bent his head toward the person on his left. I took a few more steps his way and stopped short. Abby. She sat right next to him. Super.

I told myself it didn't matter and kept pushing forward to join him.

"Hey." I'd finally reached them and stood a few feet away at the end of the row. I shifted my bag on my shoulder. "Room for one more?"

He looked me in the eyes. I played with my tie and shifted my weight, praying he wouldn't blow me off and tell me to take a hike.

A few seconds later, he nodded and moved over on the long wooden bleacher. Closer to Abby. Fabulous.

I tried to squelch the green-eyed monster as his thigh pressed tight against the side of Abby's skirt. After all, what else was he supposed to do? Invite me to sit on his lap? At least he made room for me. I smiled my thanks and sat at the end of the row next to him.

An uncomfortable silence ensued. Abby didn't so much as glance my way. Jeremy cleared his throat and stared at his shoes. Good thing it wasn't awkward or anything.

Music thundered from the speakers set up around the

gym. Cheerleaders ran from the girl's locker room door, pom-poms waving high above their heads. Several of the girls cartwheeled into the center of court. Catcalls and whistles sounded from the bleachers. The cheerleaders flashed thousand watt smiles at their adoring fans and waved and bounced some more.

I zeroed in on just one.

Jessica seemed a tad less perky than usual. Her forced smile wavered a bit, and she wasn't one of the girls doing handsprings and cartwheels. She gamely shook her red and white pom-poms in the air, all the while looking like she wanted to hurl.

No one else seemed to notice. Students stamped their feet on the bleachers, a deafening *boom-boom-boom*. When the cheer squad formed two lines and began a dance routine, I leaned forward.

I felt Jeremy's curious gaze at my rapt interest in what was going on below us. Normally, I'd be making snarky remarks.

I caught myself and jabbed him in the ribs. "Whaddya think? Will we have a costume malfunction with all that shaking?" I forced a laugh. It wasn't a potential wardrobe breakdown that had me so focused, and I had the feeling he knew it.

His jaw set. "What did you do?" His whispered accusation hung heavy in the air between us.

I twisted to face him. "I don't know what you're talking about. What? You think I rigged one of their uniforms to fall apart?" I shook my head. "I may be good, but I'm not exactly capable of sneaking in their houses overnight and ripping out seams."

He stared at me. "Sam, I have absolutely no idea what you're capable of anymore."

Ouch.

Abby glanced over, eyes wide. Great. Now she knew Jeremy and I were fighting, which gave her the perfect chance to slide right in and steal him.

I lifted my chin. "I've never done anything that wasn't completely deserved."

Jeremy's cool stare made me feel like he was looking at a stranger. He shook his head and turned to face front without bothering to respond.

I did the same, pasting a fake smile on my face and clapping along with the crowd.

Down below, Jessica looked worse. Every few seconds, she stopped jumping around and brushed her hair out of her face, or held her stomach. At one point, she bent over at the waist, clutching her midsection.

By this point, others began to take notice as well. The girls on either side of Jessica cast concerned looks her way, and a couple of kids in the stands pointed and whispered.

I acted like nothing was amiss, still clapping and giving an occasional *whoop*. I pretended not to feel Jeremy's icy glares sent my way.

The announcer called out, "Let's hear it for your Trinity Academy Titans!"

The footballs players tore out of their locker room, barreling through a large paper banner that said, *GO TITANS!* held by two cheerleaders.

The students in the stands went nuts, stamping and cheering. The players were like gods in our school. They pumped their helmets in the air, and the cheer squad danced and kicked their legs high while they shouted encouragement.

The varsity players plunked their helmets on their heads, getting ready to move to the standard play formation they always did at rallies, and that's where things got interesting. Chase Latkin's arm stuck out awkwardly at his side, trying to jerk his hand free of the hard plastic face mask on his helmet. It clung, not releasing. He shook it and grabbed it with the other hand, looking like a cartoon character.

I tried not to snort. Superglue would do that. I mentally praised Patrick and turned my attention back to Jessica. Would she get sick in front of the entire school before the rally was over and the cheerleaders flounced out of the gym? She'd be mortified. It seemed a fitting retribution for what the two of them had done to me two years ago. After all, they'd found it so amusing to publicly humiliate me that day in the mall.

The squad finished their dance and formed an elaborate pyramid. Jessica wobbled her way up to the top, arms poised above her head in a *V*. Seconds later she wavered in her perch on top of the backs of two other girls. Her eyes grew huge, and it was easy to see her fear.

One sneaker-clad foot slipped off the side of Bren's back, and that's all it took. In what almost seemed like slow motion, Jessica fell. She caught a knee on Bren on the way down, and suddenly disappeared from view behind the human tower. A collective gasp carried throughout the gym. A crack sounded, followed by shocked silence.

I jumped up, my stomach rolling. She was supposed to get sick, have to leave the rally early, maybe throw up in front of everyone. Not that.

I stood on tiptoe with the rest of the students, craning my neck to see more clearly. Teachers swarmed to the center of the gym floor, shouting commands for students to get back. Two teachers whipped out their phones, faces frantic. Probably calling 911 and wondering what the hell else could go wrong.

Jeremy's hands grasped my shoulders and turned me to face him. He looked angrier than I'd ever seen him.

"Please tell me you had nothing to do with this." His normally warm eyes were steel.

My mouth flapped open and shut. "I didn't!" I finally snapped. When he didn't answer, I jerked free and ran down the bleachers and out of the gym.

twenty-five

Tell me why all the best laid plans fall
apart in your hands.
—James Blunt

I bolted to the closest girl's bathroom and locked myself in a stall. I sat on the closed toilet lid, shaking like I was about to have a seizure. What if Jessica broke her back and was now a vegetable?

Oh my god, what if they found out I was behind it all and I got sent to prison? Like my dad. Memories of the striped locker flashed in my head, the words *Convict Society* taunting me.

What if they were right all along and I was just like him? Worse than him. My father may have threatened Mr. Wainright's life, but I may have *crippled* Wainright's daughter. Pretty sure that made me the bigger villain on anyone's scorecard.

Could the drugged brownies really be responsible? Maybe she just lost her balance, and it had nothing to do with what she'd eaten.

Beads of sweat broke out on my forehead, and I pressed my palms against my face, my eyes squeezed closed tight.

A million tiny jackhammers pounded their way through my skull.

She's fine. She probably just twisted her ankle or something.

My stomach hosted a swarm of angry insects, flapping and twisting. I leapt to the floor, lifted the lid, and shoved my face halfway into the bowl, sure I would retch any moment. But after a minute or two I realized nothing was going to come up.

Elbow on the seat, I rested the side of my face in my hand and commanded myself to take deep breaths and calm down. I needed to think rationally. I'd already made a spectacle of myself by running out of the gym. I needed to come up with a reason for my rather obvious fleeing the scene of the crime. Something believable.

The brownies.

I'd picked up Jana's brownie that she'd left behind; I could say I'd eaten it. I dug in my bag to find it and tore the wrapper off before shoving the brownie in the toilet. It looked disgusting, waterlogged and bobbing around, so I turned away and flushed.

There. Now I just had an empty wrapper…proof I'd eaten one. If anyone put two and two together and figured out what had made Jessica fall, there was no way anyone would think I'd been behind it, since I'd eaten a brownie too.

It was perfect. Logical. Well, except for the fact that none of the other cheerleaders had gotten sick, but it was better than nothing. It was doubtful anyone would be smart enough to suspect that Jessica's brownie came from its own private batch.

I'd thought I'd been so clever suggesting Becky grind up

iris leaves to mix in the batter. Simple and easily accessible. Super easy for someone as skilled in chemistry as Becky. From what I'd researched, the iris leaves would make someone ill, but they weren't even close to fatal, especially in small doses. I'd never wanted to really hurt anyone, not even Jessica.

How was I to know she would be on top of a pyramid when the symptoms hit full force? It wasn't my fault she climbed up there feeling sick. I tried to convince myself that Jessica's need to be the constant center of attention led to the accident, not what I'd orchestrated. It didn't work.

I couldn't breathe, seeing her fall over and over.

I shoved myself up from the floor and unlocked the stall door to walk over to the row of sinks. My reflection appeared flushed in the mirror. I leaned down and turned the cold water on full blast, then splashed it onto my face and neck. Inhaling deeply, I grabbed a paper towel and patted myself dry. I could do this. I *had* to do this. I had to go out there and find out what was going on.

Muted voices carried through the bathroom door, along with the sounds of footsteps. Lots of them.

Please let her be okay.

I pushed open the door and stepped out. Students swirled around me, faces slack and eyes wide with shock. Everyone whispered in hushed tones, as if using a normal speaking voice might somehow be inappropriate.

I grabbed an arm of the closest student, some underclassman I didn't recognize. "What happened? Where is she now?"

The girl didn't even try to pull away. She appeared in a daze, her pale face splotchy from crying. That can't be good.

"She's gone," she whispered.

Gone?

Gone? Gone as in *dead*?

The walls tilted around me, and the color drained from my face.

"What do you mean, *gone*?" I whispered hoarsely.

She shook her head. "I don't know where. I just know an ambulance came, and they took her."

Students pushed past us. The girl finally broke free from my grasp and walked forward in the crowd before I could get any more information from her.

I looked around for a familiar face. Everyone wore confused, scared expressions, even the teachers. I needed to get out of there. I wanted to go somewhere I felt safe, and figure out what the hell was happening.

Jeremy's face flashed in my mind, but I knew I couldn't go to his house. No way he'd want to see me after suspecting me of causing what happened, especially when he was right.

I couldn't face my aunt either. She'd see the guilt written all over me, I knew it.

There was only one other option. I pulled out my phone and dialed. "Can I come over?"

His answer was immediate, no questions asked. "Sure."

"I'll be there in fifteen minutes." I hung up the phone and walked out of school. Alone.

twenty-six

It's always darkest before it turns
absolutely pitch black.
—Paul Newman

Ransom answered the door on my first knock, his eyes widening as he took in my disheveled appearance. "Are you okay?"

He stepped forward to take my arm and lead me inside before closing the door behind us.

I sat down on the sofa, shaking my head. Mute. *What had I done?*

He left my side and walked to his small kitchen. Sounds of the faucet running carried my way. He reappeared holding a tall glass of water. "Here, drink something." When I didn't move to accept it, he set it down on the coffee table in front of us.

"Sam, what's wrong? You're starting to freak me out."

I shook my head in a daze. My skin froze and burned like fire all at once.

He moved a few inches closer to where I sat unmoving and reached out to take my limp hand. "Talk to me. What happened?"

I'd be sent away. My aunt would be so ashamed. Jeremy

would never speak to me again. And I'd deserve all of it.

What was I even doing here? I shouldn't be here. I should be at the hospital, trying to find out if Jessica was okay.

I didn't know what to do. The feel of Ransom's hand on mine finally registered. When I lifted my head to look at him, his eyes crinkled with worry.

"I think I really hurt someone." I blurted out.

His eyes widened, but he tried to cover his apparent shock at my words. "Who? How?"

I noticed he didn't ask why. Maybe he thought it didn't matter.

Beads of condensation pooled around the glass of water on the table. I picked it up; it slipped in my hand and I barely caught it before it fell. I took a small sip to cool my parched throat.

"A girl from my school. Jessica. The one I told you about. I think I may have seriously hurt her." I could barely choke out the words.

Ransom cleared his throat. "Uh, you're going to have to give me a little more detail if you want my help."

Waves of nausea crashed over me and I set the glass back down on the scarred table. "No. That's not why I came here. There's nothing you can do."

Ransom leaned back against the side of the couch. "Oh. Okay. Then what do you need?"

"Never mind." I shook my head.

Silence fell.

"Anyway, I'm not even sure what's going on with her. I ran out of the gym after it happened. I just know an ambulance came and got her and rushed her to some hospital."

He took a drink of my water. "So, you gonna tell me

what happened?"

I filled him in on the whole thing, from instructing Becky to make the drugged brownies to Jessica's free-fall during the pep rally. He nodded here and there while I talked, but didn't interrupt. When I finally finished, he folded his hands and stared at them.

"You need to find out her condition."

That made sense. "Do you think they'd give me information if I called the hospital?"

He shook his head. "Doubt it. They'd probably only talk to immediate family. All the privacy laws and shit."

"Then how do I find out?" I was getting frustrated. "I can't handle this!"

"First, you need to calm down."

He seemed pretty cavalier about the whole thing. Then again, he wasn't the one responsible.

"Look, isn't there anyone you can ask? It seems like that's the easiest option." He shrugged one shoulder. "Someone might have seen or heard something after you ran out. It could be there's nothing for you to even worry about."

"She fell off the top of a pyramid! I heard the crack!"

"Bones crack. Doesn't mean she's seriously hurt."

I shook my head. "You didn't hear it. It was so loud. And her face before she fell…" I trailed off, shuddering, remembering her look of terror.

"I don't get it." He leaned back and crossed his legs up on the coffee table.

I turned to face him. "Get what?"

"You. This. All of it. How freaked out you are." He shrugged again.

"*What* are you talking about?"

"Isn't this the same girl who made your life a living hell for years? Who helped send your dad to prison? The one you swore to get revenge on?"

"Well, yeah, but—"

"Then why do you care so much if something happened to her?" He rubbed his head. "Seems to me you'd be doing the world a favor if she'd fallen on her head and bit it."

"Ransom!" I stared at him, aghast.

"What? It's the truth." He paused. "Look, I can understand you worrying about getting caught, but I don't think that's gonna happen. You covered your bases. Let it go."

He reached out and began to play with a piece of hair spilling over my shoulder. "Sam, relax, you didn't do anything wrong. You pulled a harmless prank. You didn't know she'd go up there and fall. It's not your fault." He moved closer as he spoke, his fingers brushed the skin just inside my collar. "It's fine. You're fine," he whispered, leaning in close. "Better than fine."

My eyes drifted closed as his mouth touched the sensitive skin of my collarbone. A part of me felt disgusted that I wanted him to touch me after what happened with Jessica, but another part of me wanted to forget for a while, completely forget everything. And Ransom offered the perfect escape.

My head fell back against the cushion, allowing him easier access to my neck. I felt a slight tug on the front of my shirt, and seconds later, his hand moved across the top of my chest. I forced myself to relax. Besides, the way he was touching me didn't feel horrible; his touch was feather-soft, as if I were a fragile piece of glass. And in a way, I was. Like

I'd simply shatter into millions of pieces if one more thing went wrong in my life.

Suddenly, his lips were on mine, and his tongue sought the inside of my mouth. Even though I willingly opened my mouth, granting access, my mind went blank. I felt nothing. Not excitement, not revulsion, just…emptiness inside.

Ransom's hands were on both of my shoulders then, and I felt myself being lowered onto the sofa. His weight pressed down on me, but it wasn't suffocating, it was a welcome heaviness. I stared at the ceiling as he continued to kiss my neck. It was made of white squared tiles. They had speckles.

"You're so hot," he whispered into my ear. His hands moved from my shoulders down my body. The pads of his thumbs brushed against my breasts.

Even though the last rational part of me knew I was using him as a distraction, I didn't care. I couldn't care. If I allowed myself to open the floodgate to all of my real emotions, I might never get my head above water. I'd drown.

I began to count the rows of tiles.

He trailed kisses down my neck, and lower. His hands were everywhere. Touching, stroking, teasing. I arched against him, needing to be closer, needing to feel alive. I wanted to feel anything at all.

"God I want you," he growled. His hands moved to my bare knee, then slid higher, to my thigh. Higher.

The realization of what we were about to do crashed into me.

Jeremy's face flashed in my mind out of nowhere. I'd always fantasized that my first time would be special, exciting, something I'd always want to remember.

It's not like I expected rose petals strewn across the

bed while cheesy music played, but still. I certainly hadn't imagined it going down on some guy's beat-up sofa. I didn't want to use sex with some guy I didn't even care about as a distraction. I was through with making horrible decisions.

I pushed him off of me and stood up, pulling my sweater back into place.

"What the hell?" His eyes were wide, and it was obvious by his annoyed expression that he didn't much appreciate me putting on the brakes.

"This isn't going to happen." I shook my head, and motioned to him then myself. "You, me. It's just not going to happen."

He stared some more. "You've been putting out mixed signals from the time I met you. One minute you act like you want this, want me, then the next…" He sighed. "I mean, what the hell?"

He was right, I had been. But I knew I didn't want this, not with him. He was an escape, and it was a shitty thing to do. "You're right, so to clear up the signals, you and I aren't going to happen. I shouldn't have come here." I actually felt bad about it, until he opened his mouth again.

His face hardened slightly. "You know what? Whatever. This is why I don't have sex with virgins." He shook his head. "Oh my god, the drama." He rolled his eyes.

Who was this person?

In that second, I knew I'd made the right decision. I wanted to knock his teeth down his throat.

"Just stop. Please." I held up my hand. "Just don't say anything else, okay?" Bile rose in my mouth, sour on my tongue.

We stared at each other for what seemed like minutes,

neither of us saying a word. Although mere inches apart, there may as well have been a football field dividing us.

"Look, I'm sorry. I shouldn't have said that." His gaze didn't quite meet my eyes. "I don't know what else to say. Sorry things got out of hand."

Understatement of the year.

I stood. "I gotta go." I headed to the door.

He jumped up after me. "Sam."

I ignored him.

"Samantha, wait."

I kept going.

"Would you please hold up? Christ."

I looked over my shoulder and held up a hand to stop him. "Don't. I want to be alone right now."

"Well, do you want a ride?"

Was he serious? The thought of sitting close to him right then was too much. I needed space. I shook my head. "I'll be fine. I want to walk…clear my thoughts."

"You sure?"

I nodded, a quick jerk of my head.

"I guess I'll see you later."

That would be a cold day in hell. But I nodded again, a bobble-headed robot. "Yeah."

He stepped closer and leaned down like he was actually about to kiss me. I turned my head, and his kiss landed on my cheek instead. He sighed and pressed his lips together as he straightened up, but he didn't say a word.

As I reached the door, he said quietly, "I warned you that I wasn't your knight in shining armor."

I didn't turn around. "Yeah, you did."

I opened the door and walked out, offering a halfhearted

smile, so as not to be accused of being a drama queen, before I closed the door behind me. As soon as I heard him cross the room, away from the door, I slid down the corridor wall, and buried my face in my hands. The day simply couldn't get any worse.

I may have seriously hurt Jessica.

I'd almost lost my virginity to some guy I'd met a freaking week ago who was turning out to be a real asshole.

And I desperately needed my best friend. Only I'd ruined that too.

I sat and stared blankly across the hall, not having the energy to begin my trek home. Zigzagged cracks slivered across the dirty wall. Small flakes of paint stuck out along a huge Y-shaped crevice that ran midway down the surface all the way to the floor. It looked like someone started to repair it and gave up.

I heard footsteps and then Ransom's muffled voice carried through the door. "Hey you. What are ya doing?" His voice sounded warm, flirtatious.

Unable to add one more thing to my list of why the day would go down in history as the suckiest of all sucky days, I tried to rationalize what I'd heard. Maybe it was completely innocent. His sister or something. There was no way he'd be calling some other girl right after what just happened between us.

Too bad I didn't believe the lies I tried to tell myself. I'd been too caught up in my plan, and I'd let common sense fly out the window. The only thing I could think was that he'd played the role he'd needed to in order to gain my interest to try to get me in his bed, and I'd been too dumb to see through his false charm. Too angry at the world to really stop and think of what I was doing and more importantly, *why* I was doing it.

Footsteps sounded again, moving away. A door closed somewhere inside his apartment, and then I heard nothing at all.

The day's events were simply too much. I had to think about something else, forget worrying about Ransom, about Jessica, or even what had just happened.

The familiar numbness slowly returned. I welcomed it. I stared at the chipped wall and watched a spider cross one of the cracks and crawl down onto the floorboards. It didn't seem to be worried about anything. I envied its oblivion.

I pushed myself up like an old, tired lady and headed toward the steps to begin my long walk home.

twenty-seven

There are no regrets in life, just lessons.
—Jennifer Aniston

My aunt was asleep on her chair in the living room when I got home almost an hour later. In sleep, she looked older than I was used to seeing her…small and frail huddled under the knit afghan. I sighed. She'd probably worried when I hadn't come home after school.

I walked through the kitchen, noticing the lack of food warming on the stove or dishes in the sink. It didn't look like she'd eaten anything.

"Aunt Lor?" I shook her shoulder gently, not wanting to startle her.

Her eyes opened immediately. At first they appeared frightened, until recognition dawned.

"Samantha. What a nice surprise." She smiled. "Are your mother and father here with you too, dear?" Her wrinkled face looked hopeful.

I sucked in a breath. I opened and closed my mouth, but nothing came out.

I'd gotten somewhat used to her forgetting things. Small things, like what day it was, or if we'd eaten dinner.

But not like this.

She reached out and patted my hand. "Sit down, sweetie. I'll get you something to drink." Her small body struggled up from the chair. I stopped her with a shaking hand. "No. That's okay, I'm fine." What else could I say?

"Here. You look tired. Why don't you go lay down awhile?" I tried to smile at her, offering encouragement. She started to protest, until I convinced her I'd get myself some iced tea and watch television.

"If you're sure."

I nodded and helped her to her room and into bed. I clicked her light out, the darkness hiding my tears.

I couldn't ignore the reality that she was getting worse, much worse. And I didn't have any idea what to do about it.

I crawled into my own bed after a long, hot shower. Everything in my life seemed to be spinning out of control. Had I really ever been doing the right thing, or was I turning into all of the things that I despised the most?

Jessica had publicly humiliated me in school since the first day of classes our freshman year and hadn't let up since. But could that justify what I was doing?

I remembered back to our first day of high school, a day I'd dreamed about since I was a child and so desperately wanted to seem grown-up. I'd waited and waited for Jessica to pick me up like usual to give me a ride to school, not wanting to believe we really weren't going to be best friends anymore.

Back then, I'd still wanted to forgive her. I'd still wanted desperately for us to remain friends and get past the drama between our families.

Only, she'd never shown up. Whether initially her choice

or her mother's refusal to give the convict's daughter a ride…I never knew. And when I'd approached her by our lockers that first day of high school and asked her why she hadn't come by, Jessica had glanced around the hall at the throngs of curious onlookers and chosen sides.

"Why would I give *you* a ride?" Her pert nose wrinkled, and she looked around again to be sure she had everyone's attention. She did.

I stared at her, my eyes pleading with her to remember who we were to each other. Or at least who we'd been.

But the rules of ninth grade social climbing prevented her from giving in. "Look, Sam. The only reason people even know you exist is because you're the kid whose dad went to jail." She smoothed on some strawberry Lipsmacker and shrugged before twirling away with a catty smile.

I shook my head to clear the cobwebs of hurt and heartache. Even if Jessica *was* a bitch, I needed to find out what had happened with her. I picked up my cell.

The phone rang in my ear, and for a minute I thought he wouldn't answer.

"Hello?" His voice sounded resigned, but at least he'd picked up.

"Jer?" I wanted…*needed* things to go back to the way they used to be. I hoped he'd hear my unspoken plea. Prayed he'd forgive me and feel the same way.

"What do you want?" He sighed, a quiet sigh that spoke volumes.

I wanted my best friend back. I settled for, "How are you?"

"I'm fine, Sam. What's up?"

I closed my eyes and pulled my blanket tighter against me.

"Did you hear anything about Jessica?"

"She's gonna be fine. They took her to the hospital, and Pete and some of the other guys on the team went over too, to make sure she was okay."

My heart began beating again. My voice shook as I said, "But she fell. So far."

"Disappointed?"

"How can you ask me that?"

"Just stop lying to me, Sam. *Please*. I saw the notebook. All you want to do is destroy her."

"Bring her down, yeah. Not *physically hurt* her!" I tightened my hand around the phone so hard my knuckles turned white.

Jeremy above all people should know me better than that.

"She broke her arm, and they said she has a mild concussion. She was still in the emergency room when the guys left, but they said she wouldn't have to be admitted."

Relief shot through me, although I didn't even deserve to feel relieved. I didn't know what to say.

"Look, I gotta go. I have to help my mom with something."

He didn't. It was an excuse, and we both knew it. But I played along.

"Okay. Well, I guess I'll see you later?"

"Yeah. See ya."

He hung up.

I set my phone down on the nightstand, and leaned over to turn off the light. It was still early, but I didn't care. All I wanted to do was escape into the oblivion of sleep.

Unfortunately, my brain wouldn't cooperate. Images

continued to race through my mind. Jessica falling. Abby leaning in to whisper in Jeremy's ear. Ransom's face inches above mine as he whispered unintelligible words. Then Jessica's face morphed into my father's, and he pointed at me and cackled. Jeremy was suddenly there too, pointing and hissing.

I needed to stop the whole thing. It had gone too far and spiraled way out of control. I knew what I had to do. I got up out of bed, walked out to the living room, and stopped short.

Aunt Lor must have woken up while I was on the phone, because she sat at the kitchen table with a cup of tea in front of her.

"Samantha! Why didn't you tell me about what happened at school today? I just heard about it." She shook her head. "All these awful things going on lately, it makes me worry about you."

So at least she was back to herself again.

"I'm sorry, I didn't think to mention it. Can we talk about it when I get back? There's something I have to do quick."

She was shaking her head before I had the sentence out. "No, you're not going anywhere. I want you home tonight. With everything going on, you need a night at home."

"But, Aunt Lor, you don't understand."

"Samantha Jane, I said no, and that's final." She took my arm and led me over to the sofa. "Now you sit yourself down and watch some TV and try to take a rest."

When I opened my mouth to speak again, she gave me a firm look and shook her head. She pulled an afghan from the back of the couch and spread it across my lap like I was a child, or sick with the flu.

"Now you sit tight. I'll bring you some tea." She turned

and headed to the kitchen.

I sighed and tucked my feet underneath me, leaning my head back against the worn sofa. Aunt Lor could be stubborn when she wanted to be, and at that moment, for whatever reason, she was dead set against me leaving the protection of her watchful eyes. I didn't know if she suspected all I'd been dealing with, if it was really just worry about all the accidents at school lately, or if she was in some place in her mind that told her she needed to care for me.

I drank the strong tea she brought me and even managed to choke down a few bites of the cinnamon toast she'd set in front of me.

A few minutes later, the familiar sound of pages turning lulled me, but I fought against the exhaustion of the day I'd had. Aunt Lor sat across the room in her chair, reading. It'd grown darker in the room as evening wore on, the blackness dispelled only by the light from a small lamp on the table next to her chair. I shifted into a more comfortable position, resting my head against the pillow she'd brought me earlier. Closing my eyes, I willed my breathing to relax. In and out. In and out. She needed to believe I was asleep.

Deep, slow breaths. In. Out.

Finally, her chair squeaked. Footsteps padded toward me. Breath moved across my face right before her dry lips touched my forehead.

"Sleep, child," she whispered.

I didn't move, or open my eyes.

Slight footsteps sounded, lighter and lighter as she headed to her bedroom.

I held my breath, waiting. What if she decided to grab a blanket and come out and sleep in the living room to be near me? I counted to two hundred. Each creak and shift of the trailer caused my heart to lurch.

Finally, I decided it was safe. I slowly sat up, half expecting her thin shape to pop out of her door any second. But it didn't. I swung my legs, one at a time, off the sofa. The floor chilled my bare feet. I leaned forward, straining to see down the hall through the darkness.

I waited another minute and stood up. The blanket fell from my shoulders back onto the sofa. I crept forward and banged my toe into something solid. Sharp pain radiated from my big toe up my foot. I bit down on my bottom lip, shoving the scream back. Tears pooled in my eyes.

I froze, waiting to see if her door would open, if I'd been caught. Nothing stirred. I glanced down. Aunt Lor's heavy knitting chest rested on the floor inches from my throbbing toes. She kept needles and yarn in the cherry box. I used the side of my good foot to shove it out of the way, and crept forward toward the door.

My sneakers waited on the mat. I slipped them on, not worrying about socks, and reached for my jacket hanging on a peg. Slipping my arms through each sleeve, I considered leaving a note, but decided it wouldn't matter. If Aunt Lor woke up and saw me gone, she'd be livid with or without a written explanation. I grabbed my computer bag and pulled the door open, willing it not to creak. Just as I stepped outside, I had an idea.

I turned back around and tiptoed over to the counter. Aunt Lor's key ring lay in a shallow dish shaped like a ladybug. I bit my lip. I'd just be borrowing it. *Without permission.* I reached out and snatched up the keys and spun back toward the door.

If she knew why it was so important for me to get to town, she would say okay. *If she knew why it was so important for me to get to town, she'd probably kick me out.* I pushed the thought out of my head and held the button on the screen door with my thumb until it closed all the way, moving as slowly as possible to keep quiet.

I jumped in the Buick and shut the door behind me. Slouched down in the seat, I slipped the key in the ignition and turned it. The car roared to life.

My heart pounded. This was the first time I was driving alone, and I'd never driven at night before.

"You can do this." I chanted encouragement to myself.

I had something that needed to get done and had no choice but to hurry and get to the coffee shop. Too much was at stake if I didn't.

twenty-eight

She stood in the storm, and when the wind did not blow her
way, she adjusted her sails.
—Elizabeth Edwards

I closed the lid of my netbook and shut my eyes. I'd
done it, taken down tomorrow's tasks and written
instructions on each initiate's page to disregard the
previously scheduled assignments. Posted that there would
be no new tasks—that it was over.

Eventually the chatter surrounding me broke through
my daze. I reached for my cooled coffee and took a small sip.
I desperately needed the jumpstart the caffeine provided. My
body ached, completely beat…physically and emotionally.
Finally finished, I desperately wanted to go home and crawl
in bed, and maybe sleep for a week straight.

Jeremy had been right all along. Why hadn't I listened
to him? With everything that'd happened, all that had gone
wrong, thankfulness washed over me that no one'd been
seriously hurt. It could have been so much worse.

I shoved my computer back in its bag and slung it
over my shoulder. I almost wanted to throw it away. The
mere sight of it reminded me how far I had strayed from

who I wanted to be—someone who wasn't ashamed to look at herself in the mirror each night. Someone who was honorable in standing up for what she believed in. Someone good. I wondered how I could get that girl back...prayed I could find her again.

*F*inally home and nestled in bed under the covers, I pushed the button and held my phone to my ear. I prayed he wouldn't ignore me. It only rang once before he answered.

"Hello?"

I pressed my eyes closed tight and tried not to cry.

"Sam? You there?" His voice turned from its initial coolness to sounding worried.

I wiped my eyes. "I'm here," I whispered. I was so thankful he was speaking to me.

"Are you okay? What's wrong?" His voice went softer. "Is it your aunt?"

I felt sick. All the things I'd done...I didn't deserve his caring. I sniffed. "No. She's fine. She was bad earlier, but she seemed better after laying down for a bit." I paused. "The doctor put her on a new medicine. He said it could take a few weeks to kick in, but that it should help. I hope so anyway."

Jeremy's quiet breathing filled my ear.

What was I supposed to say now? What did I want to say? There was so much, yet I didn't have a clue how to begin.

"Can you....?" I paused once more, knowing what I needed more than anything...and afraid to ask. I pressed the phone tight against the side of my head, trying to feel closer to him that way. It wasn't the same. I took a deep breath, and prayed that it wasn't too late. "Can you come over? Please?" I was almost afraid to breathe as I waited for his response. Seconds ticked by.

"Yeah, I'll come over."

Tears burned my eyes. "Thank you."

It was his turn to pause. "I'm on my way."

My eyes still burned, yet I could breathe once more. He was coming. Jeremy didn't hate me.

*W*e sat on the front porch steps, neither of us speaking. Jeremy's arm pressed against mine, and it warmed me even through my thick hoodie. He shifted against me as he turned to face me. Even half hidden in shadows, his warm eyes made me feel safe. I hadn't felt that way in weeks.

"What's going on?" he asked.

I shook my head and looked down at my scuffed sneakers. He reached out and used a finger to lift my chin to face him again. "Talk to me." He stared directly at me, not blinking. His thick lashes framed his eyes. I loved his eyes. The saying about the eyes being the windows to a person's soul must be true, because Jeremy's eyes reflected all the goodness that he was made up of.

I burst into tears. His gaze widened for a second, and the next thing I knew he pulled me tight against him. His arms wrapped around my shoulders and he whispered, "I'm right here, Sam. I'm right here."

I remembered the last time he'd held me like that, on

these same steps. It seemed like forever ago and like it was just yesterday all at the same time. I clung to his sweatshirt, not caring that I was smearing it with mascara and tears. I held on for dear life. Jeremy let me. He didn't try to stop my tears, or tell me everything would be okay. He just held me close while I cried.

I cried for all the stupid decisions I'd made, and how I'd really hurt people. I cried for the father that had been taken from me, and for the mother who abandoned me. I cried for Aunt Loretta being sick, and I cried for the fact that I'd almost allowed myself to lose my best friend in the world.

Through it all, Jeremy held me tight and didn't say a word, like he knew I needed to finally get it all out, to release all the pain and anger and hurt I'd shoved down deep inside for way too long.

I wasn't sure how much time passed as we sat there together with my face buried in his chest, the taste of tears salty in my mouth. Finally, I raised my head. The shadows were gone from his face; the clouds had passed over the full October moon above us. He tilted his head, and smoothed the damp, matted hair out of my swollen eyes. "You're going to be okay," he whispered. "I promise."

And for the first time in a very long time, I didn't scoff inside when I heard the words. I nodded. He brushed the pad of his thumb across my tearstained cheek. "I'm right here, Sam. Always."

My heart lurched at the sincerity in his words. "I did a lot of really stupid things," I whispered.

He sat, not saying a word, still holding me close.

"I told them it was over. I'm done. I never should have

started any of it." I waited for him to say, *I told you so*. Only he never did.

"Then it's over," he said simply.

I shook my head. "But, Jer, you don't understand. You don't know what all I did." It wasn't just the stuff with the Society I was ashamed of; it was all the crap with Ransom, too.

He put a hand on either side of my head, stilling me. "It doesn't matter. We all screw up. We all do things we wish we hadn't."

He released his hold on my head, and reached down to hold both my hands in his larger ones. "The important thing is to put it behind us, because dwelling on it will eat us alive. It'll destroy us from the inside." His lips tilted into a small smile, and he shook his head. "And I won't let that happen to you."

I stared back at him, hardly able to believe someone as good and real as Jeremy wanted anything to do with me. I didn't deserve him.

"I better go inside," I whispered.

He nodded. "Okay."

We stood, and he held my hand as I opened the front door and stepped into the trailer. Our arms stretched across the threshold, neither one of us in any hurry to let go.

I glanced toward the hallway. I didn't want my aunt to wake up and find Jeremy there. He got the message, and squeezed my hand for a second before releasing his hold.

He leaned in and brushed a soft kiss across my cheek. "I'll call you tomorrow, okay?"

I simply nodded.

He must have taken my silence to mean I was tired,

because he reached out and touched my wrist. "Get some sleep, okay?" He stuck his hands in his pockets, still watching me.

I nodded again.

"Night, Sam," he whispered.

"Good night."

He turned and went down the steps and walked toward his car. Before he got in, he looked my way, smiled once more, and waved his hand above his head.

"Good night," he mouthed.

I waved back and shut the door, leaning my head against it after it closed.

twenty-nine

Life is about choices. Some we regret; some we're
proud of. Some will haunt us forever.
—Graham Brown

"C'mon, Sam. You promised." Jeremy wasn't taking no for an answer about Pete's party.

Apparently, Pete and the rest of the team had decided that with everything that had happened this week, it made for an even better reason to relax and try to have some fun. So the party was still on.

I wavered. A part of me wanted to go, just so I could spend time with Jeremy. I kind of wanted to see how things went with us when I wasn't sniffling all over his sweatshirt.

Had I misread what I'd thought I'd seen in his eyes last night? Had it only been friendly concern? Or worse yet, pity?

I wanted to curse myself for ever inviting Ransom to the stupid party. I'd been ignoring the texts he'd sent today, asking what time he should pick me up. It wasn't like he knew the location of the party and could just show up. I couldn't believe he still even thought we'd be going out tonight after what went down the last time I saw him.

I flopped backward on my bed and stared at my ceiling.

"Well?"

"I don't know, Jer."

"Look, after everything that's happened, we deserve a night out, right?" The smile in his voice carried through the phone line. "*You* deserve some fun, and I promise we'll have fun."

My resistance melted like ice cream on a hot summer day. "You promise?"

He laughed. "I promise."

He rushed on before I had a chance to change my mind. "I'll pick you up at nine. Be ready."

"Okay." I smiled as I hung up and glanced at my clock. I had less than two hours to figure out something to wear, get ready, and try to act like a normal teenager. I slapped my arm across my forehead. Things had to get better; they certainly couldn't get any worse.

*A*fter much debating, rooting in closets, hair pulling, and some muffled cursing, I'd finally thrown together a costume. I wouldn't win any awards with it, but it wasn't like Pete would really be hosting any costume-judging contests anyway. More likely the "drink 'til you're sick" type of games.

I crossed my room and sat down at my desk. I'd been putting it off too long; I needed to call Ransom and make it clear that we weren't going to the party together anymore. He answered right away.

"Hey, babe. What's up?"

Babe? Ew. I fidgeted in the wooden chair. "Hey, I just

wanted to call you because I thought we needed to talk."

"I can think of other things I'd rather be doing with you."

Double ew. My fingers tightened on the phone. "Ransom, I'm serious."

"Whoa. Okay, chill, I was only teasing you." He sounded a little annoyed. "So, what's going on?"

"I don't think we should see each other anymore," I blurted out.

Silence.

"I thought we were going to some party tonight," he said. "Is this about what happened yesterday? I said I was sorry."

"No, it's not just that," I said, shaking my head even though he couldn't see me. "This is about me. Well, and us, to be perfectly honest."

"I don't understand a word you're saying. Look, are we getting together tonight or not?"

Unreal. Where was the guy I'd thought I'd known? Maybe I'd just been seeing what I'd wanted to see, or maybe he was just done pretending. Either way, I knew I didn't want to see him again. "No. We're not."

"I kind of expected you were gonna do this." He sounded bored now. Talk about a 180. "Anyway, I gotta go." His true colors were coming through loud and clear.

"Goodbye, Ransom." My voice was quiet, and I didn't even wait to hear if he said it back before I disconnected the call. I sat staring at the phone in my hand for a few minutes.

It wasn't that I wanted to be with him, I knew now with certainty that I didn't, but it still kind of stung a little. We'd almost had sex and it was obvious I hadn't meant a thing to him. He was probably calling the next girl on his list the second we'd hung up. I felt sick that I'd even done the things I had with him—but also proud that I'd seen who he really was before I'd gotten myself in any deeper.

A part of me also felt a little guilty. Because in a way, I'd used Ransom too, so I couldn't just blame everything on him. He'd been an escape for me. A way to experience the freedom I'd craved, a way to feel desired and wanted. I'd used him to crawl out of the box I'd been hiding in to shut myself away from the rest of the world, I knew that now. And that wasn't fair to either of us. I wanted to be free on my own.

A glance at the clock reminded me that Jeremy would be there soon to pick me up. He wasn't as exciting or dangerous as Ransom had initially seemed to be, but he gave me something Ransom never offered—genuine caring. A small smile crossed my face thinking of all the times Jeremy had stood by my side through the years.

Any time I'd ever tried to thank him for it, he'd brushed it off, assuring me that I'd been there for him as many times as he'd been there for me. Once again it hit that I couldn't fathom life without him.

Maybe part of the reason I'd gravitated toward Ransom was because I felt I didn't deserve someone like Jeremy. But I was slowly realizing, true friendship and caring isn't about what we deserve…because we all screw up and make mistakes. The real measure of friendship is being there for each other through them, and loving each other anyway. Anyone can be there through the easy times; you know it's real if someone is still there after it all crashes down.

Jeremy was always there. I owed him so much, and I

resolved in that moment to be a better friend to him. He deserved it.

I hopped up from my desk and went to the bathroom to use it one final time. After I finished, I stood in front of the bathroom mirror, eyeballing myself critically. Not perfect, but it would do.

The sound of tires crunching in the gravel carried through the tiny bathroom window, even though it was closed against the chill night air. A quick peek from behind the floral curtain revealed Jeremy hopping out of his car.

I sucked in a breath. He looked hot, like, with a capital H—Hot. With his interests, I'd expected a box painted like a robot, or maybe a Stormtrooper, or the tenth Doctor in a suit and trench coat. Well, Jeremy in a suit and trench coat wouldn't be too bad, but even that image was nothing compared to the reality walking toward my front porch.

He wore dark tight jeans, and some kind of billowy long-sleeved white shirt opened at the neck. His eyes were covered by a black mask, and he had what looked like a long sword attached to his belt. Zorro, maybe?

I stared as he sauntered up the path leading to the trailer. I stood on tiptoe and tried to crane my head at a different angle so I could watch him walk up the steps, but he'd disappeared from my view. Jeremy brought sexy back in a big way in that costume. As much as I'd tried to deny it, I'd been noticing lately how cute he was, but this side of him? It made *cute* sound like a ridiculous description.

I glanced at my reflection and wished I'd chosen a different outfit. All the girls at the party were bound to be wearing sexy nurse costumes, or sexy policewoman costumes complete with handcuffs. Sexy *anything* costumes…with skirts barely covering their asses and cleavage spilling out of their tops.

I tried in vain to spot some cleavage in my reflection. It was useless. I'd need two Wonderbras on my best day to look like they did. I'd always been happy with my barely-there boobs before, but right then I'd consider making a crossroads deal for a larger cup size.

There wasn't time to do anything about it. Aunt Lor called to me, telling me Jeremy was here, like I wasn't already well aware of that fact, as evidenced by my flushed cheeks and rapid heart rate. The ribbons of curls that I'd painstakingly put in my hair now seemed stupid, childish.

I smoothed the front of my costume and fidgeted with the twined piece of thick rope I'd fashioned into a long, loose belt. I reached out to turn off the light and stepped into the hallway to meet Jeremy.

thirty

It's the end of the world as we know it.
—R.E.M.

eremy kept looking over at me as we drove to Pete's house. I played with the rope around my waist, trying not to appear self-conscious. Finally, I couldn't take it any longer.

"What?" I burst out.

His eyes widened. "What, *what*?" he asked.

"You keep staring at me."

He jerked his head away from me to face the road. "Sorry, I didn't mean to." His fingers tightened on the steering wheel, and a muscle in his jaw twitched.

I sighed. "I look ridiculous, I know, but it was the best I could come up with."

His head whipped in my direction again. "Are you kidding me?" He'd taken the black mask off to drive, and his brows rose up to meet his long bangs.

"Well, yeah. I didn't bother trying to put together a real outfit since I wasn't even planning to go after everything that happened." I crossed my arms in front of my chest and turned to stare out my window. I should have just stayed home.

"Sam, you look amazing."

Heat skittered up my neck and filled my cheeks. I bit my lip and peeked over at him. "Really?"

"Really." He nodded, and I could see him swallow.

"Thanks." I smiled shyly and my heart squeezed in my chest.

Jeremy winked.

My toes curled in my sandals and I fought to suppress a cheesy grin. Maybe the outfit wasn't as bad as I thought. I'd grabbed a sheet from the linen closet and kind of draped it around me, then pinned two of the ends over one shoulder with this fancy jeweled pin Aunt Loretta said I could borrow. From there, a piece of rope slung loose over my hips, tied in a simple knot with long ends hanging down.

A piece of thin leafy garland wrapped around my head like a crown, over the long curls that took me almost an hour to get right. I'd slipped elaborate gold candelabra earrings in each lobe, and used a deep red lipstick, kohl eyeliner, and heavy mascara.

I wasn't sure what to call the finished product, but I guess that didn't really matter. The look Jeremy gave me made the hour spent on my hair totally worthwhile.

We made it to Pete's in less than twenty minutes. Landscaping lights guided our way up the long driveway leading to his house. We had to park halfway up the drive since cars and SUVs lined the road on either side, the vehicles hanging partway over into the perfectly manicured grass.

I stepped out of the car and gaped.

Music thundered from wide-open patio doors. Kids spilled out of the house, onto the large wooden deck, and the bright lights shining inside enabled me to see the packed living room. Orange twinkle lights hung from shrubs and two tall maple trees. A stuffed man dangled from a rope from the taller tree. Someone had already wrapped a red bra around his neck.

Jeremy chuckled. "Well, when Pete finally throws a party, he *throws a party*."

I stared. Shouts and laughter rang in the night air.

He laughed at my shocked expression and slipped on his thin black mask once more. "C'mon, what've we got to lose? I don't know about you, but I can definitely use a night with no stress and just fun." He reached his hand out to me.

I raised an eyebrow but took it. "Why do I think we're going to regret this?"

We made our way up the hill. Pete's house was a huge white colonial and could easily fit five of Aunt Lor's trailers inside. Probably more. And that wasn't even including the three-car garage.

Jeremy pushed through the crowd on the steps leading up the deck, headed inside. I followed behind, being sure not to let go of his hand. After a few odd looks from some girls clustered together holding red plastic cups, I stared at my feet as we made our way in. I told myself to ignore them, but it didn't completely work.

My stomach twisted, and I self-consciously played with my belt with my free hand. Jeremy peeked over his shoulder at me and smiled, which made me feel marginally better.

"My man! You're here!" Pete walked over, painted completely green and wearing some scrap of cloth around his waist like an oversized diaper.

My eyes bugged out, and I couldn't help but crack up. He clapped Jeremy on the back, then flexed. "What do you think?"

I couldn't believe it. Mild-mannered Pete, dressed like the Hulk. Talk about priceless. Jeremy laughed along with me. "Whoa! Now that's a costume."

Pete grinned. "Yeah, I know. Blame her." He nodded his head to the left. Celia bounded over, beaming.

"Don't you love it? I got washable spray paint. It took me three coats to get it right." She ran her hand up his arm and squeezed his tricep. "I think he looks amazing."

Pete leaned down and kissed her, his eyes adoring.

Celia looked great. I guess I didn't get the memo that the cool kids were doing superhero themed. She wore a very official-looking Batgirl costume, sexy without looking slutty.

I smiled at her. "You both look fantastic."

She preened, obviously thrilled. It was nice seeing her that way, seeing both of them like that. So relaxed and happy. I turned to Jeremy and included him in my grin, glad he'd talked me into coming. He was right—tonight would be fun.

"I like your costume too," Celia said. "You too, Jeremy."

"Okay, who's ready for a drink?" Pete asked.

Jeremy squeezed my hand before letting go. "I'll help Pete. Be right back."

I smiled as Pete pulled him away into the crowd.

"This is seriously amazing." I turned back to Celia. "Did you do all of this?"

She looked around the room. Black netting draped just about every available surface. Cobwebs clung in the corners and dripped from lamps; tall electric candles dotted the tables and shelves.

She nodded. "Well, Pete helped some, but mostly he told me to do what I liked." She giggled. "And it sure made it nice that he gave me a credit card to buy what I needed."

My eyes widened.

She laughed. "It's not like he has to pay for it. It's

his mom's. She was so thrilled that he was *being social*."
She made air quotes. "She was more than willing to fund
whatever we needed."

I shook my head and laughed. "I'll feel sorry for her
when she gets the bill."

"But we couldn't get a decent band on such short notice,
so canned music it is." She pouted.

"I don't think anyone minds." I gestured to the crowd.

"Well, I better circulate a little, make sure everyone's
having a good time."

I nodded. "Go ahead. I'm sure Jeremy will be back
soon."

Celia melted into the masses, leaving me standing alone.
I glanced around, trying to spot someone else to talk to.
Kids danced at the far side of the long room. Some couples
draped all over each other, making out.

I'd been right. Most of the girls seemed to be in a
competition to see who could wear the least amount of
clothing without being outright naked. None of the guys
seemed to mind. Even though it was only a little before ten,
a lot of the kids already seemed hammered.

No one paid any attention to me. I tried to look into
the next room to spot Jeremy. All I could see were people
laughing, drinking, and having a good time. I pushed off the
wall I'd been leaning on and headed toward the kitchen. Just
as I rounded the bend, someone came from the opposite
direction and ran directly into me, spilling beer down the
front of my costume.

"Oh shit! Sorry about that."

I recognized him immediately. Seth Walters, the guy
who'd almost landed on my lap at the pep rally. I could tell

exactly when he recognized me as well. He looked stricken.

"Oh wow. I keep running into you, don't I?"

I shook my head and offered a tight smile. "Don't worry about it."

He looked down at the sticky mess on my chest and stomach and cringed. "I'm really sorry." He reached out to wipe the mess with his bare hand.

I stepped back and blocked his movement. "Um, seriously, it's fine. No big deal."

Seth apparently realized what he'd been about to do and stared at his hand before quickly dropping it.

"Well, can I at least get you a drink or something?" He shrugged, a grin popping through as he waved his now empty cup. "After all, I need one again anyway."

"Thanks, but someone's getting one for me."

"Ya sure? I don't mind."

Two guys came up behind him, shoving him closer to me. "Dude, come on. We're playing quarters over in the den."

He raised an eyebrow and motioned to his cup, mouthing, "You sure?"

I waved him off. "I'm good, thanks."

"Come *on*!" The bigger guy grabbed Seth's arm and pulled him away. He gave me a final grin before allowing them to lead him off.

The damp cotton now clinging to my skin felt sticky and cold. And gross. I looked down. Fabulous.

Where was Jeremy?

By now, I was actually more than ready for that drink, but I couldn't spot his messy hair in the crowd anywhere. I smoothed the sheet the best I could, trying to reposition the draping to cover the stain. It didn't work. I sighed. Oh well,

I'd get my own drink.

People swarmed the kitchen. Bottles of rum, vodka, and schnapps lined the slate counter, and two kegs stood next to the center island. I pushed my way through the crowd and reached to grab a cup, and I saw them.

Jeremy and Abby.

She'd gone with the Cat Woman costume after all. And as much as I hated to admit it, she looked incredible. The black leotard covered her tall lithe body like a second skin. Tiny pointed ears poked from her wild mass of hair, and delicate whiskers were drawn on her cheeks.

A long tail draped over her left arm, as her other hand reached toward Jeremy. She ran her fingers across his chest playfully as she leaned in, whispering and giggling. I hated her with a blind passion in that moment.

I hated the look on Jeremy's face even more. He was smiling while Abby practically crawled all over him.

Pain jolted through me. I knew I shouldn't have come. I didn't belong here. And it wasn't like I could walk up to Jeremy and tell him I wanted to leave. He was obviously having a great time.

I clenched my hands at my sides and tried to fight back tears.

Fine. I didn't need him anyway. I turned away before he caught me watching. Someone had lined rows of shots in small plastic cups along the bar. I grabbed one, not caring what it contained. I whipped my head back and downed it in one gulp.

It burned its way down my throat, and I swore it hit my stomach with a sizzle. I grabbed another and swallowed it just as fast. Two guys watched me, smiling and nodding.

Whatever. I drank another. The one guy cheered.

I stepped into a corner with a rum and Coke and spied on Abby and Jeremy for a good ten minutes until I couldn't take it anymore. I gulped the last of my drink and grimaced before turning away, grabbing a cup of beer setting on the counter.

"Hey! That's mine!"

I ignored the voice and kept going, headed back to the living room.

Music still blared, and if anything the room seemed even more crowded than before. Pete and Celia seemed to have vanished. Probably upstairs in his bedroom. At least someone's love life didn't suck. I stumbled over a foot and laughed. "Has anyone seen a big green guy?" I called out to no one in particular.

No one answered.

I raised my cup above my head, sloshing beer down my arm in the process. "Here's to no one!" I took a long drink. "And here's to sucky parents!" I got a few cheers for that one, so I took another giant gulp.

"And here's to girls with big boobs!" Lots of cheers for that one, so I finished the contents of my cup.

This blew. I'd lost Jeremy to a cat. And everyone had someone but me. I spotted an empty chair in the corner of the room, sank into it, and immediately wished I'd thought to refill my beer before I'd sat down. The kitchen seemed so far away to go get another.

Someone perched on the arm of my chair.

I squinted, trying to make out if I knew him or not. Both of him smiled at me.

"Hey there."

I cocked my head, studying him.

"I think we're in computer lab together."

I stared some more. "Are we?"

He laughed this deep rumble. "Yeah. You're Samantha, right?"

"Sam." It seemed like I should know him, but I just couldn't remember his name.

"I'm Brad."

I nodded. Okay.

"So, what are you drinking?" He motioned toward my empty cup.

I stared at it, and shrugged. "Dunno. Don't care."

"Well, can I get you another?" He leaned a little closer, still smiling.

"Um…sure, why not." I handed my cup to him.

He winked. "Be right back."

He stood and headed to the kitchen, where Jeremy had gone. He'd promised to be right back too.

I didn't want another drink, especially not with some guy named Brad. I sighed and shook my head. The spinning room didn't help matters any.

Music pounded and people laughed and shouted, while I just wanted to lie down, somewhere quiet. I pushed up from the chair and walked toward the wide staircase. *Please let there be an empty room.*

I made it up the stairs without any major accidents. No one spilled anything else on me, and no one bothered to ask where I was going. I thought I heard Jeremy calling my name, but when I looked back, I didn't see him, so I kept trudging forward.

The first door I tried proved locked. The second door

stood open, but I could make out two bodies pressed together on the bed despite the lack of lights. "Taken," I muttered to myself and moved down the hall.

I spied one more door on the right side. Closed.

I pressed my ear against it, but couldn't hear anything. Just as I reached out to grasp the knob, I heard a scream. I jumped back and tripped on my sheet, falling backward in the process. I stuck my hand out to break my fall, but still landed hard on my butt.

"Ow." I looked at my hand even though it was my behind that hurt.

Another scream shot through the closed door.

I leaned forward. I recognized something familiar about the scream, high pitched, a girl's. It almost sounded like…

The blood drained from my face.

I knew who was screaming. Worse, I had a good idea *why* she was screaming.

But I'd canceled it. I'd told him not to go through with scaring her. I'd put it on the damn website. I stood up, still shaky, although the situation knocked me sober instantly. I reached out my hand again, ready to turn the knob, and stopped. Maybe it was just some kids screwing around.

Why was Jessica even at the party? I didn't think she'd even be here after her fall yesterday.

I tried to tell myself it would be all right. So what if Patrick hadn't seen the new post, and did what I'd originally told him to do; it wasn't like anyone would get hurt. He wasn't even going to touch her.

The sound of glass shattering carried through the door. I trembled. He was only supposed to hide and scare her, jump out in the dark and freak her out.

Becky was supposed to be at the party too, supposed to go ahead of Jessica upstairs to hide and videotape Jessica shrieking like a baby over someone jumping out at her.

Jessica should have been coming out by now. Pissed, sure, but still. Why wasn't she coming out?

Another loud crash sounded, followed by a heavy thump. The doorknob rattled, and seconds later the door ripped open.

Jessica barreled out, her face ashen, streaked with tears. She ran right into me, and for once didn't even seem to recognize me.

"Someone's in there. He was going to kill me. *He was going to kill me!*" she wailed and ran down the hall toward the stairs, yelling for someone to call the police.

What the hell?

I froze, half afraid to look inside.

Where was Patrick? Why hadn't he followed Jessica out, laughing and busting on her that he'd gotten her good? Where was Becky?

No sound from inside the room. I tiptoed forward but couldn't see anything. The room was completely dark. I took another small step, until I was just outside the door.

I leaned in and whispered, "Hello?" No answer. "Patrick? Are you in there?" I thought I may have heard a slight groan, but wasn't sure.

I reached my hand into the room and felt along the wall—looking for a light switch. When I made contact, I flipped it up, but nothing happened. I flipped it up and down. He must have loosened the bulbs or something to make sure the room stayed dark when she came in.

I pushed the door open wider, hoping some light from

the hallway would help. I could make out a long, low dresser to my left, and it looked like a desk to my right. A large shadow across the room was probably the bed. I stepped farther in the room.

"Is anyone here?" I whispered, my voice hoarse with fear.

Something crunched beneath my feet. I looked down. Broken glass littered the hardwood floor—tiny pieces of clear, pale blue.

What the—

A body lay to my right, several feet away.

I gasped.

It didn't move.

"No, no, no, no, *NO!*" I dropped to my knees and crawled toward the body, barely able to breathe. I didn't even feel the shards of glass cutting into my hands.

I could tell it was a guy from the hair, the build. He lay face down. I reached out a trembling hand, and grasped his shoulder, trying to roll him over. His unexpected weight made turning him harder than I'd expected. The phrase *dead weight* flashed through my mind, and all the alcohol I'd drunk threatened to come back up.

I tugged with all my might. Patrick's eyes stared back at me. He didn't blink. The remnants of a shattered heavy vase lay next to him. It finally registered what I'd missed when I first saw him. The side of his head was wet. I touched his hair, and when I brought my hand back, it was sticky. Dark red blood covered my fingers.

Patrick's blood.

thirty-one

Can't wake up in sweat 'cause it ain't over yet.
—Avenged Sevenfold

omit flew from my mouth, splattering the grass in front of me as I bent over, dizzy and finding it difficult to breathe.

Red and blue lights flashed around the yard. Once again, kids cried and whispered, huddled in groups across the grass—déjà vu in the worst possible way.

It had to be a dream. Right now I was tucked in my bed, blanket tight around me while Aunt Loretta slept down the hall. No way could this really be happening.

Only…it was.

Two police officers wandered through the groups, questioning people, trying to piece together exactly what occurred.

Jessica sat on the wooden steps leading to the deck, a blanket wrapped around her shoulders. I noticed one of her arms was in a pink sling.

A strange woman in street clothing knelt in front of her. She must have been some kind of investigator, because she held a small notebook and scribbled in it furiously. I couldn't hear their words, but the lady kept nodding her head in an encouraging manner as Jessica gestured with her free arm and spoke.

I wiped my mouth with the back of my hand and turned, embarrassed, from the mess I'd made in the lawn. No one noticed.

Jeremy and Pete were nowhere around, probably still inside. Other officers had gone in the house, too.

I couldn't even begin to imagine what Pete's parents' reaction would be when they got home. They'd gone out of town overnight for some business thing for Pete's dad.

EMTs had carried Patrick out on a stretcher about twenty minutes ago, paramedics leaning over him the whole time as they loaded him into the waiting ambulance. It'd rushed down the driveway, sirens wailing, headed to St. Joe's Hospital.

I'd tried to remain calm after finding him bleeding in the bedroom. After I'd dialed 911, I'd sat next to him, afraid to move him, petrified that at any second he'd stop breathing.

He'd muttered something unintelligible seconds after I'd knelt next to him, then closed his eyes and didn't move. The only way I could tell he was still alive was the fact his chest moved faintly up and down.

While I'd sat there in shock, 911 still on the line with me, two seniors had barreled upstairs and rushed in the room. They'd told me Jessica had run downstairs screaming about someone coming after her, and how she'd clocked him over the head with a vase. Once they saw Patrick wasn't moving, one of them stayed with me while I'd asked the other to go and find Jeremy.

By that time, cops and EMTs were already bursting

in and brusquely instructed us to leave the room and wait downstairs so they could talk to us.

A lot of the kids must have taken off before the police arrived, since the room held far fewer people than when I'd gone up. Apparently no one wanted to stay in a house with a possible killer, even if he was unconscious.

It didn't make sense. I knew Patrick wouldn't have tried to actually hurt Jessica. He had no reason to. I could only guess that when she'd gone into the dark room, and Patrick jumped out to scare her, she must have lost it. She would've seen it wasn't actually Blane and freaked out. Plus, she'd probably been half wasted and not thinking straight when she hit him with the vase.

She didn't have any visible bruises, and from the little I'd been able to overhear he hadn't actually laid a hand on her. I'd been right there next to him on the floor; he didn't have a weapon. She must have gotten scared and reacted on instinct.

No way he would have actually been trying to kill her like she'd been screaming when she ran out of the room. It didn't make sense. *None of it* made any sense. It was supposed to be a practical joke. Harmless.

The only thing that kept me from running away on the spot was the fact that I needed to avoid arousing suspicion. I was petrified of what would happen when Patrick woke up, when he told police his version of what happened, all of it. When he explained that someone *told him* to do what he'd done.

What if he'd printed out the original instructions for the party, or they traced it back to me even though I'd taken them down from the site the other night? It could be done by the right person, and I knew it.

Working from the coffee shop rather than my own home might buy me some time since they couldn't track the IP address back to me directly, but it wouldn't take long until they pieced it all together. Deleting it from the site didn't make it disappear. There were plenty of ways anyone tech savvy enough could pull the information. Just because you deleted something from the web didn't mean it was gone, and I damn well knew it.

Why hadn't I bothered to check if the coffee shop had security cameras? For all I knew, an image of me merrily posting the entire website was stored on tape somewhere, waiting for police to find.

I shivered and gagged down the bile that began to rise in my throat again. *Goddammit.* Why had he still gone through with it? And how the hell had it gone so horribly wrong?

The quick flash of a lighter on the far side of the deck caught my attention. Someone huddled in the darkness, alone, smoking.

I took a few steps closer and swallowed. Becky. My first reaction was shock; I couldn't imagine sweet, innocent Becky smoking. My next: fear. What if she'd told the police the truth?

I had to know. I needed to find out how much she'd pieced together.

Becky's hand holding the cigarette trembled as I approached. A burning ember fell to the ground. An oversized straw hat lay at her feet, apparently part of some kind of farmer costume.

She didn't meet my eyes when I stopped, steps in front of her. A suspender fell down her shoulder as she shoved her other hand into the pocket of her overalls.

It all seemed so ludicrous now. It was supposed to be a way to blow off steam…dress up and hang out with friends. Laugh, party, *be normal*. Only things were as far from normal as they could get.

It's all my fault.

So what if I'd tried to stop it? I should have never fucking started it. I took a deep breath, willing my voice steady. Calm.

"Are you okay?" I asked. Stupid question.

Becky slowly raised her eyes to meet mine, her expression guarded. "I'm fine. Just shook up, like everyone else." Her voice was quiet. Too-pale skin and wide, frightened eyes belied her statement.

"So, do you have any idea what happened?"

She stared at me, cigarette forgotten, ash dangling unheeded inches from her fingertips. "I have no idea. Why would I know anything?"

Fear obviously prevented her from wanting to talk, to mention her part in getting Jessica upstairs, which didn't really make sense. She had to realize Jessica would tell the police all about it. The rose. Becky telling her Blane was waiting for her up in the bedroom.

Only of course he hadn't been there. Hell, I hadn't even seen him at the party.

Why the hell hadn't Becky stayed hidden in the room like she was supposed to? Maybe if she'd been there, none of it would have happened.

I recognized the blame-shifting…and hated myself for it. I sucked in a deep breath.

"Have the police talked to you yet? Looks like they're

questioning everyone."

Becky tossed the cigarette and stomped it into the ground with a quick movement. She walked away without bothering to answer.

"Sam!"

I turned. Jeremy stood several yards away with Pete. My stomach twisted in knots. He'd know. He'd be able to see it in my eyes somehow.

He leaned in to say something to Pete and then walked toward me. I met him in the middle of the yard.

"How is he?" I asked, motioning to where Pete stood, green shoulders slumped, shaking his head as he stared up at the second floor window.

"Not good." Jeremy sighed. "His parents are on their way home now. The police called them. They should be here soon."

I nodded.

"Can we go?" I asked. "I mean, are they done talking to us, do you think?"

Jeremy stared at me for a long moment. I knew what he was thinking. He'd seen the names in my notebook. Patrick, Becky, Zena, Jessica. The wheels had to be turning in his head, trying to figure out if I'd lied when I'd said it was over. I looked down at my feet. I couldn't bear to see the doubts and accusations I knew I'd find in his eyes. Not when he was right to blame me. Hell, I blamed myself enough for the both of us.

thirty-two

Always do right. This will gratify some people and astonish the rest.
—Mark Twain

We didn't talk much on the ride home, both of us too lost in our own thoughts. His hug didn't last long when he dropped me off with a promise to call the next day. I hoped he would, but I wasn't holding my breath.

No sound came from the dark trailer. Aunt Lor had long since gone to bed. I closed the front door behind me and stood still for a few seconds, staring out the window. Tiny orange specks from the car's taillights rounded the bend as Jeremy drove away. The reality of all that had happened crashed into me, and I slid to the floor, shaking. I'd been so stupid. So completely freaking stupid.

What if Patrick died? Tears ran down my cheeks in jagged, black splashes. I banged my head against the wall, over and over again. I welcomed the pain. I deserved it. I had no idea how long I sat on the kitchen floor crying. Long enough for pale streaks of light to creep through the window, and birds to begin calling out to each other. Aunt Lor would probably be getting up soon, coming out to make her coffee.

She couldn't see me this way.

I dragged myself up from the floor and went to my room, locking the door behind me. Sprawled out on the bed minutes later, I prayed for sleep. But it didn't come. There had to be something I could do, some way to make things right, only I couldn't imagine what.

Nausea crashed into me like a train derailing. I jumped up from the bed and ripped off my costume, pulling pieces of my hair out when I tugged the stupid leaf crown off. I rolled it all up in a messy ball and shoved it in the trashcan next to my desk. Just as I'd finished throwing on sweats and a hoodie and sat back down on my bed, my phone chirped.

You awake?

Jeremy.

I rolled to my side and answered him. *Yeah. Can't sleep.*

Wanna go for a drive?

Indecision tore at me. I desperately wanted to see him, be near him, but fear held me back, fear that he'd see me for what I really was—a monster who hurt people.

Seconds ticked by until the need to be close to him won.

Okay.

Pick you up in twenty.

I prayed it wouldn't be the last time he wanted to be around me, because I'd decided to ask him to take me somewhere, and once I told him where, it might push him away for good.

"You want to go *where*?" Jeremy's eyes grew wide, while the dark smudges beneath them hinted that he'd probably gotten about as much sleep as me. Translated—none.

I sucked in a deep breath. "The police station."

His fingers tightened on the steering wheel. "Why?" His voice barely rose above a hoarse whisper, and he stared straight ahead, refusing to look at me. We sat parked behind my aunt's car.

"I…I need to talk to them," I mumbled.

"Why?" he repeated, still facing forward.

I closed my eyes and pulled on the last ounce of courage I possessed to answer him. "Patrick didn't try to hurt her. I have to tell them that. I don't want them believing he tried to kill her like she said."

"You don't know that for sure. Who knows what happened before you got there? He could have—"

"He didn't."

My calm assurance finally made him look at me. His jaw tightened a fraction, and furrows formed between his eyes.

"He was trying to scare her…jump out in the dark and freak her out," I said.

Jeremy's throat moved as he swallowed. A few more seconds passed. "And you know this because…"

I tightened my hands on my lap. "Because I'm the one who told him to do it."

It was his turn to close his eyes. "Sam," he croaked. His fear came through; I could tell how scared he was for me.

He didn't say anything more, just opened his eyes to watch me, silent. His eyes were sad. I sighed, emotions spent. "Jer, please say something."

He shook his head. "I don't know what you want me to say."

"Say I was wrong, I was stupid. Say I deserve whatever they throw at me." *Say you'll be there for me and still be my best friend no matter what.* "Say anything."

"You *were* stupid. And wrong." His voice wasn't mean; it sounded more like he'd given up.

My lips pressed together as I tried not to cry. I didn't think I had any tears left anyway. "I know," I whispered, head bowed. "Trust me, I know."

His breath whistled out as he swore.

"Don't tell them," he burst out.

I raised my head to stare at him. "*What?*"

"Don't go. Don't tell them. Just leave it alone. Maybe they won't find out you had anything to do with it. Maybe—"

I shook my head as he spoke. "Jeremy, I have to. I have to try to fix this."

"Do you realize what can happen to you? Do you realize they could find out *everything*?" His fist pounded the wheel. "They could arrest you!"

His face drained of color. "Hell, Sam, I don't know all of what happened exactly, but I can guess enough of it. And if the police find out, who knows what will happen to you. And I can't…I can't lose you."

I reached out and took his hand from where it still rested in a tight fist against the steering wheel. He resisted at first, but then his fingers gripped mine tight.

"I need to do this." I spoke softly, firmly.

He squeezed my hand and sighed. "I know," he finally said.

"I'm scared," I whispered, staring at our fingers twisted together.

Jeremy reached out his other hand to cover our joined hands. "I know," he whispered back. "Me too."

The plastic chair was hard and uncomfortable. I shifted in my seat, while Jeremy sat stone still next to me, waiting for someone to come out and talk to us. To me.

We'd arrived at the police station about twenty minutes earlier. The cop behind the counter had taken our names and instructed us to take a seat and wait, then disappeared in the back room for a few minutes. He didn't so much as glance our way again when he'd returned and went back to work sorting papers.

Shouldn't they be more interested in what I had to say? I'd told him that I needed to speak to a police officer about what happened at Pete Rogers' house, explained that I had information about it. Yet we still sat, watching the hands on the clock slowly inch ahead, minute by long minute at a time.

I pulled at the drawstring of my hoodie and tapped my sneakers restlessly under my chair. Jeremy glanced over at me and offered a halfhearted smile. A door opened across the hall and a very large, scowling policeman immediately filled it. His rumpled shirt strained against the belly hanging over his waistband, but my eyes were more focused on the gun holstered on his hip. I swallowed, and raised my eyes to meet his squinted ones. He didn't look especially happy to see us.

"I hear you have some additional information for me?" His deep voice came out brusque.

Oh shit. *That* was the person I had to hope would be understanding and show me mercy after I spilled my involvement in the whole mess? He looked like he ate small children for breakfast. And enjoyed it. I shot Jeremy a quick glance before standing up. "Um…yes, sir."

He looked me over for a moment, taking in my beat-up sweatpants, messy hair in its ponytail, and my Trinity

Academy sweatshirt. His one eyebrow rose slightly, as if surprised to see that someone who looked as sloppy as I currently did even went to Trinity. Maybe I should have worn my ball gown. I stamped down my annoyance and shuffled my feet. Jeremy rose to stand next to me.

"Fine. Come on back." He turned and walked through the door without waiting to see if we followed.

I looked at Jeremy again. He motioned for me to go first.

The open door led to a narrow hallway. We passed several closed doors to the left, and then the guy we were following rounded a corner and opened a door on the right-hand side. He flipped a switch and the room filled with a bright, fluorescent light. A brown rectangular table sat smack in the center of the small room, and two metal folding chairs hugged either side of it. The far wall held a large mirror. I'd seen enough movies to know it was probably two-sided.

The officer stood against the wall, arms crossed.

I hesitated.

His raised eyebrows made me think he was waiting for me to do something, so I pulled out a chair and sat down, hoping that was what I was supposed to do. Jeremy sat next to me. I cleared my throat and looked up, waiting for him to ask me questions. He stared at me, and then finally spoke.

"So, you said that you have information about what happened." He raised his eyebrows yet again and uncrossed his arms to loop his thumbs behind his wide black belt.

I shifted in my chair nervously. "Yes, sir, I do."

He glanced at Jeremy.

"Um…I'm just here with her." Jeremy sounded as nervous as I felt.

"Statements indicate you were *both* at the party last

night." His tone made it clear he thought we were a couple of spoiled rich kids who thought we could do anything. His eyes narrowed as he waited for our responses.

Jeremy swallowed and nodded. "We were. But, uh…I just meant I wasn't upstairs when it happened."

The police officer shifted his steel eyes back to me. "I'm Officer Meyers." His voice turned formal. "I'm one of the officers assigned to this case. I've reviewed the records and they indicate you were both at the party last night, is that correct?"

I nodded, half afraid to speak. Didn't we just cover this?

"In fact, Ms. Evans, you were the one who called Emergency Services reporting you discovered Mr. Shaw."

Was that a question? I nodded again, more nervous than ever. Did he think *I* was the one who really hurt Patrick? He looked Jeremy's way again.

"I, uh, came up later. I didn't see what happened," he said.

Officer Meyers stepped forward. I involuntarily leaned back a little in my chair as he approached. He sat down across from us and folded his meaty hands on the scarred surface of the table. He watched me for a few seconds, not saying a word. Then he pulled a recorder from his pocket and motioned to it.

"Do you mind?"

I shook my head. Did I have a choice? I glanced around and spotted a small camera mounted in the corner of the room. A tiny yellow light blinked on top of it. I swallowed.

He pressed a button and leaned back, crossing his fingers behind his head. "I'm speaking with Samantha Evans and Jeremy Ellis regarding the party at their classmate, Peter Rogers' residence at 2125 Ridge Road in Cloverfield." He paused. "Have you both come in of your own volition?"

We both nodded.

He pointed at the recorder. "You have to actually speak up." I leaned in a little. "Yes." I glanced toward the camera again. Myers' gaze tracked my own, but he said nothing.

"Yes," Jeremy said.

"Tell me what happened," Meyers said.

Jeremy's knee began to bob up and down inches away from my leg. I shot him a pointed look. He stopped.

"I don't think Patrick tried to hurt Jessica." I looked directly at Officer Meyers as I spoke, refusing to be intimidated.

His dark eyebrow rose. I began to wonder if it was some weird tic, he did it that often. Or maybe it was his way to make me feel off-balanced, let me know he didn't trust a word I was telling him. If so, it was working.

"And what makes you say that?" He uncrossed his fingers and leaned forward.

I hesitated. *Did I really want to go through with this?* I could still just say it was because I'd been outside the door and hadn't heard any sounds of a struggle or fighting. I didn't have to tell him all of it. Another thought burst in—should I be asking for a lawyer? His level gaze didn't leave mine as he waited for me to answer.

Jeremy reached under the table and placed his hand on my leg, pressing down a little. I could almost hear his unspoken plea for me to keep quiet.

Only…I couldn't. I refused to become any more like my father than I already had. I would tell the truth. I would come clean and face the consequences…whatever they were.

So I opened my mouth and began to talk. And I told him. Everything.

thirty-three

You are never as broken as you think you are.
Sure, you may have a couple of scars, and
a couple of bad memories, but then
again all great heroes do.
—Unknown

"What do you think's gonna happen?" I sat cross-legged on my bed, plucking at loose strings on my indigo comforter.

Jeremy shook his head and sat down next me. I scooted over so he could fit, and we both leaned back against the headboard.

"I honestly don't know." He paused. "I hope they look at the fact that you went to them, and told them all about what you did. And the fact that you'd told Patrick *not to do it* seems like it should count for something."

It seemed hard to believe it'd been a month since the party. I'd freaked out when I'd learned Patrick was in a coma, but thankfully, he'd woken up two days later. He had a pretty nasty cut and needed seventeen stiches. They'd held him in the hospital a few days to make sure nothing more serious was going on since it was a head wound. Thank God, there wasn't.

I leaned my head on his shoulder. "At least he isn't facing charges since he didn't really do anything. But I feel bad for Becky. It's my fault." I bit my lip and squeezed my eyes closed tight to prevent the now way too familiar tears from falling.

"You can't take all the blame." Jeremy shifted, his leg pressed against mine. "She made the decision to go through with making drugged brownies all on her own. She knew what she was doing."

"But still, I told her to do it." I sighed. "And the rest of it, I'm afraid they can use all of that against me too."

"The whole picture thing with Zena doesn't mean squat. Really, like the courts care that Blane's a horn dog who cheated on Jessica." He shook his head. "It's not like they're gonna press charges for that. And the fire had nothing to do with you. Patrick didn't even do his task with the whole Dumpster thing, it was a gas leak. But yeah, orchestrating it all…" He paused. "I checked with my Aunt Christine who's a lawyer out in California. She says there's a good chance they'll try to charge you as an accessory and base your sentencing off that."

He reached over to hold my hand, his fingers warm against mine. We didn't speak for a while. After all, what was there to say, really?

I'd told the police every single part of the whole shitstorm. About the website I'd created, the fake invitations to rush the Society, the tasks…all of it. It hadn't been easy. Not the first time, nor the multiple other times I'd had to sit through rounds of questions. I'd had to hand over the notebook with all my plans spelled out as well as my laptop.

On top of my guilt about what I'd done with the whole

fake tapping the initiates and the tasks I'd engineered, I also felt like crap for putting my aunt through all of it with me. She didn't deserve any of it, and I knew I'd broken her heart, despite her reassurances that we would get through it together. Her health had finally begun to improve, and I'd thrown the whole mess at her. I reached over and grabbed a notebook sitting on my nightstand. Jeremy's eyebrows rose when he saw what I was holding.

"Would you read this?" I asked.

"What is it?"

"A letter." I paused, shame filled me once again as I thought about all I'd done. "It's to Jessica." I shook my head. "I tried calling, and even went to her house, but no one answered. I think she's purposely ignoring me, and I can't say I really blame her."

He reached out to take the spiral notebook then looked me straight in the eyes. "I'm proud of you. I know that couldn't have been easy."

It hadn't been, but it was also something I knew I had to do. I couldn't just act like what I'd done hadn't hurt people. I'd learned that lesson from everything that happened with my father.

He flipped it open, and I leaned over to read the words that I'd so painstakingly written the night before.

Jessica,

I know you probably don't want to hear a word I have to say, and I can't say I blame you. I was so wrong for everything that I did to hurt you and also know that simple words could never make up for the mistakes I've made...for the people I've hurt.

We were friends once, do you remember? I do.

I remember the nights we spent at each other's houses, sharing secrets, and how we always swore to be there for each other.

I was so hurt after my father's trial when we lost that. I was hurt about what you did before the trial, and since then. But that doesn't excuse what I did. And I'm so sorry.

I hope one day you can forgive me, and even if you never want to speak to me again, please know that I regret each of my actions. I was wrong.

Since I'm not going to Trinity anymore, I don't know if our paths will ever cross again. But I want you to know that I don't regret the friendship we once shared. I could never regret that.

Although if I'm being honest, I also can't forget all you've done to me through the years, the pain and all the tears I cried at your hands. I wish we'd been able to make up that day I'd come to see you years ago. We've both made mistakes.

Maybe one day you'll feel the same. I hope so, anyway.

Sam

Jeremy closed the notebook, and pulled me in a tight hug. We sat that way, not speaking, for a few minutes.

I looked across the room and stared at the new computer on my desk, the one I needed now for school since Aunt Lor pulled me out of Trinity. Even though I missed seeing Jeremy in class every day, I was kinda glad I wasn't there anymore. It wasn't like it really mattered about getting a fancy diploma from the Academy to look good on college applications anymore. Heck, I doubted any college would even accept me after what I'd done.

That more than just about anything made me sick inside. Would I ever be able to really start my life over? My aunt and Jeremy tried to assure me things would work out, but I wasn't so sure. And I couldn't imagine facing everyone in the halls or class since word had gotten out about everything that'd happened. So now I went to an online charter school instead.

"When's your hearing?" Jeremy asked quietly. "Did they tell you yet?"

He played with my hair absently as we sat together. He'd been coming over just about every day, even if only for short visits. I always appreciated when he stopped by; it helped me not feel so isolated and alone. Being with Jeremy made me feel safe, cared for.

"Yeah, I found out today." I cleared my throat. "Two weeks. December second."

His eyebrows rose. "That quick? It seems awfully fast. I thought these things usually take forever."

I nodded and shrugged. "I think because it isn't a real trial. Like, with a jury and stuff, I mean. And it isn't like they really have to prove anything. It's more them deciding what to do with me since I confessed." I yanked a loose string from my comforter. "It's a sentencing, since my guilt's already been established."

His thumb stroked my hand, stilling my nervous movements. "It'll be okay. I have a good feeling about it."

I glanced up and gave a small snort. "Right."

"I do." He tugged my hair and swung his legs off the side

of the bed. "Come on, let's go for a walk."

"But Aunt Lor's making dinner. It'll be ready any minute."

"I'm sure she won't mind if we're back soon. It'll be good to get outside a little."

I knew he meant it would be good *for me* to get outside. I'd been spending most of my time cooped up in the trailer, afraid to go into town or anywhere I might run into anyone from school.

I wavered.

"C'mon," he said. "Just a short one."

"Fine." I sighed and stood up.

I grabbed my jacket and followed him to the kitchen. Aunt Lor stood at the stove, mixing something in a large pot. The air smelled delicious, and I sniffed appreciatively. She turned and smiled, clearly happy to see me with a coat on since that meant I'd be venturing into the great outdoors.

"I'm making vegetable soup. I thought it would be nice given the chilly weather we've been having." She nodded toward the oven. "And I have some garlic bread to go with it."

I smiled, and crossed the room to wrap her in a gentle hug. "Thanks, Aunt Lor. It smells great."

She held me close, and I tried to ignore when her eyes glassed over with unshed tears. My stomach twisted, knowing all the pain and heartache I'd caused her. She'd never once yelled at me. She'd just sat me down and asked me to tell her everything. We'd talked for hours, both of us crying at times. She'd told me she loved me and was sorry for how much I must have been hurting inside.

I patted her thin shoulder a final time, and pulled back.

"Is it okay if Jeremy and I go for a quick walk before we eat?"

She nodded, and covered the pot with a lid. "You two go on ahead. This can keep until you get back, don't you worry." She made shooing motions at us. "Go, have fun." She included Jeremy in her smile. "Will you be staying for supper with us?"

"I'd love to, but I have to leave pretty soon. I have a ton of homework." Jeremy grinned at her. "But thanks anyway. Maybe another night?"

"You know you're welcome any time." She wiped her hands on her apron.

"We won't be long," I said as we headed out the door.

The evening air bit into me, and I wrapped my heavy pea coat tighter around my body. I inhaled deeply, reveling in the hint of winter approaching.

"Do you think we'll get snow soon?"

Our feet crunched in the fallen leaves alongside the edge of the road. Most of the trees were bare, with just a few still grasping tightly to the last remaining brightly colored leaves above us, like mothers not ready to release their children into the world.

"The weather this morning said there was a chance of flurries this weekend." Jeremy's boot snapped a twig as he stepped farther off the road and pulled me next to him when a car raced past.

"I hope so. That would make one thing in my life that doesn't actually blow right now."

Jeremy glanced my way with a sad smile, and I immediately felt bad.

"It's...I love the snow. That's all I meant." I'd hurt his feelings. I leaned my head back to stare at the sky, pink streaks mixed with deep reds to form a kaleidoscope of color in the waning light.

Jeremy nodded, gentle understanding filling his face. "I know."

We walked a little farther, until he suddenly reached out to stop me, and turned me to face him.

"I *am* really proud of you." His face became serious, his gaze intense.

I cocked my head. "For what?" I hadn't done a whole lot to make anyone proud of me.

"For coming forward, for telling the truth."

His bangs fell into his eyes behind his glasses when he shook his head. "I know that was hard to do."

I went silent.

"Especially when you had me telling you not to do it at first." He dropped his hand from my arm and shoved it in his coat pocket. "That was wrong of me. My only excuse is that I wasn't thinking straight, and I was freaked that I'd lose you if you told them." He paused. "I was a coward."

"No. *No*, Jer, you weren't." I reached out to touch the sleeve of his dark jacket.

He shook his head. "Yeah, I was. But you?" His eyes traveled over my face. "I think you're the bravest person I've ever known."

Brave? What a laugh. I was afraid of everything.

"I'm not brave at all." I looked down. A wayward maple leaf blew across my red high-top sneaker.

"Yeah, you *are*. Through all the crap you've been through, you've held your head up. Sure, you did something kind of..."

"Stupid."

He grinned. "Not so well-thought-out," he said. "But you didn't run or hide from it. You did all you could to make it right."

"I can't ever make what I did right."

He tipped his head. "You faced it head-on. That's what I mean. I admire that."

A few lone crickets chirped around us as Jeremy stood in front of me, silhouetted by trees against the darkening sky.

"Thanks, Jer," I whispered.

He smiled, and brushed my hair back as it blew into my face. "Anytime."

We stood that way, inches from each other, for several seconds. A look crossed his face, one filled with what I could only describe as yearning. It made me wonder if Jeremy and I could ever have more than friendship—or if that would mess things up between us.

I glanced down again.

"Come on." He took my hand and we fell into step, side by side once again. We didn't talk, but the comfortable silence wrapped around us like a favorite blanket.

The fall colors littering the path reminded me that Thanksgiving would be here in less than a week. I had a lot to be grateful for—Aunt Lor, Patrick being okay, things not going down even worse than they had with the mess I'd created. But I was most thankful that I had my best friend back and knew he wasn't going anywhere.

thirty-four

Sometimes love can descend, gentle as a first snowflake.
Or it can build and build like a mighty blizzard.
—Samantha Evans

*J*eremy's prediction was wrong.

The snow held out until the following week, and we didn't get flurries, we got eleven inches. It started Thanksgiving Day and carried into Friday morning. I peeked out my bedroom window. Snow covered everything in a blanket of pristine white. Nature in its purest form... beautiful. I hurried into my clothes and headed to the living room to find my aunt.

"Did you see it?" I plopped down on the sofa and bounced up and down.

"Rather hard to miss, sweetie." She sipped her coffee.

"I'll go out and shovel the walkway," I said.

"Just be sure you dress warmly."

"I will." I leaned over and stole a piece of toast from her plate, biting into it as I stood.

"And wear gloves!" she called out, as I walked to the closet to grab my winter boots.

"I know," I yelled back, and shook my head. You'd think

by now she'd realize I could dress myself without direction. I shoved the rest of the toast in my mouth to free my hands and rooted through the back of the hall closet trying to find my boots. And she said *my* room was a mess; this closet beat it hands-down for clutter. I finally found them and pulled the second Timberland onto my foot just as a knock sounded on the front door.

I paused mid-tug. I hadn't heard a car. Probably Martha. I finally got both boots on and finished tying the laces before reaching in the cardboard box where we stored gloves and hats.

"Samantha! Jeremy's here!"

My head jerked up in surprise. I grabbed the first hat I came across, some old green and white thing with frog eyes, along with a pair of blue ski gloves.

"Samantha?"

"Coming!" I yelled. I stuffed my arms through the sleeves of my coat and shoved the hat over my messy hair. Crap. I hadn't even brushed my teeth yet, let alone put any makeup on to try to cover my zombie look.

I raced to the bathroom. After brushing my teeth, I grabbed mascara and brushed a little on my lashes, praying it would help make up for the fact that I had bags under my eyes the size of small moon craters. The past month or so I'd been lucky to get four or five hours of sleep a night. I blew the bangs off my forehead in exasperation. Oh well, good enough. He'd seen me looking worse.

Jeremy stood in the kitchen with my aunt, his hands wrapped around a cup of steaming coffee. His cheeks radiated bright red, and fog tinted his glasses as a result of coming into the warm kitchen from the cold. They both turned when I walked into the room.

"Hey! What are you doing here?"

He leaned against the counter and took a sip before answering. His windblown bangs spilled into his eyes from beneath his beanie.

"I figured you guys would need some help shoveling out your aunt's car."

My eyebrows rose, and I glanced out the window. His black Acura was nowhere in sight, and no tire tracks cut through the thick snow, only footprints.

"How in the world did you get here?"

Aunt Lor rubbed his arm. "He walked all this way just to help us. Wasn't that nice of him?" Her face shone pride wreathed in smiles over his generosity.

I gaped. "You *walked*? In *this*?" I stared out the window again. It didn't even look like the township had plowed the roads yet. Plus, flurries had begun to come down again since I'd woken up.

Jeremy set down his cup and reached out to grab his gloves to pull them back on. "Nah, not the whole way." He clearly wanted to downplay his role as the hiking hero. "The roads are better in town. I drove most of the way, but kind of got stuck once I hit Sauderton Road. They haven't gotten there yet, I guess."

I shook my head and laughed. "You're crazy."

He grinned. "Yeah, I know." He turned to my aunt. "Thanks for the coffee."

"You're welcome. And I have muffins in the oven for when the two of you finish out there."

"Sounds good." He walked to the sink to rinse out his cup, and turned back to me. "So you ready to do some digging?"

"Sure." I pulled on my gloves then paused. "Oh, wait! I don't think we have an extra shovel." I waggled my eyebrows. "So does that mean I get to watch while you do all the work?"

He barked out a laugh. "Nice try. I brought my own."

"You carried your own shovel here? Through the snow?"

"Well, I thought it would make more sense in the snow than waiting to bring it in the spring." He smirked.

I swatted him on the arm. "Smart-ass."

His eyes crinkled with his chuckle. God, he had a great smile. It'd been a while since I'd allowed myself to appreciate it; my mind had been way too busy with tiny things like my impending sentencing. We headed out, and I gasped when the frigid air hit me full force.

"I still can't believe you walked in this." I stuttered, my teeth chattering and my breath coming out in white puffs in the early morning air.

"Aw...don't be such a baby. It's not that cold."

"For a polar bear maybe." But I grinned back at him.

I walked to the end of the lot where Aunt Lor kept a giant outdoor storage container. My gloves made it impossible to open the latch, so I pulled one off with my teeth and pried the lid open far enough to grab the snow shovel from inside. As soon as it was out, I slammed it closed and pushed my fingers back in the welcome warmth of the heavy glove.

Jeremy had already begun working, digging through banks of snow behind the Buick. The morning light brought out golden highlights in his mahogany hair. He looked strong. And gorgeous. I couldn't believe it'd taken me so long to really notice.

I smiled as he ferociously attacked the piles of snow,

clearly on a mission.

He turned and caught me watching. "You going to just stand there?" He reached down and grabbed a handful of snow and patted it into a ball.

"Don't you dare!"

Thwack. It pegged me straight in the belly. That was all it took. I dove behind the storage container and prepped an arsenal. Every couple of seconds a snowball flew over to land nearby. It felt good—to be normal, not chained down by thoughts of what I'd done, or what might happen. I packed another snowball together.

"Chicken! Come out and fight!" he yelled.

I popped my head up and whipped two in a row in his direction. They both missed.

"You throw like a girl!"

"I'll show you throwing like a girl!" I shouted back.

I lobbed another one his way, finally managing to make contact.

"Lucky shot!"

He ran toward me, arms filled with snowballs, yelling a guttural battle cry as he approached. "Aaaaahhh!"

Oh crap. I looked for an escape route. Too late, I attempted to make a break around the side of the trailer. I wasn't quick enough. He pummeled me, one after the other. Laughing, I covered my head with my hands and tried to run the best I could, hunched over. Just when I thought I had a chance, he leapt toward me and tackled me into the soft snow. His upper body pinned me down.

"Say mercy."

I whipped my head side to side.

"Say mercy," he repeated in a warning tone.

"Never!" Snow crept up the back of my coat, which had inched up when he'd flipped me over. It was freezing cold against my skin. I desperately tried to grab handfuls of snow to shove in his face, but he blocked me.

His triumphant face hovered inches away, and he grinned. A hint of coffee carried my way as he leaned down even closer. I was suddenly glad I'd taken the time to brush my teeth.

"Do you give up yet?"

My heartbeat double-timed as his weight pressed down on me, his chest right against my own; our legs tangled together.

I licked my lips and stared at him, and could tell the exact second his attention shifted from our snowball battle to something else, something way more intimate. His eyes darkened, and he swallowed. He stilled, until finally, with aching slowness, his hands moved from where they'd been holding my arms out on either side of me, and traveled up to rest on my shoulders. Our eyes never broke contact.

"Hey," he whispered, the tiniest of smiles peeking through.

"Hey," I whispered back. My mouth felt incredibly dry, and I couldn't imagine how he couldn't feel my heartbeat pounding in my chest.

His familiar eyes traced the contours of my face while I lay immobile, not wanting to move one inch beneath him.

I love him.

It hit like an avalanche. I loved him. I loved Jeremy. The realization freaked me out while at the same time filled me with an utter sense of...*rightness.* Something in my expression must have changed, because his smile softened, grew even tenderer, and he used his teeth to pull off his gloves, one at a time.

My eyes widened. "What are you doing? Your hands will freeze," I stuttered.

"I don't care." He tossed them aside.

I shifted my gaze, unable to face him.

"Look at me," he said softly, reaching out to turn my face back toward his.

"I can't." I whispered.

"Why not?"

I bit my lip, still refusing to look at him. "Because I'm afraid if I do you'll see inside me…the real me."

"Oh, Sam," he whispered. "Don't you get it? I already do. And that's why I could never, ever lose you."

I turned then, and he smiled at me, his smile that glowed from the inside. And I gave in.

He reached out and ran his palm against my cheek, his hand warm and gentle. My breathing hitched at even that simple touch.

"Jeremy?" I whispered, barely able to get the word out.

"God, you're beautiful."

My eyes widened.

"You are. Your skin, your smile, your little turned up nose." He tapped me on the tip of my nose. "Do you have any idea how beautiful you are?"

I shook my head slowly, petrified if I opened my mouth I'd blurt out something stupid like, *you're beautiful too.*

"I watch you sometimes, like in class or whatever. You get this serious expression when you're thinking or trying to solve a math problem. This little crinkle right here." He smoothed a finger between my eyes.

I fought away a mad giggle.

"Then other times, when you're reading, I can tell you're a million miles away. In this world all your own. It made me wish I could be there with you."

I'd always believed the saying 'my heart melted' was idiotic...until that precise second, because mine melted into a giant puddle of goo. It wasn't humanly possible to feel more alive than I did right at that moment, until he leaned down and kissed me.

And my world changed forever.

thirty-five

To forgive is to set a prisoner free and discover
that the prisoner was you.
—Lewis B. Smedes

"**A**re you sure you want to do this?" Jeremy looked at me from behind the wheel of his car. *Was I sure?* No. Not in the least. For the past week, since our kiss, Jeremy had been there for me in every way that mattered—someone to talk to, or spend time with and just laugh while trying to push the thought of my impending trial out of my mind. And I loved him for it.

But now, sitting in the parking lot of the Eastern NY Correctional Facility, I'd begun to wonder if even his quiet strength was enough to bolster me for what lay ahead—seeing my father for the first time in three years. I hadn't so much as spoken to him on the phone since the day I'd watched him walk out of the courtroom. I hadn't known what to say, hadn't wanted to hear anything he might say. My anger and resentment and hurt had built a wall up around me that I'd used as a shield to hide behind...partially so I didn't actually have to face my feelings. It was easier to shove them down and pretend they didn't exist.

But denial probably wasn't the healthiest option. Finally facing that truth was what led to me sitting in Jeremy's car, staring out the window at the massive stone building. Tall barbed wire fence surrounded the structure, but what totally struck me as odd was the fact that the prison almost looked like an old castle, complete with several multi-colored flags hanging from a front entrance and odd towers sticking off the side. It looked more like something you'd find plunked down in a Scottish field than maximum security housing for male prisoners.

Off to the left, a pathetic excuse for an exercise yard was empty. Something inside me tightened thinking of my father only being allowed to go outdoors at specified times. I wondered what that would feel like—to be so contained, caged up. Sweat beaded at my hairline as I sat frozen, staring.

Jeremy reached out to gently take hold of my trembling hand. "If you're not ready, or if you think this will be too hard, it's okay. We can come back another time."

I shook my head. This was something I needed to do; I had to face him. "No, I'm fine. Let's go." Before I could lose my nerve and change my mind, I opened the car door and stepped out. Wind bit my cheeks and blew my hair across my face, temporarily shielding my view of what lay ahead.

We walked together to the entrance marked for visitors. Once inside, a uniformed guard directed us through a tall doorway that served as a metal detector. Another guard stood inside the archway. His somber expression, along with the gun holstered to his waist, made me swallow. I turned to Jeremy, and he must have read the terror in my eyes, because he squeezed my hand and mouthed, *I'm right here.*

When it was our turn to enter the visiting area, panic

hit me again. My legs trembled so much that I worried I couldn't make it across the worn floor to sit at the scarred wooden table. The room was large, and uniformed guards flanked the edges, watching to ensure no one stepped out of line. We sat down, and waited for my father to enter the room. My chest tightened, and I desperately wished I had something to drink to ease the dryness in my mouth.

A minute later I saw him. Tears filled my eyes as he scanned the room, seeking me out. When our eyes met, it was as though someone punched me in the stomach, knocking all of the air from my lungs. Whether it was a result of seeing how much he'd aged in just three years, or the hurt rising to the surface reminding me of all I'd lost, I wasn't sure.

He made his way across the room and sat down across from us at the table. He was thinner than I remembered, and his shoulders stooped in a way they never had before. It was like looking at a ghost of the strong man I'd once known.

"Samantha." He reached across the table as though to take my hand, but I pulled back. I swallowed down the burning lump in my throat and stared at him.

"Why did you do it?" The words escaped before I could stop them. All the time I'd spent planning what to say to him, and I couldn't remember a single thing I'd come up with. I just needed to understand *why*…why he'd chosen greed over his family. Over me.

He closed his eyes for a moment, and if possible, his shoulders slumped even more. When he looked at me again, tears filled his eyes.

"I'm so sorry." He shook his head. "If I could take it back, change the mistakes I made, I would. In a second."

I stared at him. A piece of me broke inside at his words,

the part of me that missed my dad and remembered the man he'd once been to me, my hero. But a bigger part of me felt nothing but anger, fury at what he'd done.

"Saying I'm sorry doesn't change what happened," I whispered hoarsely. "It doesn't make things right or put our family back together again."

"No, you're right, it doesn't," he said.

My hands balled into fists on my lap, and I was ready to spring from the chair, to rush out the door, when Jeremy laid his hand on my own, offering silent support.

My father glanced at Jeremy then. "Thank you for coming with her, for being such a good friend to Samantha."

"I didn't do it for you. I did it for her."

A sad smile crossed my dad's face. "I know, and I appreciate that." He looked back at me. "How have you been? How's school?"

I barked out a laugh. "Seriously? We're going to sit here and you're going to ask me about school?"

"I…I just want to know how you've been doing. I want to know you're okay."

"No, Dad, I'm not okay. I'm not okay at all." My voice rose. "I've been ostracized and ridiculed and had to put up with being the butt of jokes since I have a convict for a father."

He sucked in air like I'd punched him. I knew I was being horrible, but I'd needed to get it out, to vent the pain I'd kept bottled up since I was thirteen years old.

I wanted to tell him about how badly I'd screwed up, and blame it all on him. Until it hit me that I'd made all of the choices to do what I'd done, just as my father had done three years ago. The blame rested squarely on my own shoulders, and no one else's. Tears rolled down my cheeks as we stared at each other. I saw my pain mirrored in his eyes.

"I'm so sorry," he whispered. "I'm sorry for all the ways that I failed you and your mother. For all that I've missed, and all the hurt I've caused you."

My lips trembled, and my chest felt like something heavy was weighing me down.

"I'm sorry for not being there to see you grow into such a beautiful young woman."

I wasn't ready to do this; it hurt too damn much. "I have to go." I stood suddenly, the chair making a loud scraping noise as I jumped up.

"Samantha, please." My father's face looked anguished. Jeremy stood beside me.

"I…I just need some time." I shook my head. "I'm sorry. This is just hard, harder than I thought it would be."

"Will you come back again? Can I see you again?"

I nodded but then couldn't help the words that tumbled out of my mouth. "You really hurt me. You were my hero, Dad, did you know that?"

He bowed his head.

"I'm sorry. I just…" I brushed my hands across my face; they came away wet. "I need time," I repeated.

He nodded. I noticed gray in his hair that hadn't been there before. We'd both changed, in different ways.

"I understand. But please know I love you, Samantha. That's never changed."

I couldn't form an answer, couldn't tell him the words I knew he wanted to hear, so I stared at my shoes for a few seconds before looking up at Jeremy.

"Do you want to go?" he asked softly.

I jerked my head up and down.

"Okay." He took my hand once more, before looking to my father. "I hope you're doing well."

I didn't look back as we turned to leave. I didn't have the strength to face my dad again. The short time we'd been there had wiped me out, had ravaged pieces of my soul that I'd fought so hard to keep locked up.

Steps away from leaving the visiting area, I heard my father's voice call out, "I love you, no matter what. And I'm so proud that you're my daughter."

My spine stiffened, and tears rolled down my face, but I didn't stop.

Once inside the warm safety of Jeremy's car once again, I broke down. Shaking sobs convulsed me and I pounded the dashboard.

"I hate him."

"No you don't." Jeremy wrapped his arms around me.

He was right, I didn't. And that was why it hurt so much. I leaned into him and cried. "I thought I'd know what to say, what to ask, but it was so hard, harder than I'd imagined."

"But you did it. You saw him."

"There's so much I want to say to him. And I couldn't."

Jeremy lifted my face toward him, and brushed away the tears spilling down my cheeks. "That's okay, too. Today was a big step. You can come back again to see him when you're ready."

I hiccupped. "Do you think it makes me a horrible daughter that I didn't tell him I love him back?"

"No. I think it makes you human." He touched the side of my face. "Sam, you're amazing and strong, and your heart is so big. Sometimes when a person feels things as deeply as you do, it's tough." He ran his fingers through my hair, never breaking eye contact. "I'm here for you, whatever you need."

He leaned in, and pressed his lips to mine. I kissed him back, needing to feel close to him.

"Thank you," I whispered.

"Always," he whispered back. "I'm not going anywhere."

thirty-six

*Every new beginning comes from some
other beginning's end.*
—Seneca

The days leading up to my sentencing passed way too quickly. I'd crossed large red *X*s on my desk calendar, marking down the days leading to the date that I had circled in thick black Sharpie. There were no more squares to *X* out. Tomorrow at nine fifteen a.m. I would have to face the consequences of what I'd done.

Waves of fear crashed over me, even though Jeremy kept telling me to be strong, and to keep faith that everything would work out fine. My lawyer said the same thing. As much as I liked the young attorney, I wasn't sure how much faith I had in her ability to make everything okay.

Ms. Gibbons had been assigned to my case through the courts, some kind of free legal representation since Aunt Lor certainly didn't have the money to pay someone over a hundred dollars an hour to argue my defense. Not that there'd be much of a defense since I'd flat-out told the police what I'd done. It was more a matter of waiting to see what the judge decided to do with me. And the lawyer would be there to try to convince him to be lenient.

I stepped out of the shower and wrapped an oversize blue towel around my body, shivering in the chilly bathroom. Or maybe my rattled nerves caused me to shake. A glance in the mirror revealed purple smudges beneath my eyes, and it looked like I'd lost weight over the past few weeks. The bones of my shoulders jutted out above the towel, and my cheeks sunk in at a weird angle. My hands shook where I grasped the towel at my chest, and I looked away.

I wanted to believe everything would work out…that I wouldn't be going to jail or juvenile detention or wherever, but I couldn't help but worry. Nighttime was the worst. When darkness fell and I was left alone with my thoughts, it became next to impossible not to give in to the fears and doubts, especially with only fourteen hours until I had to stand before a judge in a courtroom.

At least there wouldn't be a ton of people watching like at Dad's trial. Since mine was closed, there wouldn't be any curious classmates or whatever. Just the lawyers presenting their case, and the judge who would decide my fate. I prayed that whoever was assigned to the case would be merciful, and not someone wanting to make a lesson out of me.

I flashed back to my father's trial, and paled as the terror of that day washed over me like it was just yesterday. I closed my eyes, and my mind transported back in time, remembering the jurors steely eyes, their frowns. Remembering my father in his jumpsuit walking away from me.

A soft knock on the bathroom door pulled me back to the present.

"Sweetheart? Are you all right in there?" Aunt Lor had been extra watchful over me the past few days. I didn't know if she thought I was going to freak and try to off myself or what.

"I'm fine," I called. "I'll be right out."

We'd rented a movie earlier and planned to make popcorn and watch it together. She'd insisted on something funny. I knew it was because she wanted to do everything she could to keep the mood light, upbeat.

I slipped into a pair of soft fleece pajama bottoms, and pulled a thick, long sleeved T-shirt over my head. After combing out my hair, I twisted it into a single long braid spilling over my shoulder and stepped into my comfy slippers. Everything was set up when I padded out to meet her in the living room. She'd arranged popcorn and napkins on the low table in front of the sofa and even set out sliced strawberries and mango—my favorites. I grabbed a bottle of water and joined her.

"You didn't have to do all this." I motioned to the snacks on the table.

"Oh, it was no trouble." She waved away my thanks and reached over to gently pat me on the arm as I passed her chair.

I smiled my appreciation and sank into the sofa before tugging the old afghan down from the back of the couch to tuck across my lap.

The doorbell rang. Joy mixed with gratefulness when I saw the familiar car parked outside near the lamppost. I ran the few remaining steps, ripped open the door, and jumped across the threshold to wrap my arms around a smiling Jeremy.

"I thought you couldn't come over tonight." My words muffled against the collar of his jacket.

He held me tight, rocking me slightly as I clung to him.

He pressed his lips to the side of my head, then my cheek, and finally my waiting mouth when I turned to face him. I closed my eyes and kissed him back for a few seconds, not even caring that Aunt Lor was right in the next room, before pulling back to look at him.

He unzipped his jacket, and pulled off his winter beanie. "I tried calling you about forty-five minutes ago but you didn't answer, so I called your house phone."

That must have been while I was in the shower. I reached for his coat and hung it over the back of a kitchen chair. He tossed his hat on the seat.

"Anyway, your aunt invited me over. Didn't she tell you?"

Without thinking, I reached out for another quick hug before raising my voice so she'd clearly hear me too. "No. She must have wanted to surprise me." I grinned.

Jeremy chuckled. "So were you surprised?"

"You have no idea how happy I am to see you," I said softly, tracing the pattern of his flannel shirt with my fingertips.

His hands moved across my back. "Ditto," he whispered into my neck.

We walked into the living room, and he sat next to me on the sofa.

"So now that the gang's all here, are we ready to watch this movie or what?" I smiled at each of them in turn.

Jeremy nodded, and Aunt Lor settled back in her chair. I grinned and picked up the remote to press play.

"*I*t's getting late; I think I'll be headed to bed."

I paused the DVD and looked up at her in surprise. "But the movie isn't even over. And it's only a little after eight."

She nodded, her gray curls bouncing a little with the movement. "I know, dear, but these old bones need rest. It's been a long day." She yawned. She left off adding that it would be an even longer day tomorrow. I suspected the real reason she was heading to bed so early was to give me a chance to spend some time with Jeremy. I again thanked whatever gods might be listening for bringing her into my life.

I stood and crossed the room to help her up, and we walked together a few steps down the hallway. "Thanks, Aunt Lor," I whispered. "For everything."

Her face gentled and she touched my cheek with her tiny, wrinkled hand. "No, Samantha. Thank *you*. You being here with me these past few years brought more life and joy into this house than you could ever possibly imagine."

My eyes misted, and I leaned in to kiss her soft cheek. "I love you," I whispered. I didn't tell her that enough, didn't thank her enough for always being there for me.

She patted my cheek again. "I know, dear. I love you too." She glanced into the living room where Jeremy sat, patiently waiting. "Now you go back to your young man and finish the movie."

I nodded.

"Just not too late."

I nodded again. We had to be up early to get into town on time.

"Good night, Jeremy," she called down the hall.

"Good night, Ms. Evans," he answered with a wave in our direction.

She walked slowly down the remainder of the hallway before turning into her room. I chuckled when she left the bedroom door open a few inches.

Once I'd sat back down next to Jeremy, he scooted closer and wrapped his arm around my shoulder, pulling me toward him. I rested my head on his shoulder.

"Thanks for coming over." I smiled up at him.

"I'm glad dinner was cut short so I could." He played with my braid. "I knew you'd be worried, and I wanted to be here for you."

All the pain, the heartache and tears, were worth it if only for the fact they made me realize it was okay to let my guard down…to let people in. My aunt, Jeremy. I'd even spoken briefly to my mother last week. It hadn't quite been a Hallmark moment, but it was the first time we'd talked in ages. Aunt Lor had called her to let her know what was going on, and my mom called back the next day to talk to me. She'd even offered to come back for the sentencing, but I refused. I wasn't quite ready to see her yet; the hearing would be enough to handle.

It wasn't like I was suddenly the poster child for positive mental health…but I was taking baby steps in the right direction, between the phone call and the visit to see my father. I'd even begun to see my counselor again. Aunt Lor and Jeremy both told me more than once how they were proud of me, but more importantly, I was finally starting to feel the first embers of pride in myself.

I lifted my legs to tuck my feet beneath me. "Are you still able to come tomorrow?" I peeked up at him.

"Of course I'll be there, silly." He brushed a kiss on the tip of my nose. "Where else would I be?"

I smiled at him gratefully.

"Sam, I don't think you realize how important you are to me." He stared into my eyes, and I couldn't look away. My stomach did all kinds of fluttery things at his expression.

"I'd do anything for you." He reached out and took my hand, rubbing his fingers gently over mine. He swallowed and looked suddenly nervous; his jaw twitched, and he blinked rapidly several times. He leaned in, and I felt his breath on my face for the briefest moment before he kissed me. Soft, like I was something precious, something he cherished. His touch almost brought tears to my eyes.

When he ended the kiss, he pulled back until he was inches away. I knew this was what it was supposed to feel like when you were with someone. Real love wasn't a power trip like I'd felt with Ransom—it made you feel safe, strong, like together you could do anything. And not just together—it made you realize you were strong in your own right too. Jeremy made me feel that way. I felt beautiful and…happy. The word sounded so simple when it was anything but.

His eyes didn't leave mine as he stroked the hair that had fallen loose from my braid back from my face. I held my breath.

"I love you, Samantha Jane Evans," he said softly.

Three simple words, written and sung about for ages… and they still slammed into my heart like nothing ever before. I shook my head.

"How can you possibly love me? All I've done, the mistakes I've made." I looked down.

He gently lifted my chin so I faced him again. "Don't

you get it? I don't love you for your past, or even who you're going to be. I just love you."

I bit my lip, tears forming when I whispered, "I love you, too."

His face lit up, like I'd given him some priceless gift, then he leaned in to kiss me again.

We never finished the movie, which was more than okay with me. Instead, we spent the next two hours talking and kissing and holding each other. They were the best two hours of my life.

thirty-seven

*It takes courage to grow up and
become who you really are.
—E.E. Cummings*

No seventeen-year-old should ever have to sit in a courtroom, scared and silent, waiting to hear if she's going to jail. But nevertheless, there I was. I glanced back to where Jeremy and Aunt Lor sat side by side in the row behind me and Ms. Gibbons, my defense attorney. They both looked at me with encouraging smiles, their warm faces letting me know how much I was loved.

I turned back around to face the judge. Both sides had delivered their arguments, and now it was up to Judge Lewis to decide my fate. Becky's hearing was held separate from mine, so besides the lawyer for the commonwealth, we were the only ones in the room. I was grateful they'd allowed Aunt Lor and Jeremy in the room during the proceedings. I'd been deathly afraid they'd have to wait outside until it was all over. I took a deep breath and tried to sit up straight and tall, mentally preparing myself for whatever was to come.

Please don't let him send me away. Please, God.

The judge leaned forward, hands clasped in front of him as if in prayer. He peered over his glasses toward our table, his eyes commanding. I swallowed, and Ms. Gibbons reached over her files to pat my hand.

"Counselor, while you've reiterated that Ms. Evans showed good faith in approaching the police to confess to her part in what happened, the reality is that her actions resulted in injury to two different individuals, as well as psychological duress to many others. This can be construed as gross negligence on her part." My stomach flopped hearing the ominous sounding legal jargon, while Ms. Gibbons tipped her head in acknowledgment. She looked professional in her stylish navy suit, with her hair pulled back into a neat twist. I prayed she'd done her job well and convinced Judge Lewis that even though I'd initiated the acts, I myself hadn't performed them, and that I'd had no serious ill intent.

"Furthermore, she performed several of her actions on school grounds and sullied the reputation of a long-standing school organization in the process."

I fought to keep from grimacing at that part. It's not like the Musterian Society was some humanitarian organization. I held myself still, not allowing any expression that could be remotely considered disrespectful to cross my face.

"Because of this," he continued, "I have no choice but to take these facts under serious advisement when making my decision as to the level of Ms. Evan's accountability in the situation. Even though she did not personally execute either of the actions that led to Mr. Shaw or Ms. Wainright being injured, the question here is whether or not her actions do constitute conspiracy to commit a crime."

I was going to be sick. My chin trembled, and I fought

to keep control and not run from the room, crying and screaming. He couldn't send me away from Aunt Lor and Jeremy. *He just couldn't.*

"Ms. Evans." The judge looked directly at me as he addressed me personally.

"Yes, sir. Your Honor I mean." I stumbled over the words, voice shaking.

"Do you understand the seriousness of the actions you've confessed to?"

Oh God.

"Yes, Your Honor." My voice barely rose above a whisper. I clenched my hands into fists beneath the table.

He stared at me a moment longer, gray brows furrowed together.

"And do you admit to each of the actions the opposing counsel has set forth in this courtroom today?"

I nodded. Ms. Gibbons nudged me with her leg under the table.

"I mean, yes, Your Honor, I do." I stammered, a blush creeping up my neck.

Judge Lewis leaned back in his chair, and nodded gravely.

"I'm ordering a fifteen minute recess, after which time I will return and render my verdict on this case." He stood, black robe flapping as he turned and exited through a door behind the podium to enter his chambers.

My shoulders slumped. I would be sent away, just like my father. Ms. Gibbons reached over to rest her hand on my shoulder. "Stay strong, Samantha. It's not over yet."

Only even she sounded doubtful.

I couldn't turn around, couldn't bring myself to face

Jeremy and Aunt Lor, to see the expressions I knew would be on their faces. So instead, I put my head down on the table and went to the faraway place in my mind I'd learned to escape to long ago.

*T*his was it. Judge Lewis re-entered the small courtroom. The room spun slightly, and my legs shook under my long black skirt as I waited to hear his verdict. As before, he faced me directly when he spoke.

"Ms. Evans, I have taken the severity of your actions into consideration. Even though you did not intend to harm either party, you did intend for others to do so."

He rested his palms flat on the tall podium.

I was going to faint. *Here it comes.*

"However, given your age, I am not forced to try you as an adult in this case." He looked at me sternly. "But this does not mean that I take this situation lightly. Individuals cannot be allowed to manipulate others into criminal misdeeds and walk away with no punishment."

I heard someone suck in a deep breath behind me.

Just say it. Just tell me what's going to happen to me. I couldn't bear waiting any longer. I nodded at the judge to show I understood.

"I've reached my decision."

Ms. Gibbons motioned for me to stand to receive my sentencing. I wasn't sure I could. I rose in slow motion to stand next to her and grasped the edge of the table so tightly that my knuckles turned white. A dull ringing filled my ears as I waited to hear his next words.

"Based on the fact that you have no criminal record, it is my intention to attempt to rehabilitate rather than simply punish."

Hope rose inside me. Maybe I wouldn't be sent away. *Please, please, please, dear God.*

Judge Lewis continued, "I hereby sentence you, Samantha Jane Evans, to one hundred hours of community service."

I wavered against the table, half afraid I was dreaming.

"In addition, you will be placed on juvenile probation until your eighteenth birthday. As part of which, you will be required to abide by a curfew and report regularly to a juvenile probation officer."

Tears filled my eyes, and I wanted to turn around and jump over the bench and hug Jeremy and Aunt Lor. I forced myself to stay still, to listen. Ms. Gibbons reached over and rubbed my arm, smiling. I smiled back at her through my tears.

Judge Lewis wasn't done. "Do you understand your sentencing?"

I bobbed my head up and down. "Yes, Your Honor. Thank you, Your Honor, sir."

His eyes finally lost their firm look and gentled somewhat. He looked almost grandfatherly. "Thank me by never showing up in my courtroom again. Learn from this, Ms. Evans."

"I will." I nodded again. "I promise. Thank you, sir. Thank you, Your Honor."

He rapped his gavel down and announced, "Court is dismissed."

I covered my face with my hands and sobbed tears of

relief and joy. Moments later, arms pulled me into a tight hug. I moved my hands to see Jeremy beaming, with what looked suspiciously like tears glistening in his own eyes.

"I'm so happy for you." He crushed me against his chest once again.

I twisted to search the room for Aunt Lor. She stood several steps behind us, arms held open toward me. I launched at her and fell into her embrace. She held me, running her hands down the back of my head over and over as I cried.

I sniffled and looked at her, unable to find the words for all I wanted to say. "Thank you." I hugged her tighter. "Thank you for always believing in me, and being there for me." I shook my head. "I'm so sorry for what a pain in the ass I've been."

For once she didn't reprimand my language. She stroked my back. "Sh…there, child. It's over. It's all over now." Her bright blue eyes smiled up at me. "I love you. I told you, we're family and always will be."

I nodded and wiped my eyes with the sleeve of my shirt. Aunt Lor reached her hand out behind me to include Jeremy. He stepped over and stood close to me, his presence comforting, reassuring. It was real…things were going to be okay, just like he'd said. I smiled at him through brimming eyes.

"Come on now," she said to both of us. "Let's go home."

Jeremy took my hand as I clung to Aunt Lor with the other. He leaned down and kissed my temple, mouthing the words, *I love you.*

I glowed. I had everything I needed, and the rest of my life stretched out before me, wide open and full of possibilities. I finally believed that now. It'd been a hell of a road to get here, but I could finally see past the bend that'd always blocked my view before.

We opened the courtroom door and walked into the bright morning sunshine, headed home.

Home. It was my *home*, not just Aunt Lor's trailer.

I broke free to run ahead a few feet, holding my hands out and spinning wildly. I couldn't erase my past or the memories of everything that'd happened in my life, but that was okay. All of it made me who I was. The good *and* the bad.

The familiar weight on my chest lightened, and I reached out for Jeremy's hand once again. Aunt Lor joined us as we turned and walked forward, *home*…together.

epilogue

Sometimes we have to leave home in order to find out what we left there, and why it matters so much.
—Shauna Niequist

"Sam, are you almost ready?"

Jenny, my roommate, leaned her head through the open doorway.

I jumped up from my desk, where I'd been hard at work for the last hour or so. They never really warn you about the reading and papers and studying you have to do in college. Or maybe they did, but I hadn't listened. But despite the workload, I loved it.

I smiled at her. "Yep. Just gimme a minute to throw some shoes on."

Jenny nodded and disappeared. We'd been roommates for two years now, ever since my freshman year of college began. NYU may not have been where'd I'd envisioned myself years ago, but I couldn't be happier. I loved everything about the campus, the teachers, and the classes. The decision to study journalism here was the best choice I'd ever made. Well, almost the best choice.

As if on cue, Jeremy walked into my dorm room. "If you

don't hurry up, I think Jen is going to leave without us."

I walked over to meet him and offered him a quick kiss. "No she won't. I'm driving."

He winked. "Well, in that case…" He bent his head to kiss me, longer than the brief peck I'd given him. The touch of his lips, the feel of his hands on either side of my face, melted me inside. His touch never got old. I once again thanked my lucky stars that I was gifted with someone as amazing as Jeremy in my life.

After the kiss, he rested his forehead against mine. "Hey," he whispered.

"Hey back." I smiled, and wrapped my arms a little tighter around him.

"You're beautiful."

I no longer contradicted him when he said things like that. He made me feel beautiful, even in sweats and a hoodie like I was currently wearing. "Thanks." I kissed him again.

He nodded his head toward the door. "Are you all packed?"

"Yep." I pointed to the edge of my bed, where a small suitcase waited. He walked over to grab it. "Aunt Lor is so excited that I'll be home for Thanksgiving. She said she's already baked three pies."

Jeremy rubbed his stomach. "I hope one of them is cherry."

"I'm sure it is." I chuckled. "She knows they're your favorite." I glanced around to make sure I wasn't forgetting anything I'd need over the long weekend. I grabbed the hobo bag lying on my bed. "I think I'm good. Lets grab Jen." We headed out the door together.

For the second year in a row, Jenny was headed back

to Cloverfield with us to spend the holiday with Aunt
Lor and me since her parents went on a cruise for the
holiday. Jen said she didn't like spending Thanksgiving
with hundreds of strangers on a ship. Her parents were
fine with that, and Aunt Lor loved it. It gave her one
more person to dote over and feed. Jeremy usually came
over sometime after dinner to share dessert while we all
watched a Christmas movie. It had become our tradition
in a way. I liked that—the idea of forming new traditions.

The three of us piled into my car, an old beater Aunt
Lor bought for me when I'd gone off to college. I loved it;
the paint was kind of chipped in places, and tiny pieces of
rust peeked through above the tires, but it still ran well.
It reminded me a little of myself. A little beaten in small
places maybe, but still going strong with some TLC.

Things couldn't have worked out any better. Since
Jeremy attended the New York Culinary Institute, we
got to spend time together every week. Even though we
were both busy with school, we talked on the phone or by
text every weekday, and usually spent weekends together
exploring the city.

The three of us talked and laughed as we made the
drive home. It was only about an hour later, when we passed
Trinity Academy, that my thoughts visited the place I rarely
went anymore. Memories—of Jessica, the fire, Pete's party,
and finally...of the courtroom I'd sat in waiting to hear
my fate—filled my mind. They'd been some of the hardest
weeks of my life. I'd done so many stupid things that I was
ashamed of. But at least it had served a small purpose, even
if I should have gone about it in a better way.

The Society was defunct. After news of what I'd done

came out, other investigations had begun. Probes into the favors by school alumni afforded to Society members. Lines crossed or blurred. Trinity hadn't wanted to chance that anything would mar its golden reputation, so the school board and trustees had denied any knowledge of the Society ever existing, which was a joke and everyone knew it.

But at least it halted future generations of students from being placed in molds of the Society's choosing. It stopped the Society from handing out preferential treatment to only those it deemed worthy.

I wasn't naive enough to believe that it wouldn't start up again after interest waned and prying eyes stopped digging. But for now, I was happy. I had school, friends, family who supported me, and a boyfriend who loved me.

Minutes later, we turned onto Sauderton Road, and I could see my aunt open the door to stand on the top step outside the trailer. Her smile was huge as she waved a dishtowel at us. I grinned.

As soon as the car stopped, I hopped out and ran toward her to wrap her in a hug.

"Samantha." Her blue eyes crinkled into a loving smile. "Just look at you." She smoothed my hair back, and it was impossible to miss the tears of pride shining in her eyes. She waved to Jeremy and Jenny as they climbed out of the car. "Come on in; get those bags later. Let's have some pie."

Jeremy caught up with me and took my hand as we headed inside my home, where the air smelled like cinnamon and brewed coffee. The door closed behind us as we entered the warmth of the kitchen. I looked around at my family and friends and sighed in happiness.

Life was good.

note from the author

Bullying is a very real epidemic going on both in schools and online. If you are being bullied, don't be afraid to reach out and talk to someone about it. Report it. Fear of reprisal from the bully may make you hesitate to reach out, but it is important to not allow bullying to continue. If you see someone else being bullied, take a stand. Silence strengthens bullies. Show that it isn't funny and won't be tolerated in your school, or anywhere else.

If you are depressed, anxious or having thoughts of hurting yourself or others, there is help. Please reach out. You can call the National Suicide Prevention Hotline at 1-800-273-TALK (8255) or find them online at http://www.suicidepreventionlifeline.org/ Counselors are available 24/7.

You can also text "hi" to 741741 to get in contact with a trained crisis counselor who will immediately respond to your text and message you back.

Some other resources if you are in crisis are:

http://hopeline.com/ - Offers a Chat Now option to speak with a trained professional.

https://twloha.com/ - Offers chat with a trained professional.

Remember, you are not alone. There are supports to help you through whatever crisis you may be facing. You are strong, and you matter.

acknowledgments

This book would not exist without the support of so many people around me. First and always, thank you to my readers and to the fabulous book bloggers out there. You make this all worthwhile. I also owe a huge thank you to my Entangled family—Alethea Spiridon, Melissa Montovani and Jasmine, Liz Pelletier, Sharon Johnston, Heather Riccio, Melanie Smith, Meredith, Jessica, Stacy, Christine, and the whole team! None of this would be possible without you. Thanks also to Heidi R. Kling and Brenda Drake for being with me as I began this wonderful journey and cheering me on. And a huge shout out to the #WO2016 crew…you guys rock! I love each and every one of you. And last but never least, to my family, especially to Corey and Hope…Thanks for believing in me. I love you with all of my heart.

GRAB THE ENTANGLED TEEN RELEASES READERS ARE TALKING ABOUT!

LIFE UNAWARE
BY COLE GIBSEN

Regan Flay is following her control-freak mother's "plan" for high school success, until everything goes horribly wrong. Every bitchy text or email is printed out and taped to every locker in the school. Now Regan's gone from popular princess to total pariah. The only person who speaks to to her is former best-friend's hot-but-socially-miscreant brother, Nolan Letner. And the consequences of Regan's fall from grace are only just beginning. Once the chain reaction starts, no one will remain untouched...

THE FOXGLOVE KILLINGS
BY TaraKelly

I work at Gramps's diner, and the cakes—the entitled rich kids who vacation in Emerald Cove—make our lives hell. My best friend, Alex Pace, is the one person who gets me, but he's changing. And then one of the cakes disappears. When she turns up murdered, a foxglove in her mouth, a rumor goes around that Alex was the last person seen with her. When Alex goes missing, it's up to us to prove his innocence and uncover the true killer. But the truth will shatter everything I've ever known about myself—and Alex.

LOVE ME NEVER
BY SARA WOLF

Seventeen-year-old Isis Blake has just moved to the glamorous town of Buttcrack-of-Nowhere, Ohio. And she's hoping like hell that no one learns that a) she used to be fat; and b) she used to have a heart. Naturally, she opts for social suicide instead...by punching the cold and untouchably handsome "Ice Prince"—a.k.a. Jack Hunter—right in the face. Now the school hallways are an epic a battleground as Isis and the Ice Prince engage in a vicious game of social warfare. But sometimes to know your enemy is to love him...

ROMANCING THE NERD
BY LEAH RAE MILLER

Until recently, Dan Garrett was just another live-action role-playing (LARP) geek on the lowest run of the social ladder. Cue a massive growth spurt and an uncanny skill at basketball and voila...Mr. Popular. The biggest drawback? It cost Dan the secret girl-of-his-dorky dreams. But when Dan humiliates her at school, Zelda Potts decides it's time for a little revenge—dork style. Nevermind that she used to have a crush on him. It's time to roll the dice...and hope like freakin' hell she doesn't lose her heart in the process.